Reckoning at Lost Hope

A BILLY YOUNG AND HUGO DORLING NOVEL

Reckoning at Lost Hope

Robert D. McKee

THORNDIKE PRESS
A part of Gale, a Cengage Company

Thorndike Press, a part of Gale, a Cengage Company.

Thorndike Press® Large Print Western.

The text of this Large Print edition is unabridged.

Other aspects of the book may vary from the original edition.

Set in 16 pt. Plantin.

LIBRARY OF CONGRESS CIP DATA ON FILE.
CATALOGUING IN PUBLICATION FOR THIS BOOK
IS AVAILABLE FROM THE LIBRARY OF CONGRESS.

ISBN-13: 978-1-4328-7114-7 (hardcover alk. paper)

Published in 2021 by arrangement with Robert D. McKee

Printed in Mexico
Print Number: 01 Print Year: 2022

For Kent and Jessica

Chapter One: Hugo Sometimes Forgets Himself

Deputy United States Marshal Billy Young shoved his nose against the front glass of Sweet Sorrenson's confectionary shop and spotted what he was looking for: his friend and fellow deputy, Hugo Dorling. Billy wasn't surprised. The afternoon hour was late, and since Hugo had not been at the Half-Moon Saloon, which was the first place Billy looked, he expected to find him at Sweet's.

As Billy stepped into the shop, he said, "I swear, Hugo, when you're not drinking whiskey, you're eating candy."

"Just my Hubs, boy. Just my Hubs."

A few months earlier, Hugo decided he spent too much money on tobacco and rolling papers and began eating candy in an effort to cut back on cigarettes. It hadn't worked. The old coot smoked as much as ever. The only thing Hugo had accomplished was to acquire another bad habit to add to his already extensive list.

"That'll be a nickel, Deputy Dorling," said Sweet, taking a roll of Hub Wafers off the shelf behind her counter.

The woman's real name was Dorothy, but years before moving to Casper she'd opened her first candy shop in Deadwood, Dakota Territory, and folks there began calling her Sweet. Some said Hickok himself gave her the nickname, but since Wild Bill had been murdered eight years before Sweet moved to the wild Dakota mining town, Billy was skeptical.

"Or," Sweet added, "since you're now such a fine and steady customer, I'll sell you three tubes for thirteen cents. How does that sound?"

The ever-frugal Hugo jumped at the opportunity to save a couple of pennies. "Why, it sounds fine," he said, digging into his pocket for the money. "I've been enjoyin' these little rascals off 'n' on since I was a kid."

According to Hugo, the sugary wafers were manufactured by some confectionary company in New England that had started selling them way back in the 1840s.

"Pa brought a bunch home from the war. It's just here lately I remembered how much

I like 'em."

"I'm glad you did, Hugo," said Sweet with a smile. "You eating that candy has caused my income to soar."

Hugo handed over the coins, and, following Billy out the door, he said, "Catch you next time, Sweet."

"I'll be here," she promised, as she dropped Hugo's money into her till.

Hugo tucked two of the rolls in his vest pockets and peeled open the third. "Care for a Hub?" he asked, extending the candy to Billy.

"No, thanks," Billy said. Despite a sweet tooth, Billy was not as fond of the chalky confection as Hugo. "I haven't eaten since breakfast. I need something heartier than a round piece of fruit-flavored sugar. I came looking for you to see if you wanted to get some supper."

"Sure. Where'd you have in mind? The Wentworth?"

"Sounds good."

They both liked the food served in the dining room of the Hotel de Wentworth. When they were home in Casper rather than working in other parts of Wyoming, Billy most often ate at his ranch at the foot of Casper Mountain. As far as he could tell, though, Hugo survived on nothing more than the few meals he ate every week at the Wentworth and the boiled eggs and dill pickles he dug from the Ball jars atop the Half-Moon's bar.

As the boys rounded the corner from First Street onto Center, they came upon a noise that might have been music, but Billy wasn't sure. "Do you hear that?" he asked.

Hugo craned his neck and turned an ear toward the unusual sound. "Yes, I do, but what the hell is it?"

After a few seconds of listening, Billy said, "Sounds like fiddle playing. Sort of." If what they were hearing was music, the music was unlike any Billy had encountered.

They followed the sound, which led to a short man standing in the street in front of the hardware store. Dressed in a dark, dusty suit, the man wore no tie, and his dingy white shirt was buttoned up to his small but protruding Adam's apple. A white handkerchief — even dingier than his shirt — was tucked between his chin and the body of a violin. With a furrowed brow and clenched eyes, the little man played the fiddle so fast the notes shot forth like bees swarming from a hive.

A boy of about eleven, also wearing a grubby shirt, stood next to him. He held a short-billed canvas cap extended in both of his small hands in the hope, Billy assumed, of collecting money as payment for the man's speedy fiddling.

As they watched, Hugo's mouth fell agape, and Billy suspected his had, too. The man's left hand was a blur as his fingers darted up and down the instrument's fingerboard.

"*Damn*-Sam," said Hugo, "the little fella's quick, ain't he?"

Billy agreed. "He is, for sure. His fingers're dashing about like chickens chased by a fox."

Even standing right in front of the man, Billy wasn't sure what he heard could be called music.

"It's fast, all right," said Hugo, "but if whatever he's playin's supposed to be a tune, it doesn't make you wanna dance, does it?" Hugo fancied himself quite the dancer.

The old deputy was right. The music was not the sort to make a man tap his foot or whistle along, but *damn.* Though strange, fast, and loud, Billy was impressed.

Not everyone agreed.

"My *God,*" bellowed Earl Whitson, in his rough, raspy voice. Whitson was a well-known big mouth. He and another man pushed their way to the front of the small group of onlookers. "Shut that racket down.

It sounds like a bobcat's got his testes tangled in a meat grinder." Whitson nudged an elbow into his companion's ribs, and they shared a chuckle.

The fiddle player either didn't hear the remark or chose to ignore it. From the intense expression on his face, Billy guessed the man was lost to everything in the world but the scurry of his fingers and the saw of his bow.

"I said shut the caterwauling *down.*"

The violin player continued to ignore Whitson's demands, but the boy did not. He ducked away from the shouting man and stared into his empty cap. Billy guessed the fiddler was the boy's father by their resemblance.

Whitson, who would not be ignored, ripped the violin from its player's hands and screamed, "Stop that goddamned *noise.*"

The fiddler's eyes popped open in startled surprise. When he was jerked away from whatever remote air castle his playing had taken him, he grabbed the boy and pulled him closer.

Whitson, holding the violin up for a better inspection, said, "I'm gonna do the whole town a big favor and smash this thing." Turning to his friend, he smiled and added, "It'd be a public service to everybody in earshot."

The friend, a ne'er-do-well Billy had seen around town but whose name he didn't know, let out a guffaw and shouted in a high-pitched squeak, "Do 'er, Earl. Bust 'er up."

Whitson crossed to the hitching rack and lifted the fiddle above his head. As he was about to crash the thing down onto the post's crossbar, Hugo pulled his forty-four and slammed its barrel into the top of Whitson's skull. When the Colt's blue steel landed, every muscle in Whitson's large body turned to pudding, and he melted into a puddle. As he went down, the violin went sailing. Billy, like an outfielder diving for a long fly ball, caught it a half second before it hit the ground.

Dumbstruck, the group of onlookers stared at the unmoving Whitson.

After a bit, the silence was broken by Whitson's friend. "By god," he said. "I think you killed 'im." He pointed to the stack of dirty laundry piled at Hugo's feet.

"He ain't dead," said Hugo. Turning to face the man, he asked, "What's your name, mister?"

The man was not as large as his unconscious companion, but he was bigger than Hugo, and he puffed out his chest in an effort to appear even bigger. Billy suspected Hugo was not impressed. The man's size was more blubber than sinew.

"Who wants to know?" asked the puffed-up man. The high tone of his voice sounded as though it should be coming from someone smaller.

Hugo pulled back his vest and tapped his shooter's muzzle against the star pinned to his shirt.

Deflating some, the man answered Hugo's question. "Jones," he said. "Evelyn Jones."

"*Evelyn?* Ain't Evelyn a woman's name?" asked Hugo with a smile.

The man's eyes narrowed. He had no doubt heard the question before. "It ain't a woman's name. It's my name." The puffy man's bravado fell flat against Hugo's toothy grin.

"Well, Evelyn, I'll make you a deal."

"What kinda deal?" Evelyn sounded skeptical.

Hugo jerked the forty-four toward Whitson. "If you'll haul this here heap of cow droppin's off the street, I won't arrest the two of you and toss you in the city jail."

"Arrest us for what?"

"I'd like to say for bein' a pair-a sons-a bitches —"

Billy grimaced and glanced at the women

who were among the onlookers. "Sorry, ladies," he said. Most of the women tittered and brought their fingers to their lips. A couple of them appeared incensed at Hugo's harsh language. And a couple wearing men's clothes and toting side arms showed no reaction at all. "Hugo," Billy added, "sometimes forgets himself." Billy knew Hugo forgot himself more often than a mere "sometimes."

"But, I'm sad to say," continued Hugo, ignoring Billy's interruption, "there ain't no law against bein' a son of a bitch, which might be all right 'cause the jails'd be plumb full if there was. I could arrest you, though, for disorderly conduct, public nuisance, the attempt to destroy property not your own, and, knowin' the never-employed Whitson as I do — and also judgin' by *your* seedy appearance — I'd say I could add in a couple-a counts of vagrancy to boot. So how does that sound to you, Evelyn? You wanna go to jail, or do we have us a deal?"

Billy guessed Evelyn was stupid, because the man's jaw tightened as he took a couple of steps closer to Hugo and stared down into the deputy's eyes.

Jabbing a finger into Hugo's chest, he asked, "Since when did United States Marshals start arresting folks for petty stuff like that? It ain't hardly in your jurisdic—"

Before Evelyn Jones could make his point, Hugo's left fist shot out and caught him square on the tip of the chin. In an instant, the chubby man was on his back next to his partner. Jones wasn't knocked out, but his eyes were crossed when he said, "You're a fella quick to bust a strap, ain'tcha?" He gave his head a shake in an effort, Billy guessed, to get both eyeballs aimed in the same direction. "Okay," he said, "I'll take your damned deal."

"By golly, Evelyn —" Hugo showed real pleasure in using the man's given name — "I'm happy to hear it. Me and my young partner Billy here've got supper waitin' at the Wentworth, and takin' time to lock you two scoundrels up'd be an inconvenience."

Jones pushed himself onto his wobbly feet and with difficulty dragged Whitson off the street and into an alley. "Wake up, Earl," Jones said, as he gave his friend a shake. When the shaking didn't bring the man around, Jones smacked the unconscious man a couple times on the cheeks. "Wake up," he repeated.

Hugo wore a big smile as he watched Evelyn's futile efforts in the alley. The smile did not surprise Billy. Knocking a loudmouth unconscious never failed to cheer Hugo up.

Chapter Two: Aboard a Long-Eared Critter

"If Evelyn wants Whitson to come around," said Hugo, "it's gonna take more than a few shakes and a couple-a cheek pats. He needs to dump some water on his head. A bucket of chilly water should get him movin'." Hugo had bashed enough skulls to know the amount of effort necessary to rouse his victims.

Pointing to the violin in Billy's hand, the old deputy said, "Nice catch there, Billy-boy. The fella's fiddle would-a busted to smithereens if you hadn't grabbed 'er just in the nick-a time."

"Which would've been a shame," said Billy. "It appears to be a good one." He crossed to the little man and handed it to him.

"Thank you," said the man, looking the violin over. When he was satisfied it had survived the ordeal, he cradled it as he might a puppy. "Thank you, very much."

Billy smiled and nodded toward Hugo. "You have this fella to thank. He's the man in charge of whacking folks on the head."

Hugo laughed. "He's right, mister. There's nothin' I like better than givin' a good whack to bullies and their bootlickers."

Billy extended his hand. "Name's Billy Young. And the short-tempered, elderly gent is Hugo Dorling." Billy was twenty-one, and Hugo was twenty years Billy's senior. The difference didn't make Hugo elderly, but the deputy was sensitive about his age, and since his vanity was as puffed up as Evelyn Jones's chest, Billy enjoyed giving it a jab.

Everyone shook hands.

"I am Ivan Kradec. My young companion is Abraham." Mr. Kradec squeezed the boy's shoulder and motioned toward Billy and Hugo. The kid stared at his cap.

"Hello, Abe," said Billy, with a smile. The boy was a handsome tyke, with black hair and dark-blue eyes, but he was unwashed and had a wary look about him.

He offered Billy no response.

"Looks like you got interrupted before you made any money for your fiddlin'," said Hugo.

"Yes," agreed the small violinist, sounding disappointed.

"What was the name of the tune you were playing?" Billy asked. "It's not a thing I've heard before."

"It's the *Winter* concerto from Vivaldi's *The Four Seasons.*"

A touch of the old world colored Mr. Kradec's speech. He sounded like a man who was foreign born, but who'd been speaking American for a long while. Though slight, his accent was noticeable, but Billy couldn't place its origin. He knew Mr. Kradec was not an Englishman, a Frenchie, or a German. Those accents Billy had encountered even in Wyoming. So, he decided, wherever the man started out, it must have been in one of those big empires on the far side of the European continent, a distant location Billy admitted with shame he knew little about.

"So, it's called *Winter,* eh," said Hugo. "I believe it, 'cause it sure left everybody cold." Hugo was the only one who laughed at his joke.

"Well, sir," Billy said, "it's fast moving, and you played it with skill. But Hugo's right. You might've had better luck getting silver in the boy's cap with a lively ditty like *Turkey in the Straw* or *Great Big Taters in Sandy Land.* There's not much demand for the fancy stuff around Casper." Nor, he told himself, many other places between the Missouri and the San Francisco hills.

"I expect you're right," agreed Mr. Kradec, rubbing his right hand over the top of the violin's polished wood.

"I don't believe I've ever seen you around town," Hugo said. "Are you and Abraham travelers passin' through?"

Billy could tell if they were travelers, they were traveling on the cheap.

The man had left his violin case atop a bench on the far side of the boardwalk, and he walked over and tucked the instrument and its bow into it. The violin was fine and elegant. The case was not. Scuffs and scrapes covered it from one end to the other. Large patches of leather had peeled away from its edges.

Mr. Kradec motioned toward a white mule tied to a rail in front of the barber shop. "We've been riding for thirty-one days."

"My God," said Billy, "you two've been aboard that boney, long-eared critter for thirty-one days?" Billy realized too late his denigrating the man's animal came off as rude. But the idea of a month astride that churlish-looking monstrosity caused Billy's tailbone to ache.

Mr. Kradec nodded. "Pearl is not a fancy

car on the Burlington, but she's a willing ride." With a shrug he added, "Most of the time, anyway."

"Have you and young Abe been sleepin' on the ground all them nights?" Hugo asked.

"Yes." Mr. Kradec provided his answer in a tone implying Hugo's question was a bit half-witted. *Where else would they sleep?*

"When was the last time you and the boy had yourselves a full meal?" asked Billy.

With obvious embarrassment, Kradec admitted, "It's been awhile." He turned his eyes away from Billy and down to his beat-to-hell violin case.

Billy aimed a finger at a large two-story building a block away on the corner of Center and Midwest. "We're headed to the hotel to get a bite," he said. "Care to join us? It'll be my treat."

Mr. Kradec glanced at Abe, cleared his throat, and said in a soft voice, "Yes, thanks. You're very kind."

Billy said to Hugo, "I'll even buy *your* supper, you ol' skinflint. I'm feeling generous." Hugo's habit of poor eating caused Billy concern even if it didn't worry Hugo. "Since you were such a big loser at cribbage last night, my pockets are heavy with your money." Penny-a-point cribbage was a game the boys played whenever they had the chance.

"The reason you won is because you kept movin' your peg when I wasn't lookin'."

Billy laughed. Hugo had no evidence to back up his accusation. "A fella needs no trickery to beat you," he said. "Beating you's so easy it's stopped being fun."

As they headed for the Wentworth, Billy glanced over his shoulder in time to spot Evelyn Jones dump a pail of horse-trough water onto the face of Earl Whitson. When he did, the big man came out of his stupor sputtering and spewing.

Hugo had been right. Shaking the man wouldn't do it. The job required a bucket of cold water. When it came to bashing skulls, ol' Hugo knew his business.

Chapter Three: Our Situation Is Awkward

Conversation was sparse during the meal of beef steak and boiled potatoes. Ivan Kradec and the boy ate with eager appetites, which gave Billy pleasure. He figured it made for a good day if a man could feed a couple of hungry travelers, especially if one was a kid. Hugo ate with vigor as well, which was no surprise. When the last morsel was gone, Hugo dug into his vest and came out with the opened roll of Hubs.

Turning to Abe, he asked, "Are you, perchance, a candy eater, young fella?"

The boy stared without responding. Billy doubted the kid had much acquaintance with sweets. Hugo extended his arm and poked the roll a couple of times in the boy's direction. After a bit, Abe raised a small hand and lifted a flat, round disk from the tube. The one on top was lemon yellow. He sniffed it and slipped it into his mouth. When he did, the wary expression Billy had seen earlier eased, and the boy's young, fresh face came close to blossoming into a smile. But not quite.

Hugo's not-so-fresh, weathered face did blossom into a full-blown smile, and he thumbed out a green one for himself. "Yes, sir," he said. "It's hard to beat the Hubs." He offered the roll to Billy and Mr. Kradec, but they both waved him off. "Suit yourself," Hugo said with a shrug, and tucked the roll into his pocket.

"So, tell me, Mr. Kradec," said Billy, "where are you headed in your travels?"

The Wentworth was busy, and Kradec's eyes darted among the tables of diners before he answered. "To the west and south. I have a sister who has a small cattle operation on the Sweetwater, not far from Independence Rock."

"Where'd you start out from?" asked Hugo. The candy in his mouth could not have yet melted. Even so, he produced his makings and rolled a smoke.

"East of here," Kradec answered.

"Thirty days east of here," Hugo said, "would put you . . ." He scratched behind his ear. "Well, sir, let me try to recall my Nebraska geography . . . I suppose somewhere on the Niobrara, past the Sand Hills and Valentine." He took a guess. "Maybe around Springview?"

"No, sir, south of there. Kearney. We got here following the old trail along the North Platte."

"What were you and the boy doin' in that country?"

Mr. Kradec blotted his mouth with a napkin. A large urn of coffee sat on a table against the room's far wall. At crowded times when the waitresses were swamped, the patrons were encouraged to help themselves.

"Abraham," said Kradec, lifting his empty cup toward the boy, "fetch more coffee, if you would, please. Perhaps the deputies would care for more as well."

Billy smiled at the lad, placed his palm over the mouth of his cup, and shook his head.

Hugo said, "Why, sure, little fella. I always enjoy an extra cup or two with my after-supper smokes."

When the boy left the table, Kradec said, "We're not from there. But Kearney is where we bought the mule and started west. Abraham was living near Albion, Nebraska." Kradec looked toward the boy, who stood in line waiting his turn at the urn. "He is my nephew — my sister's child."

Billy was surprised. He had them pegged

as father and son. Although being the boy's uncle would also explain the resemblance.

"The sister who lives on the Sweetwater?" asked Hugo.

Kradec nodded. "Our situation is" — he fumbled for a word — "awkward."

"What d'ya mean?"

"There's a small community where my sister, Marlene, and Abraham lived," he said with a woeful smile. " 'The Community' is what its residents call it. It's on the Boone County tablelands not far from Albion. A year ago, Marlene was" — again he searched for what to say or how to say it — "excommunicated."

"Excommunicated? Was she part of some sort of religion?" Billy asked. He'd heard of off-shoot groups from more conventional religious denominations popping up at various places around the West.

"There is an element of religion. Or was. What it is now, I would describe as nothing more than a cult. Marlene was married to its leader, Martin Glatt. Mr. Glatt is a vile and dangerous man. He has convinced his followers that he is a prophet and was sent by God to lead them and to show them the 'way.' Once he has them convinced, they're required to donate all their wealth and worldly possessions to the Community."

Kradec looked down at his empty plate and rubbed the back of his neck. He appeared tired. "My sister's misfortune with Mr. Glatt and his group is a long and sordid tale, and not one I have been privy to for the last two years, except through my sister's letters. I can say Glatt's behavior toward her is the reason Marlene sought the friendship of . . ." He paused.

"Another man," offered Hugo. "In my experience, it's a common story."

Billy assumed Hugo didn't mean in his *personal* experience, but rather in his long experience as a marshal. Although, with Hugo, who could say?

"Yes," admitted Kradec, "another man."

"Is she now with this man on the Sweetwater?" asked Billy.

"She is. The place belonged to his father. Both he and Marlene were exiled from the group. When Glatt cast them out, he would not allow Marlene to take Abraham with her. Over the last year, she has maintained contact with some of the women who are there, and she was informed that many in the group had turned their eccentric ways and beliefs toward Abraham. After receiving that information, she wrote me and begged for my help."

Mr. Kradec struggled with the telling, and

Billy coaxed him on. "What did you do?"

"I live in St. Louis. I give violin lessons to children in the area. On occasion, I play in a string quartet and with a choral group. At the time, I also cared for our invalid mother. But since Mother's passing six months ago, I found myself at something of a crossroads. I had considered moving west, but had made no effort to do it until I received Marlene's letter asking for help. And I knew Glatt. He and Marlene were also living in St. Louis until his ideas became so unconventional that he moved his group to a less populated bit of country. Upon receiving Marlene's most recent letter, I knew I had to help. I scraped together what few funds I could and purchased a railway ticket to Albion."

"Where you got the boy and headed west?"

"Yes." The little man swallowed hard. "By stealth and luck, I located Abraham, and we made our escape." Kradec lifted his eyes. "But I fear I was seen and that Glatt has sent a man by the name of Elijah Thorn after us. I have not met him, but from my sister, I understand Thorn to be an evil, heartless, violent man. A murderer whom Glatt refers to as his Enforcer. If Thorn finds us, he will kill us." Kradec looked away. "It pains me to admit it, but I am not a brave man, and I fear Thorn is not far behind."

"Do you figure Mr. Thorn knows you're in Casper?" asked Hugo.

"He knows we are following the North Platte. We stopped at that little settlement along the river where Fort Laramie used to be. Abraham and I camped off to ourselves for a night and part of a day. One afternoon a storekeeper there told me he'd spoken to someone who was looking for a man and a boy who matched our description. But he told the man he'd not seen anyone. The shopkeeper said he is not in the business of providing information to men who appear to make their living chasing other men. Marlene had mentioned Mr. Thorn was competent, but I was surprised he had already caught up with us. We planned to rest for a few days, but instead, we left right away. I'm in hope that Thorn did lay up a day or two. I doubt he would take the time for himself, but perhaps he would for the sake of his animals."

"Do Glatt and Thorn know your sister is on the Sweetwater?" Billy asked.

"I don't know. Perhaps. Perhaps not."

"It's possible he lost the trail at Fort Laramie and has given up the chase."

Kradec looked doubtful but said, "I suppose it's possible."

"Even if he kept on upriver," offered Hugo, "he's gotta stop along the way and ask around about you and the boy."

Billy agreed. "I expect he'd stop at Charlie Guernsey's place, and for sure he'd stop at Probity." Probity was a town also on the North Platte about forty miles downstream from Casper. "I'm guessing he'd have to be at least two or three days behind you, if he's kept on your trail at all."

"I hope you gentlemen are right," said Kradec.

Abraham returned with the coffee. His hands looked even smaller carrying the two large cups, and conversation lagged as Hugo and Kradec drank their coffee. Once they were finished, Mr. Kradec said to the boy, "We must go." And to Billy and Hugo he added, "We need to settle in for the night. I saw a likely spot outside of town along the river."

"Heck," said Billy, "there's no need to make a camp. I have a ranch house full of empty beds." Since the passing of his parents and brother, Billy's house was a big, lonesome place. "I'd be pleased to put you up for a while."

Hugo smacked his hands together. "By

golly, now there's a fine idea. After more than a month on the trail, I expect the ground gets pretty hard."

When Mr. Kradec paused and looked with sorrowful eyes toward his young companion, Billy knew he was about to receive some guests.

Chapter Four: Well, Here You Are

By the time they left the Wentworth's dining room, Abe's eyelids were flying at half mast, and, though early, Billy told Hugo he was going to take Kradec and Abe to the ranch so they could clean up and get to bed.

"All right-y, boy," said Hugo. "I think I'll head to the Half-Moon for an evenin' bracer. Maybe two."

Before he left, he slid another Hub into his mouth and handed the roll to Abe. The boy took one, and when he offered to return the roll, Hugo said, "Nah, you keep 'em, son." He reached into his pocket and dug out the other two tubes and handed them to the tyke as well. When he did, Abe's logy blue eyes took on a sparkle.

Before leaving, Hugo looked to Mr. Kradec and again suggested next time the man fiddle a different tune. "You need somethin' snappy," he said. "Folks 'round here wanna *dance.*" And, right in the middle of Center

Street, Hugo began to kick his legs in the exaggerated steps of some old-fashioned jig. Hugo's cavorting would have looked ridiculous even if there'd been a band in the street hammering out a raucous rendition of *Cotton-Eyed Joe.*

When Hugo did his dance, Abraham watched with more interest than he'd shown toward anything since Billy and Hugo met him and his uncle two hours before.

Mr. Kradec appeared surprised.

Though the boy had dropped his head, Hugo gave the kid a wink, and as he took off toward the Half-Moon, he hopped a couple more feather-brained steps. Billy thought Hugo's crazy gambols might again catch the boy's attention, but they did not.

They did cause Ivan Kradec to chuckle. "Deputy Dorling has an interesting way about him, doesn't he?" he said.

"Yes, sir," agreed Billy, "he does."

Billy pointed toward the barn as they rode into the yard at the Young family ranch. "Mr. Kradec," he said, "if you'll take care of the animals, I'll go inside and heat some water for baths. How does that sound?"

"Good. How does it sound to you, Abraham?"

Avoiding his uncle's eyes, the boy answered with a quick nod, which Billy found curious. Abraham hadn't said a word since they met. Billy wondered if the boy was incapable of speech. But he didn't ask. That question would be even ruder than his remark about the mule.

Billy dismounted and handed Kradec his reins. "We keep Badger in the first stall on the right." He patted his big gray's shoulder. "Feel free to put your mule in any of the others. I give Badger some oats after I brush him down." Nodding toward the white mule, he added, "I expect Pearl would appreciate a few oats herself."

After cleaning up, Kradec and Abe went to the room Billy had provided. Rather than taking the time to wash their grimy clothes, Billy, in the hope of locating something for them to wear the next day, went to the attic and explored the contents of an old cedar chest of his mother's.

For Abe, Billy ran across a pair of pants and a shirt that had belonged to Frank, Billy's older brother, when he was a kid. Rounding up something to fit Kradec was more difficult, but Billy dug deeper and found some denims and a tow linen shirt that had been his. His mother had stowed the items away after his teenage growth spurt.

Pleased with himself, Billy headed down the hallway. As he approached the travelers' room, he could hear violin music. Placing the clothes on a hallway table outside the room, he stopped and listened. As before, the music was fancy — the sort not often heard around Wyoming, but this time the piece was slower, more melodic, and rendered with . . . what? More feeling, maybe. Billy couldn't put a finger on it, but whatever Kradec was doing, Billy liked it better than what the man was playing when they first met. Billy suspected if Kradec had fiddled this tune on the street, they would not have had trouble with the bully Whitson and some silver would have landed in Abraham's cap.

Billy considered knocking on the door and giving them the duds, but he decided against it. He assumed Kradec was playing in an effort to help the boy get to sleep. Abe's bath had given him new energy, but the kid had to be tired. It wouldn't do to disturb them. Billy would make sure they found the fresh clothes in the morning.

Before turning in himself, Billy went downstairs with the intention of reading another chapter in the second novel about the strange but clever English detective. He'd read the first book and liked it. The story in this one was more complicated, but Billy was enjoying it, too. The brainy detective made for an interesting character; but, for reasons Billy didn't understand, he felt a special fondness for the narrator, Watson. He'd heard rumors that a new book had come out last October, but Billy was certain it had not yet made its way from London, England, to Casper, Wyoming.

Billy tugged his suspenders off his shoulders, dropped onto the parlor sofa, and made himself comfortable. Taking up the book, he flipped to his bookmark. When he'd left off, the great detective and his doctor pal had a dog on a leash, and the dog was leading them through the streets of London. Before Billy could finish the next chapter's first sentence, the back door opened, and in clumped Ivan Kradec wearing his heavy brogans and the white nightshirt Billy had loaned him. Although Billy had placed a chamber pot in his room, he guessed Kradec had gone to the privy.

"Ah, Mr. Kradec," Billy said with a smile. "You gave me a start. I figured you were in your room. I've placed something for you and the boy to wear tomorrow on the hallway table. We can give your clothes a washing in the morning."

"Thank you, sir. You are too kind."

"When I was upstairs, I heard violin music."

"That was Abraham," Kradec said in a matter-of-fact tone. He traversed the room with his hands behind his back and sat in the wing chair across from the sofa. Once settled in, he said, "Earlier you mentioned you had a bottle of Scotch."

"Yes, I did." Billy had offered Kradec a drink before his bath, but the man had declined.

"Is the offer of a dram still open?" Kradec asked.

"Yes, yes, of course it is." Billy stood. "I keep it in a cupboard in the kitchen. Make yourself comfortable. I'll be right back."

Billy fetched the whisky and a couple of glasses. When he returned, Kradec was tucking something between his right hip and the arm of the chair. The move was furtive, but Billy didn't think much of it. He poured their drinks and had a seat.

"Most of the time I keep a bottle of American around as well," he said, "but Hugo was here last week and polished it off. He has a fondness for Kentucky corn juice."

Kradec took a sip of his drink. "Ah, yes,

Deputy Dorling. It appears Abraham, in his own way, has taken a liking to the man."

"I expect," said Billy, "plying a young-un with candy is a good way to win his favor."

"No, not with Abraham. Abraham is unique."

"He is a handsome little fella," Billy said. "I listened in on the violin playing coming from your room a bit ago. He's good. I thought it was you."

"No, not me. Abraham is twice the violinist I will ever be."

"Well, sir, that's saying something," said Billy, remembering the speed with which Kradec's hand dashed about the fiddle's neck. "How old is the child? Eleven, twelve, maybe?"

"Turned eleven two months ago."

Billy chuckled an amazed little laugh and took a sip of whisky. "I find it a wonder that a boy of such a tender age could play so well."

"As I said, Abraham is unique."

"He does look to be a smart one, but, if you don't mind me saying, I find it odd at how little he talks. I don't believe I heard him say a single word since we ran into you two fellas in front of the hardware store."

"He seldom speaks. I doubt he has said five words since I stole him away from the

Community."

"You're saying he's said only five words in the last thirty days?"

"Yes. It is hard to believe, I know, but it's true. Abraham began talking at an early age. He spoke his first words before his first birthday. He was forming sentences by the time he was — Well, I'm not sure, but a year and a half, maybe a little older."

Billy's knowledge of what age kids started to talk was limited, but if Mr. Kradec considered Abe's starting to speak when he did impressive, Billy couldn't argue.

"The boy was reading by the time he was three — not *Moby Dick,* to be sure, but he had a fine command of McGuffy's. Remarkable, I'd say, for such a youth."

"Yes," agreed Billy, not wanting to admit he had not made it through the whale book himself. As he recalled, he set it aside during the long, tedious lesson on the rendering of blubber.

"Despite his intelligence, at three or four, Abraham's behavior became . . . different. He would move a chair within two feet of the parlor wall and stare at it for hours at a time, not reacting to anything. Glatt used to say at such times a howitzer could be fired next to the boy's ear, and he'd not even blink." Kradec lifted his drink toward the light, and, examining the whisky, he tilted the glass first one way then the other. After a bit, he voiced a cryptic "Hummph" and took a sip. "At the age of six," he said, "Abraham shut down."

"How do you mean?"

"He stopped talking. He would not look anyone in the eye. He would scream whenever he was touched. My sister was terrified."

"Was there nothing to be done for the boy?"

"Marlene took him to the best doctors in St. Louis. They were of no help. They agreed the boy's condition was rare, but not unheard of. Their consensus was Abraham would either outgrow it, or" — he finished off his drink — "he would not."

"I guess he has," Billy said. "At least some." He poured another drink for Kradec and added a splash to his own.

"Things with Abraham continued as they were. About six months later, I introduced him to the violin." Kradec smiled. "And whatever interest Abe found in the bare wall of Glatt's parlor, he transferred to the instrument. He'd have more of his screaming fits whenever anyone tried to take it from him. I taught the boy the basics of fingering and reading music, but soon he didn't need me. He'd listen and watch me when I played. He would then emulate what I did and go his own way with it. His skills were amazing. Even a fool like Martin Glatt was amazed."

"What sort of man is this Glatt?"

"I once thought him to be a good man. Not well educated, but intelligent and well spoken."

"Is he a preacher?"

"No, not always. I suppose he became one — of a sort. He had been a deacon in a small church in St. Louis, but he and a few of the other congregants had a parting of ways with the church's leaders, and they formed their own church. Glatt was the *de facto* minister to this small group. A group which, under his leadership, grew to dozens. They had stern, harsh beliefs, which in time became so stern and so odd that the church drew the attention of the authorities."

"And that's when everybody picked up stakes and moved to Nebraska?"

"Yes. After they left St. Louis, what little I know about it is what I've learned from my sister's letters."

"It's strange she'd leave without her son."

"Glatt promised if she took Abraham, he would order his man Thorn to track her down and kill her. Marlene feared Thorn would even kill the boy. When it became known she was with another man, they barely escaped with their lives, but she didn't take Abraham. I assume because of that, Glatt has not searched for her. Until now, anyway. Since Thorn appears to be close, I am questioning the wisdom of taking the boy to her. If Thorn finds us, he will kill us all."

"How did you get Abe away from the Community?"

"Kidnapping, pure and simple. In the summer, between the hours of three and five, the children are allowed to play on Beaver Creek, a hundred yards or so away from the main settlement. Abe would go along, but instead of playing, he would move away from the others and sit by himself. I came to him when he was alone and told him I would take him to his mother. He was eager to go, and we left. A simple plan."

"Well, here you are," said Billy with a smile. "So, simple or not, your plan has worked."

Kradec looked down into the golden swirls of his whisky. "We'll see," he said without conviction. "We shall see."

Chapter Five: The Hour Was Late for Callers

Before they had finished their drinks, Billy heard what sounded like the nicker of a horse. That was strange. The hour was late for callers.

Kradec's eyes went wide. "Are you expecting someone?" he asked.

"No." Billy lowered the wick on the table lamp and crossed to the large cabinet where he kept his firearms. Since pinning on his star the year before, he had become cautious. A deputy tended to make enemies, and the dark of night was a fine time for those enemies to drop by. He reached inside the cabinet and lifted his short-barreled Colt from its holster.

Billy expected what they'd heard was nothing more than the wind soughing through the spruce trees out back, but he wasn't sure, and the sound was such that it deserved a look.

He cracked open the front door and

peered outside. The moon's silver light sheathed the yard, corrals, and outbuildings. Seeing nothing suspicious, he stepped onto the porch. He again told himself that what he'd heard was nothing more than the wind. At sunrise that morning, the rowdy crew who was hired every summer had left the home place with Orozco Valdez, the man who last year had purchased Billy's cattle operation. Rosco and the boys were moving cattle to higher grass on Casper Mountain, and without the normal ruckus coming from the bunkhouse, things were quieter than usual.

Billy no longer heard whatever he'd heard earlier, but he decided to look around. He stepped off the porch and headed for the barn. He found nothing unusual there or at the cook shack. He peeked in a bunkhouse window. The long narrow room was empty.

Yep, he told himself. *My imagination.*

He turned and headed back, but halfway there, he heard movement at the side of the house and pulled up short.

Staying in the shadows, Billy held his breath and cocked an ear. He also cocked his forty-five just in case, and, dropping to a crouch, he scuttled toward the porch. He stopped below the cover of the porch's railing and listened again.

As he did, the front door opened, and Ivan Kradec stepped outside. The breeze caused his nightshirt's hem to flutter around his thin calves. In his hand, Billy saw a pistol and realized that was what he'd spotted Kradec stuffing between his hip and the arm of the easy chair.

Billy placed his index finger to his lips and motioned for Kradec to come forward. When the little man tiptoed down the porch's steps and came Billy's way, Billy caught a better look at the fiddler's handgun. The unimpressive piece was a small, nickel-plated twenty-two caliber revolver. Billy couldn't tell much about it, but, judging by its spur trigger, he guessed it to be another of the many cheap, small-frame pocket guns that manufacturers by the dozens had begun churning out once Smith and Wesson's Rollin White patent expired.

Again, listening for the sound, Billy could hear furtive movement coming from around the corner of the house. He leaned toward Kradec's left ear and whispered, "Stay here." The man started to say something, but this was no time for debate. Billy felt his eyes go narrow, and Kradec gave a nod. When Billy stood, Kradec remained in a crouch at the porch.

Billy stepped into the moonlight and

rounded the porch. As he did, he saw a man lift his head to the parlor's window and peer inside.

"Hold it right there," Billy shouted.

The man spun and, seeing the Colt aimed at his chest, shouted back with a genial laugh, "Whoa, there, partner." He lifted his arms straight out from his sides and stepped forward. "No need for the shooter, friend," he said. "I mean you no harm."

He was of average height and build and, with his broad smile, appeared harmless enough. His features were sharp and angular, and on his head was a dusty derby hat. Above the smile was a thick, blond mustache. The mustache was not as bushy as Hugo's soup-strainer, but to Billy, who needed to shave no more than twice a week, the thing was impressive. The man wore his gunbelt high around his hips. The holster on his left slanted toward the right and hung more in front of his body than on his side. His shirt was a dark shade of red or maroon — the moonlight made it hard to tell — and over the shirt was a brown corduroy vest. The vest was a handsome thing with leather buttons and wide lapels.

"Let me show you something," the man said, "and then we can talk." With his right hand, he made a slow move toward his left.

"Sorry about skulking about like this, but I was told in town you might be in the company of . . ."

Before he could finish, Ivan Kradec stood from his hiding place at the porch, leveled his revolver, and fired a shot into the smiling man's back.

The man gave a jerk, and his smile disappeared. He made an odd gesture with his right arm as though trying to reach behind in order to feel what had struck him, but before he could get it done, his knees lost their sand, and he dropped.

Kradec stepped forward and aimed his pistol at the man's head.

"Drop it," shouted Billy.

Kradec paid him no attention.

"Drop the gun, goddamn it." When Kradec continued to ignore him, Billy knocked the pistol away, grabbed a handful of nightshirt, and shoved Kradec backward. The little man tried to catch his balance, but, having no success, he hit the ground hard enough to clatter his teeth.

"What the hell are you doing?" Billy screamed. "Get yourself in the house right now, and be quick about it." He pointed to where Kradec's gun had landed. "And leave that where it is."

Kradec pushed himself up, took another

look at the man on the ground, and did as he was told.

The man who now lay at Billy's feet did not look familiar, so Billy assumed he was not one of Billy's own potential enemies. As far as Billy could see, that left one possibility: Martin Glatt's man, Elijah Thorn. Billy guessed he'd been wrong. The Enforcer was not two days behind Kradec and the boy as Billy had guessed at supper. Thorn was already in Casper, and he now lay in Billy's yard shot and maybe dying.

Billy tucked his short-barreled into his pants at the small of his back and bent to tend to the man.

"Mr. Thorn," he said, "you've been shot. I'm going to roll you over and take a look at your wound." The man was conscious but made no response as Billy turned him onto his stomach.

The bullet hole, three inches below Thorn's right shoulder, was small and did not produce much blood.

He was lucky, Billy thought. If Kradec's pistol had been of a higher caliber, at such close range, Billy suspected the man would already be dead. He would be soon anyway, if Billy didn't get him some treatment.

"You're not in any more danger. The man

who shot you is gone. I'm going to get you to the doctor, but first I need to hitch a wagon. I'll be right back."

Though he didn't say anything, Billy could see from the man's eyes that he understood.

Billy retrieved Kradec's gun. Along with the spur trigger, the pistol had a bird's head grip and was marked "Defender." This was the first of these Billy had come across, and he could see its poor quality; but, even so, the damned thing had accomplished what Kradec had intended it to do. Billy took the gun with him into the barn, where he slid it onto a shelf behind a jar of nails.

A seldom-used, antiquey old Goddard buggy was stored in the back of the barn. Billy would have preferred the buckboard for the job, but since the buckboard's bed was loaded with hay, he chose the Goddard. He pulled off the buggy's canvas tarp and tossed it into a corner. He then brought in a mare from the corral and had her hitched and the buggy in front of the house in less than ten minutes.

The Goddard was not ideal for carrying an injured man. Billy could not lay him flat, but Doc Waters's place in Casper wasn't far, and the buggy would do.

Thorn had not lost consciousness. Billy

took that for a good sign. When Billy had spoken to him earlier, the man had shown no indication of pain, but now from the glassy, vacant look to his eyes and the tight clench of his jaw, Billy saw the pain had arrived in force.

"All right, Mr. Thorn," Billy said. "Hang on to me the best you can. I'm going to heft you into the wagon."

Thorn's build was solid, but he was lean and not heavy. As Billy placed him onto the Goddard's seat, the man let out a soft groan — not much considering he had a bullet lodged in his back.

Kradec had described Glatt's Enforcer as an evil and heartless killer. That may be, but it appeared to Billy the man possessed some grit.

Chapter Six: Who Is This Poor Soul?

Billy and Hugo sat on the front porch of the clinic waiting for news from the doc regarding his back-shot patient.

Earlier, once Billy had left Thorn with Dr. Waters and Abigail, the doc's wife and surgery nurse, Billy went to the Half-Moon Saloon and located Hugo, who was playing blackjack with a few of his rambunctious pals. Billy described the evening's many events to Hugo, and they rode to Billy's place to confront Ivan Kradec about what the little man had done.

When they arrived, Kradec and young Abraham were no longer there. Neither was their mule. Kradec's cheap pistol was still tucked behind the jar of nails, which meant Kradec had been unable to find it. If he had, it would be gone, because he'd taken about everything he could carry, including his and Abe's filthy clothes, a Winchester from the cabinet, a smoked ham that had been hanging in the pantry, and Billy's bottle of Scotland whisky. The mule was gone, but, to Billy's surprise, none of the horses were missing. He found that odd. Kradec had proven to be a thief. Why not replace his bony mule with a horse or two?

After discovering the absence of his house guests, Billy unhitched the mare from the buggy, saddled Badger, and he and Hugo rode back into town to await word as to whether Elijah Thorn would live or die.

"I find it hard to believe," said Hugo as he puffed on a smoke, "that a violin player'd have the stuffin' to shoot a fella down like that."

"It doesn't take much stuffing to step out of the dark and put a bullet into a man's back." Billy had seen some horrific things in the last couple of years, but such a display of pure cowardice was rare. "If I'd had more time," he said, "I might have beat out of Kradec what little stuffing he does have." The more he and Hugo discussed the shooting, the more furious Billy became.

"We ought-a chase that little weasel down and charge 'im with attempted murder," Hugo said.

"I hope *attempted* murder is all it is," said Billy. "As for chasing him down, we need to run the idea past Gardner first."

Skip Gardner had bested the worthless Dale Jarrod in the election the previous November and been sworn in as county sheriff a few months later. Neither Billy nor Hugo knew the man well, but they could already tell that Gardner was a damned sight better at the sheriffing profession than Jarrod had ever been.

Hugo nodded. "I suppose we should," he said. "Though I doubt Sheriff Gardner'll have a problem with us handlin' this one. He's plenty busy these days huntin' them rustlers out on Poison Spider. There's a lot of pressure on 'im, 'specially after what happened to Joe Broom."

There had been a half-dozen rustlings along Poison Spider Creek in the last month. A few nights earlier, Broom, one of Ben Cahill's hired hands, had been murdered. The cowboy must have confronted the thieves as they were moving cattle off the Cahill ranch. He was found the next day shot dead.

Billy agreed. "Skip's plate is full, all right. I'm sure he'd be glad to have us go after Kradec."

In the past, crimes that occurred off federal land were not in the marshal office's jurisdiction, but, in addition to the county's acquiring a new sheriff, the state had acquired a new United States Marshal. The new marshal was a practical man, who felt his office should assist what few lawmen were scattered around the state. His first month on the job, the marshal had written letters to the state's thirteen county sheriffs suggesting they exercise concurrent jurisdiction. The sheriffs were every one quick to agree. So were the judges, both state and federal. The decision was made that, when a crime took place in the local sheriff's jurisdiction, if he chose, he could request the assistance of the marshal's office; if a crime took place on federal land, the U.S. Marshal, if he chose, could request assistance from the local sheriff. It made sense in the vast empty spaces of Wyoming for all of law enforcement to work as a team.

Though "team work" was not the sort of thing Hugo did best, even he considered the idea a good one.

Dr. Ezekiel Waters pulled his watch from his pocket as he stepped through the door and onto the porch. His clinic and surgery were located on the street-side of the building. He and Abigail lived in rooms at the back. A lamp burned on the table where Billy and Hugo sat, and the doctor tilted the watch toward the light.

"Three fourteen," he said in a raspy,

exhausted voice. He looked toward the east. "What the hell time is sunrise these days?"

"Couldn't tell you," said Billy. "Since I've given up raising cows, I try my best to avoid sunrises. Now I expect Hugo here sees the sun come up every morning of the week as he staggers home from the barrooms and bawdy houses."

Doc Waters smiled. Hugo did not.

"I gotta say, boys, I'm whipped." The doctor plopped onto a bench snugged against the porch rail. "I had to probe around longer than I like trying to locate the bullet. It had stayed in one piece, which is good. That's not always the way it works, especially with the smaller calibers. The damned slug had glanced off his shoulder blade and headed south. It traveled up close to the rib cage, so the internal damage was minimal. No damage at all to any of the organs. This fella is one lucky *hombre*."

"I get your point, Doc," said Hugo, "but I consider it odd to hear a man who's been back-shot described as lucky."

Billy gave the matter some quick thought and decided it must be possible to calculate a thing as mysterious as luck in multiple ways.

"So you figure him to live, do ya?" Hugo asked.

The doc shrugged. "He's a strong one, though because of how long things were taking with the surgery, I had to give him more ether than I wanted to. That's always risky."

"Is he still out?" asked Billy.

"Yep, he is. He will be for another two or three hours. The gunshot and the surgery aren't going to kill him. Except for a little pain, I expect he'll be up and about in a day or two. But," he added, "we have to worry about an infection." The doctor looked down at his hands and said more to himself than to Billy and Hugo, "Infection's always a thing." He spoke of infection the way a sailor speaks of sea storms or a farmer speaks of blight. The doc cleared his throat and went silent. After a full minute, he asked, "Who is this poor soul, anyhow? Why is he in town?"

"Well, sir," said Billy, "we didn't have a formal introduction."

"He got the bullet put in him by a fella named Kradec," Hugo said. "Kradec told me and Billy that he was bein' chased by a mean Nebraskan by the name of Elijah Thorn. We take this fella to be that Nebraskan."

"We can't figure who else he could be," said Billy.

Hugo squinted through his swirling smoke

and asked, "Did he happen to say anythin' to you before you put 'im under?"

The doctor closed his eyes and rubbed the back of his neck. "No, he wasn't too talkative, but it's my experience that bullet holes tend to extinguish conversation in most men." Lifting an eye toward Hugo, he added, "Even the chatty ones."

"Like Hugo was saying," said Billy, "Kradec told us that your patient's a killer who aimed to hunt him down."

"Kill him and maybe a young boy he's traveling with," added Hugo in a flat, cold tone.

"Our contact was brief," said Billy, "so I couldn't say whether he's bad or whether he isn't. He was good-natured enough, considering I caught him red-handed in the dark of night peeking into my parlor window."

"A window peeker, eh," observed the doc. "A nefarious sort of activity, to be sure, but, in my opinion, the act does not warrant getting shot. That could just be me. I'm a progressive, as you know, and feel that shooting folks should be kept to a minimum."

"We expect," said Hugo, "Mr. Kradec shot him for reasons other than bein' a Peepin' Tom."

The doctor looked at the glow of Hugo's cigarette. "Do you have your makings on you, Deputy?"

"I do. Would you care for a shuck, Doc?"

"Seeing as how I left my pipe way back in the house, and I'm too bushed and lazy to fetch it, that would suit me fine, if you don't mind."

Hugo tossed over his tobacco and papers, and the doc rolled himself a smoke. As he returned Hugo's makings, he said, "I don't believe I ever heard anyone but you call these little rascals shucks, Hugo. Where'd you get that?"

"When we was kids, we didn't have papers, so we'd roll whatever tobacco we could find in corn shucks. We kept callin' 'em shucks even after we could afford paper."

"Makes sense." The doctor stuck his cigarette between his lips and pointed to the tip.

Hugo produced a match, popped it alight with his thumbnail, and touched it to the doctor's shuck.

Blowing a stream of smoke as he talked, the doc asked, "What do you boys know about this Kradec, other than he's a back-shooter?"

"Not much," Billy said and related a quick version of Kradec's story of whisking Abraham away from the Community in Nebraska and Thorn's tracking them to Kearney and on to the area around old Fort Laramie.

When Billy was finished, the doc said, "That's interesting."

"What is?" asked Hugo.

"This Martin Glatt's Community must have more money available to it than most places of the sort."

"Why do you say that?" Billy asked.

"When Abbie and I were undressing Mr. Thorn, I found this." He lifted something out of his pants pocket. "The thing was pinned to the underside of the left lapel of his vest."

Doc Waters leaned forward and gave what he held to Billy.

"From what I hear," said the doctor, "those fellas don't work cheap."

Billy turned what the doctor had given him toward the lamp. "Good Lord," he whispered. To Hugo he said, "A solid silver shield." When Billy said that, Hugo's bushy eyebrows popped up a notch.

Engraved on the shield's face were the words Pinkerton National Detective Agency.

Chapter Seven: Nobody's Fool

The doc provided the boys a room that held a couple of beds, and, despite Hugo's snoring like a snorting bull, and the many tensions of the previous evening, Billy fell into a deep and dreamless sleep. But he awoke with a start less than two hours later when he felt the touch of a hand on his shoulder.

"Easy now, Billy," soothed a soft voice.

Billy rubbed his eyes and looked into the handsome face of the matronly Abigail Waters.

"You told Zeke you wanted us to wake you when the man you brought in was conscious; is that right?" Abigail gave him her comforting nurse's smile.

"Yes, ma'am, I did. Has the fella come around?"

"He's groggy, but he's awake enough to keep down a few tablespoons of chicken broth. If you want to talk to him, you need to do it now. He's in some pain, and I want to give him something." She turned for the door leading into a hallway. As she left, she said over her shoulder, with another of those smiles, "I'm going to let you rouse Hugo. I expect he wakes up surly."

Before Billy and Hugo came into the room, Nurse Abigail had assured them her patient was awake — more or less. But once the boys had taken up places on either side of his bed, the man's even breathing and closed eyes told them otherwise.

Hugo said, "The Pinkertons say they never sleep. I guess that ain't true."

When Hugo said that, the man's eyes fluttered, and he came awake. The sight of two strangers staring down at him caused his brow to furrow. Focusing on Hugo, he said in a weak voice, "I've always imagined the angels in charge of greeting newcomers would be beautiful women with golden harps."

"That ain't me," said Hugo.

"I see that. Could be I didn't end up where my Sunday school teacher promised I would. That's troublesome."

"You ain't dead," Hugo said. "Not yet anyhow." Hugo's bedside manner was not ideal.

The man's angular features tightened into

a severe look.

"No," assured Billy, "you're not dead."

The man turned away from Hugo and squeezed the bridge of his nose between a thumb and index finger. He ran his other hand through his disheveled blond hair and said, "The not-being-dead part sounds good. As I drifted off after my soup, I had doubts that I'd wake up."

"Well, sir, you are awake. And we're thinking you're going to be fine."

"Maybe," the man said as he leaned back and stared at the ceiling. "The truth is I don't feel as bad as I figure I ought to, considering I took a bullet not so long ago. What sort of gun was I shot with, anyhow?"

"Small caliber pocket gun. A twenty-two."

"That sounds good, too, I suppose. Of course, the bad thing about gunshot wounds is even if they don't kill you outright, they have a way of coming back on you."

Recalling the doc's comment about infection, Billy recognized the man before him was nobody's fool.

"Do you remember me, Mister?" Billy asked.

The man took another look at Billy and blinked a couple of times trying to focus. "I do," he said with a nod. "You're the young gent who hauled me into the doctor's clinic."

"That's right. The name's Billy Young. The fella to your left is Hugo Dorling. Nurse Abigail is going to give you something for your discomfort here in a bit, but, before she does, Hugo and I would like a few words."

It appeared Billy's saying that increased the man's discomfort, but he recovered fast. "A few words about what I was doing at your place?"

"Yes, sir, that's part of it."

"I was looking for a scoundrel by the name of Ivan Kradec."

"What made you think he was at my place?" asked Billy.

"A man in town wearing a big knot on his skull named Earl and another man named Evelyn told me that a fella looking like Kradec was last seen walking off with you and another man they described as one dirty son of a bitch."

"I'm the dirty son of a bitch," said Hugo with a hint of pride.

"I guessed as much." Turning again toward Billy, the man added, "It did not require much effort to figure out you had taken Kradec and the boy to your place south of town."

"The person you're looking for, and, by the way, the man who shot you, told us he was being followed by a known killer named Elijah Thorn, and Thorn's intention was to murder him and his young nephew as well."

"Is that so?"

"That's what he said. I have to admit at first Hugo and I had you pegged as this fella Thorn."

The man's blond eyebrows rose an inch. "Me? Thorn?"

"I expect Kradec thought that as well, and that's why he shot you."

"Makes sense, I guess."

"But a couple of hours ago, we discovered you're with the Pinkertons, and that has put some doubt on your being the man sent to murder Kradec and his nephew."

"Some doubt, maybe, but not enough to discount the possibility," said Hugo. "What the hell's your name, anyhow?"

The Pinkerton answered in an icy voice. "It ain't Thorn."

"You know," said Hugo, "I don't have much use for a man who skulks about houses in the dark of night, peekin' into windows. Especially if that man is a strike-bustin' Pinkerton."

The man's eyes turned to slits. "Gee whiz," he said, "that makes me real sad to hear an intelligent fella like you say such a thing."

Billy doubted Hugo would beat the hell out of a wounded man as he lay in his sick bed, but when he saw Hugo square his shoulders, Billy wasn't so sure. In a more polite manner than Hugo had used, Billy asked, "What is your name, sir?"

The Pinkerton held his stare locked on Hugo for another fifteen seconds before he turned toward Billy. "Warren. Dub Warren. I'm out of the Pinkertons' St. Louis office."

"Are you familiar with a man named Martin Glatt?" asked Billy, "and a place he runs a few miles south and east of Albion, Nebraska? It's called the Community."

"I'm familiar with Albion. Kradec's trail led there. I knew when his sister and her group left St. Louis, they moved to that area of Nebraska. When I figured out Kradec had purchased a train ticket to Albion, I expected he planned to hide out at his sister's. I followed him to Albion and went to the Community and sniffed around a bit."

"What's the place like?" Hugo asked.

Ignoring Hugo's question, the man asked Billy, "Could I get a drink of water?"

"Sure." A glass was on the table next to the bed. It contained water and a sipping straw. Straws were quite the novelty. As far as Billy knew, the clinic was the one place in town that had any. Dub Warren was familiar with them, though, and made use of this one without hesitation. Sipping straws, like English detective novels, made their appearance in lots of places long before they were common in central Wyoming.

"Thanks." Warren handed the glass back to Billy and answered Hugo's question without looking at him. "Strange. The place is strange."

"How do you mean?" asked Billy.

"There are lots of women. Quite a few more women than there are men."

"Polygamists," Hugo said.

Warren looked surprised. "Could be you're smarter than I thought."

"I bet I am."

"Though not in large numbers," said Warren, "the men who were there looked to be a rough bunch."

"Did you talk to Glatt?" asked Billy.

"He's who I did talk to. I got the feeling he's the one who does all the talking for that group."

"What's he like?"

"I'd say he's a fella with a big personality. Lots of charm. Lots of words. But a pleasant fella and an intelligent sort."

"Did you tell him you were hunting Kradec?"

"I did. He said he hadn't seen his brother-in-law since the Community left St. Louis. I didn't get much out of him. He's a smooth one."

"How did you figure out Kradec left Albion and headed to Kearney?"

"As I was riding back, I ran into a couple of women from the group who were returning from town. They were driving a small cart and said they'd been selling vegetables on the square. I struck up a conversation with them. They filled me in on plenty. The women are quick to talk even if the men are not. They told me about Glatt's wife being driven from the Community, and if she had taken her son with her, Glatt had promised that she and her new beau would be struck down."

"Sounds like quite the fella," said Hugo.

"The women hadn't seen Kradec but guessed if he came through there looking for his sister, he'd head west. I gave the ticket agent at the depot a half eagle, and he was happy to tell me a man looking like Kradec had purchased tickets to Kearney for himself and a boy. The agent was a talker. He was so eager to tell me about

Kradec, I expect I could've gotten the information for a dollar."

Billy looked at Hugo. "It appears a bunch of folks are on the hunt for Ivan Kradec. There's Mr. Warren here, Elijah Thorn, and, once we visit with the sheriff, maybe we'll be chasing him, too."

"Why are you after him, Pinkerton?" Hugo asked.

"As a rule, we don't discuss our cases, but I'd say I'm indebted to young Mr. Young, here, for saving my life."

Billy gave a dismissive shrug, but he had to agree.

"I always repay my debts, and I repay them with interest." He looked at Hugo. "It's a matter of honor." Warren turned and nodded toward the water on the table. Billy handed it to him, and he took another a sip. "I'm not after Kradec," he said, "not exactly."

"You're not?"

"No, sir. Oh, I suppose once I catch him, I'll haul him in. I might even beat hell out of him for shooting me."

"I would," allowed Hugo.

"Or," said Warren to Billy, "maybe I should thank him for shooting me with such a puny and worthless little gun."

"So, what do you mean when you say

you're not after Kradec?" Billy asked.

Hugo leaned forward and fixed Warren with a steely glare. "Are you after the boy?"

The Pinkerton, ignoring Hugo's question, answered Billy's. "What I'm after," he said, "is the violin."

Chapter Eight: My Spirits Are High

In unison, Billy and Hugo chorused, "The *violin.*"

Dub Warren nodded. "My reaction, too, when I first heard about it. Kradec gave violin lessons to the children of a few of St. Louis's finer families. One family, I reckon, was a notch or two finer than the others. They owned some fancy violin their kid used."

"How fancy could a fiddle be?" asked Hugo. "If you've seen one of the durned things, you've seen 'em all."

"No, I don't think so. This one was special. It'd been made by some Italian fiddle maker about two hundred years ago. I was told it's worth thousands of dollars."

"Good god," Billy said, "how is that even possible?"

"You got me, friend," said Warren. "But some folks take their fiddle playing and their fiddles more serious than regular folks do.

This man Kradec was part of the orchestra that played for the St. Louis Choral Society. Joseph Otten, the fella who started the society back in '80 and has run it ever since, introduced Kradec to some of his highfalutin' acquaintances and encouraged them to have Kradec teach their kids how to play. At the end of one lesson, Kradec switched a violin of his for the Italian one. I guess he put his into the fancy violin case, and the fancy violin into his case. Then he lit out for parts unknown. It didn't take long for the switch to be noticed, though. The owner and Mr. Otten hired us to get the violin back. They'd like to see Kradec brought to justice, but what they want more is their fiddle."

The door to the room opened, and Abigail came in carrying a spoon and a small vial.

"Ah," said Warren, "the laudanum lady has arrived."

Abigail held the bottle to what little early morning light came through the window behind Hugo and said, "There looks to be one dose left."

"I figure one dose'll do it, Nurse. I'm feeling good, and my spirits are high. Deputy Young figures I'll live."

"The doctor figures that, too," agreed Abigail.

"Well, then, ma'am, there's some more good news."

"It looks like you're about as close as a fellow can come to being bullet proof."

"That's nice to know. I'll bear it in mind the next time some miscreant is taking potshots at me."

"I wouldn't get too cocky about it, if I were you," said Abigail. She set the spoon and vial on the table. "You can take this, once these two wrap up their business" — she turned to Billy and Hugo and added — "which'll be soon, I'm sure."

"Yes, ma'am," Billy said, "it will be. I promise."

Abigail left, and Warren said, "The sad thing about this is before I took Kradec's bullet, I damned near had the little snake caught."

"We might be able to help you catch up with him again," said Billy.

Warren looked pleased. "You can? How so?"

"Kradec told us he was taking Abraham back to his mother."

"So, she's in Wyoming?"

"That's what Kradec said. She and her new fella have a small operation on the

Sweetwater River somewhere around Independence Rock."

"Independence Rock. I've heard of that place. How long a ride is it from here?"

Billy looked toward Hugo. "Oh, a day, I'd say."

Hugo nodded. "A long one."

The Pinkerton asked, "Is the sister's place right on the river?"

"On it or close to it, I'm sure," said Billy. "A fella by the name of Tom Sun owns a big spread around there. His headquarters are located at Devil's Gate, not far past the Rock. It's easy to find. Either Mr. Sun himself or a ranch hand'll be able to point you toward the sister's place. I'm sure they'll know. They keep real close track of what's happening on the Sweetwater."

"That's for damned sure," agreed Hugo.

"Tom Sun, eh?"

"That's right."

"Thanks for the lead, Billy. I appreciate it. Now, if you don't mind, in my effort not to die, I expect I need to get busy getting rest." He gave Billy a wink and reached for the vial of laudanum.

Billy cut into his over-easy eggs and scooped a bite onto a biscuit. They'd walked to the Wentworth for breakfast after they left the clinic. "The Doc'll set Dub Warren loose here in a couple of days," said Billy. "And he'll be heading after Kradec as soon as he's able. It wouldn't hurt for us to help him out. What do you think? Should we approach him with the offer?"

"I figure if Warren needs any help, he can go to the sheriff, either here or down in Carbon County. If one of them sheriffs needs us to be a part of it, he'll let us know. Besides, I don't wanna work with that Pinkerton unless I have to."

Hugo had developed a quick dislike of Dub Warren. When Billy asked him about it, Hugo said, "Every Pinkerton I ever met had shifty eyes."

"Every one?"

"Every single one. That must be the sort of man they look for — shifty-eyed ones. Did you know, boy, that you can gauge the character of a man that fast" — he snapped his fingers — "by lookin' right into his eyes." When he said it, Hugo leaned forward and waggled his index and middle fingers three inches from Billy's face.

Billy batted Hugo's hand away. "Hell, Hugo, this Pinkerton's eyes were glassy from pain and maybe that stuff Nurse Abigail was pouring down him. He didn't look shifty to me. I'd say he's a fine and affable man. I could tell that when I caught him peeking in my parlor window. You're saying what you're saying because of your never-ending prejudice against every Pinkerton you ever met or even heard about."

Hugo'd had harsh words for the Pinkertons for as long as Billy could remember, and over the years he'd been quick to share those words with whoever would listen.

"I liked the fella, myself," Billy added. "It appeared to me that he sized you up pretty fast, too. I wonder if he did it by looking into your rheumy old eyeballs."

Billy offered Hugo a big grin, which Hugo ignored by cutting a piece from his ham steak and shoving it into his mouth.

Once Hugo had chewed and swallowed, he gulped a drink of coffee and went into what Billy feared would become a typical Hugo, long-winded taradiddle. This one was about how a poet somewhere — Hugo couldn't remember who, for sure — had said that eyes were like windows. "Windows lookin' right down to the bottom of a fella's soul," he said, nodding with satisfaction as though a poet's putting it to paper had to make it true. "So how do you like that, Mr. Smart Aleck?"

Billy didn't answer. He'd not been paying much attention, because he was busy trying to picture the old buzzard reading a book of poetry. An image that was slow to come.

They were on their third cup of coffee when a boy dashed into the dining room and up to their table. "Deputy Dorling, Sheriff Gardner sent me to fetch you." The kid's breathing was heavy as he gasped out, "He also sent me for Mr. Teasdale, the undertaker. I told Mr. Teasdale I had to find you, too, and he figured this time of day, you'd be here at the Wentworth having your breakfast. Looks like he was right."

The words spewed from the boy.

"Slow down," said Hugo. A pitcher of water sat on the table, and Hugo poured a glass, which the kid accepted with thanks.

"Now, you need to go easy," Hugo advised. "You'll pop a vessel. What does the sheriff want, anyhow?" Hugo took a sip of coffee. He seldom got excited about anything before he'd finished his morning coffee, and he was peeved when those around him did.

"The sheriff wants you and the undertaker to meet him out by where that old Reshaw Bridge used to be. Mr. Teasdale's on his way there now." As an afterthought, the tyke jerked a thumb toward Billy and added, "The sheriff said you could even bring along Deputy Young, if you wanted to."

Hugo looked to Billy and smiled. "My *word,* could the problem be so dire that we'd need Deputy Young?"

"Maybe," said the boy. "The sheriff was pretty het up."

"Did you run into town from the Reshaw?" asked Billy. "That's quite a ways."

"No, sir, from the sheriff's office. Then I ran from the undertaker's after I gave him the message." The boy looked at Billy's and Hugo's unfinished breakfasts. "The sheriff wants you out there fast."

"Why?" Hugo asked. "What's goin' on?"

"Mr. Carson came in and told the sheriff that he'd found something." Norm Carson was a rancher who had a place east of town.

"What did he find?"

"If Mr. Teasdale was called, it must be a body," said Billy.

"According to the sheriff, Mr. Carson was so upset he was about to be sick right there on the sheriff's floor."

"Well," asked Hugo, "did Carson ever let the sheriff in on what he'd found?"

"Yes, sir, he told the sheriff, but the sheriff wouldn't tell me."

"Why not?" Billy asked.

"Because he said the way Mr. Carson described it, what he found was something real horrible."

Chapter Nine: A Sense of Apprehension

They left their breakfasts half finished, collected their horses from the White Star Livery, and headed east. The spot where the old Reshaw Bridge had been was five miles downriver from where the town was later built. A shrewd businessman of French ancestry, John Baptiste Richard — or Reshaw, as the pilgrims pronounced it — erected his bridge across the North Platte in 1853 to capitalize on the heavy traffic along the Oregon-California Trail. It replaced the ferry operation the Mormons had begun a few years earlier. The bridge was gone now, dismantled in the mid-1860s and used for firewood and other construction; but in the old days, it had been a famous landmark, and people remembered it still.

The summer morning was mild and trotting along the river would have made for a pleasant ride if it weren't for a sense of apprehension about what the sheriff wanted them to see.

"I expect some poor soul got hisself murdered," said Hugo as they rode. "I doubt Skip Gardner would call us out for anythin' less."

The river took a bend to the south, and, as they came around, they spotted where the bridge was once located. Billy had not been out here in a while, but he knew it well. He and his brother used to hunt geese along this stretch of river. The area was historic, but it showed little sign of the bustling community of old. In addition to the bridge, which Billy had been told was eighteen feet wide and a thousand feet long, the place had consisted of a blacksmith shop, a trading post, and as many as twenty log buildings. The army even set up a garrison to protect the travelers as they trudged their way west.

It had been impressive in its time, but now it lay empty and remote.

Billy and Hugo saw the sheriff's strawberry roan and Barnett Teasdale's hearse in a stand of cottonwoods. They pulled up at the place where the others had tied their animals, dismounted, and tied off their own. They couldn't see anyone, but they heard voices. As they followed the sound, Hugo called out, "Sheriff, where are you?"

Gardner shouted back, "Come to the river. We're downstream a ways."

Billy and Hugo stepped through the brush and on to a grassy area that ran between the trees and the river. They spotted the rail-thin sheriff and the three-hundred-pound undertaker thirty yards away. Their backs were toward Billy and Hugo, and the two men stood looking toward something at their feet.

"What're you fellas lookin' at there?" asked Hugo.

Both men turned without answering and stepped aside as the boys walked up. When they did, Billy let out a gasp and turned his head away. Even Hugo, who had seen about every bad thing a man could imagine, winced. "Good Lord," he whispered. Then louder he added, "I see why Norm Carson about tossed it on your office floor, Sheriff."

The body of a disemboweled man lay with his feet lashed to stakes in the ground. His hands were cuffed behind his back. The flies were thick.

"We haven't touched anything," said the sheriff, "except to take off the blanket Norm covered him with. I guess some animals got to him in the night, and vultures were circling when Norm found the body. Mr.

Teasdale got here a little before you fellas." The sheriff looked pale and his eyes big. "This is my first time with something like this, and I wanted to wait to do anything 'til more experienced hands arrived."

"You did right, Skip," Hugo said.

Billy, who had stepped to the river and taken in a couple of deep breaths, returned to where the other men stood and again looked at what had been found.

"How old do you figure this fella to be, Barney?" asked Hugo. "Thirty-five or so?"

Barnett Teasdale, who was the one man in this part of Wyoming who had seen more dead bodies than Hugo, nodded. "Yes, I suppose." He bent lower and pulled his spectacles onto the tip of his nose. "There looks to be some gray streaks in his hair, though, so maybe a bit older."

The dead man's black hair was bloodied and matted, so the gray streaks were hard to see, but Billy could tell Mr. Teasdale was right.

"How long do you figure he's been dead?"

"Twenty-four hours, I'd say. Maybe a little less."

In addition to the evisceration, the body bore multiple knife wounds — dozens of slices across his face, shoulders, chest, and belly. Some were superficial. Some went to the bone. One eye had been plucked from its socket and the ears had been cut off. To Billy, in a way, what was the most horrific was that neither the ears nor the eye were anywhere around. Billy guessed the night scavengers had gotten them.

"It doesn't look like any of those knife wounds would've killed him," said Mr. Teasdale.

Hugo took off his hat and ran his fingers through his hair. "Which means," he said, "the fella was alive when he got opened up."

Teasdale swallowed and said, "Yes, I expect he was." His voice was raspy. He cleared his throat and spit, but it didn't appear his dry mouth could produce much spittle.

"Sweet Jesus," said Gardner, "who around here could be capable of such a thing?"

No one answered.

As with Billy earlier, the sheriff stepped toward the river and sucked in a couple of deep breaths. He looked back over his shoulder and said, "The poor fella was tortured."

"That's for damned sure," agreed Billy.

"There's just two reasons to torture a man," Hugo said. "Either for information or sport."

"The cuts look to have been done in a

methodical way," said Teasdale. "Which makes me think the killer did it for information."

Hugo nodded. "I'm thinkin' he did it for both."

The sheriff rejoined them. He had a tad more color in his ashen complexion than he'd had before he stepped away. "Have any of you fellas seen this man before?"

They all answered no.

Hugo pointed to the remains of a fire. "He'd made camp. I doubt he was from around here."

"Why would he camp so close to town?" asked Billy. "Why not ride on in and get a room? Look at his boots." He pointed to a pile of clothing lying in a heap ten feet away. "It doesn't look like he needed to save money." The boots next to the dead man's clothes were of a high quality and close to new. The dead man had been no saddle tramp or pauper.

On the far side of the fire, part of a bedroll was laid out. The blanket Norm Carson used to cover the body had no doubt come from there. Hugo shrugged. "The summer evenin's've been nice," he said. "This place right here by the river made for a topnotch camp site. Why go into town when you got somethin' like this? There's lots-a water and grass for his horse. To me it looks to be a better place than some stuffy ol' hotel room. Maybe this fella felt the same."

Hugo walked to the clothing. "You haven't looked at this stuff yet, Skip?"

"I looked, but I didn't go through them or move them around any. Like I said, I was waiting."

Waiting for Hugo, Billy thought. Which, he had to admit, made sense. Skip Gardner was not yet thirty, and, though smart and capable, he was green.

"Well, let's see what we got here," said Hugo as he squatted next to the clothes. He picked up a boot, turned it over, and stuck a hand inside. Finding nothing, he put it down and did the same with the other boot. He found nothing there, either, and he set it aside as well.

He lifted the shirt. "It looks like this was cut off 'im," he said as he held it up for the others to see. "Same with the trousers." Hugo rummaged through the pants pockets and pulled out some cash. " 'Bout twelve dollars in paper and silver."

"Must not've been a robbery, then," said Sheriff Gardner.

"No, a robber might shoot a man down, but I doubt he'd take the time to do what this killer did."

Next, Hugo lifted a narrow-brimmed hat from the pile. The hat was dusty but otherwise in good shape. Better shape than Billy's and far better than Hugo's old sweat-stained Stetson. Hugo turned the hat over, and, after running his finger around the inside of the sweatband, he tossed it back on the pile.

There were a couple of large saddlebags next to the bed roll. Hugo crossed to them and dropped to one knee. The others followed him over. He opened a bag and dumped its contents onto the bedroll. There were three pairs of socks, a bar of pumice soap wrapped in waxed paper, and a razor.

He opened the other bag, and said, "Nothin' in here but a bunch of dirty clothes. Like we said, it doesn't look like the killer was lookin' to steal anythin'; but, even if he was, I doubt these bags ever held much worth stealin'."

Digging into the bag with the dirty clothes, Hugo pulled out two shirts, a couple of pairs of BVDs, two pairs of dingy trousers — one canvas, the other denim — and a striped woolen vest with what looked to be a coffee stain down its front. Hugo held up the shirts, took a look at them, and dropped them onto the bedroll. The canvas pants had no pockets, but the denims did. Hugo searched them, found them empty, and dropped them as well. The vest bore two slit pockets, one on either side. He stuck an index finger and thumb into the pocket on the right. When he found nothing, he checked the left-side pocket and retrieved a folded piece of paper.

"What do you have there?" asked Billy.

"Well, let's see." Hugo unfolded the paper. "It's a copy of a telegram sent from the Probity Western Union."

The sheriff asked, "What does it say?"

"Not much. It looks to be a list of expenses."

The sheriff stepped around the bedroll and stood behind Hugo. "Who to?" he asked.

"Well, sir, it's to the St. Louis office of the Pinkerton Detective Agency." Raising his eyes to Billy, he added, "And the fella who sent it was an agent by the name of Dub Warren."

Chapter Ten: The Go-Ahead

Billy, Hugo, and the sheriff searched the area around the campsite and into the trees for anything else of interest, but they found nothing that would shed any light on things.

They did determine that the killer had stolen something — the horse Agent Warren would have been riding and maybe a pack horse as well. *Also,* thought Billy, *the killer had stolen the Pinkerton's badge.*

They helped Barnett Teasdale load the body into the hearse. The dead man's hands had been manacled using his own handcuffs, but no key could be located. Mr. Teasdale said he'd get a local blacksmith to cut the cuffs off. Which, to Billy's thinking, would be a difficult and gruesome task.

Once the body was loaded, the sheriff said he would wire the Pinkerton office in St. Louis and let them know what had happened and make arrangements to get their agent home.

"If you'll give us the go-ahead, me and Bill'll get to the clinic *pronto* and have a visit with the *other* Agent Warren."

"Thanks." Gardner checked his watch. "I was supposed to ride to the Poison Spider first thing this morning."

"The rustling's bad out there, I hear," Billy said.

"It's not only out there. They hit the Henshaw place up north a couple of days ago, and then last night they got Brewster down south. Cal came to my house about midnight raising all kinds of hell. I fear if I don't make some headway on this thing, these men are going to form an old-fashioned vigilance committee and start hanging folks to send a message."

"While Dale Jarrod was in office," said Hugo, "there wasn't much sheriffin' goin' on around here, and things got pretty wild. It's gonna take a while to get the place under control, but I expect you're up for the job, Skip."

"Well, I guess we'll see, won't we?" He didn't sound too sure.

"Me and Billy'll look into this mess here." He nodded toward the hearse and the dead man in it.

"When I first took office, I went to the county commissioners and asked to hire a deputy, but they wouldn't even consider the idea. So thanks, fellas. I could use all the help I can get."

The boys got to the clinic in half the time it had taken earlier to get to the Reshaw. They tied their reins around the rail and rushed inside. Not seeing either the doc or Abigail, they headed straight to the fake Agent Dub Warren's room.

"If he's sleepin'," said Hugo, with a hint of a smile, "let me be the one to wake 'im up."

Billy guessed the man was about to receive a rude awakening, but, when they opened the door, they saw the room was empty, and the sheets had been taken from the bed.

As they shared a confused expression, they heard someone coming down the hall and turned to see Dr. Waters. He wore a heavy look of concern. "Agent Warren," he said, "is gone."

"Gone?" asked Billy. "Did you tell him he could leave?"

"Nope," said the doc. "He didn't ask. While you boys were talking to him, Abbie and I went to the residence to have breakfast. When we came back into the clinic, we saw he'd taken his clothes, boots, and gunbelt from the wardrobe where Abbie had stored them. Looks like he got dressed and left. Before he did, though, he took three vials of laudanum out of the cabinet in my private office. I had five vials in there. He left two, which I thought was curious. I don't mind telling you, I find Agent Warren to be a strange one. Another thing he did was leave two double eagles on my desk with a note that read 'for services rendered, plus interest.' Forty dollars is a third more than he owed."

"Hummph," grunted Hugo. "An honest liar, thief, and murderer. My, my." Hugo headed for the front door.

The doc looked to Billy. "Murderer?"

"It's a long story," said Billy, following Hugo. "We'll fill you in another time."

"What d'ya figure we're looking at here, Hugo?" Billy asked.

"I'm thinkin' we must've been right, that the fella Kradec shot is the killer, Elijah Thorn. What was done by the river was bad — vicious bad. And that's pretty much the way Kradec described Thorn. Our fake Pinkerton knew things he could've learned nowhere but from the real Pinkerton. So, it stands to reason that our fake is the one who did the killin'."

Billy agreed. "He did know things only

the Pinkerton would have known, like that the Pinkerton was after the violin. And he knew how Kradec went about stealing the violin back in St. Louis."

"And the man we talked to would have no reason to make that stuff up. I figure it had to be the truth, considerin' the way he got the information."

"Also," Billy added, "he knew Warren's name, and he ended up with the man's badge."

"That's right. He's got the badge. That's pretty good evidence, I'd say."

"But why would he kill the Pinkerton? What did he have to gain? And why torture the man?"

"Like we said. Tortured 'im for sport and information. I expect he wanted to find out what the Pinkerton knew about Kradec and if he knew where Kradec was headed. Also, he might've figured he was gettin' close to his prey, and he didn't want the Pinkerton gettin' in his way."

"So, the fake Pinkerton murdered the real one yesterday before he came to my place looking for Kradec."

"Yes," agreed Hugo. "But when he left the Reshaw, first he came back to town."

"Right, at about the time we met Kradec."

"Had to've been, since he said he talked

to Earl Whitson and Evelyn What's-his-name. That's how he knew Kradec was with us."

Billy looked down at his boots and rubbed the back of his neck. "It's hard to picture the man I brought to the clinic last night and the man we talked to this morning doing what we saw at Reshaw Bridge."

"Maybe," allowed Hugo, but he didn't sound convinced. Billy knew the old deputy had stopped being surprised by a deceitful world long ago.

Hugo stepped off the clinic porch, untied his reins, and climbed aboard his bay. "Our man'll know we'll be lookin' for him, so if he's able to travel, he'll be gettin' out of town — maybe even headin' to the Sweetwater."

"I might be wrong, but I don't think he knew where Kradec's sister's place was when we talked to him this morning. So either the Pinkerton didn't know where Kradec was headed, or, even with the torture, he refused to tell. I was the one who provided the killer with that tasty morsel of information." Billy had been chastising himself for that fool's blunder ever since they left the Reshaw.

"Don't feel bad. If that Pinkerton knew where the sister's place is, he told. He might've even known the part about askin' Tom Sun for the particulars on where she might be stayin'. If he did, he told that, too."

"Maybe." Even if the Pinkerton did tell, it didn't change anything. Billy had not hesitated to hand out the information, and he couldn't keep from feeling bad about it.

"Do you think he'd be able to travel after getting shot and having the doc dig around inside him a mere few short hours ago?"

"He looks to be a tough one, and if he slurps down enough of that smiley juice, maybe he could at least get out of town and hole up for a while."

"But he didn't have a horse," said Billy. "Although he must've had one when he came out to my place last night."

"It'd be a long walk, if he didn't."

"Yet last night when you and I went back to the ranch looking for Kradec, we didn't see any unfamiliar horse trotting around."

"Kradec must've taken it and put the boy on the mule."

"So Mr. Thorn's afoot, which means if he wants to get out of town, he'd have to go to the livery to either buy a horse, rent one, or pick up one he'd boarded earlier."

"He could steal one," said Hugo. "But I doubt he'd want to draw any more attention to himself than gettin' shot and killin' a man has already done."

"So that leaves the livery." Billy stepped over to Badger and slipped a foot into his stirrup. "Let's get to the White Star and have a word with Thirsty Joe."

Chapter Eleven: Thirsty Joe Was a Stickler

The White Star was a large, busy operation that sat on the corner of Second and David streets and took up most of the block. The retail portion of the business was conducted in the main building, where they sold feed, seed, tack, and tools. Out back was a large barn and stables, a couple of work sheds, a blacksmith shop, privy, and two corrals. At one time, there had been a small one-room shack behind the place, but it burned to the ground the previous winter. Had it not been for the speedy response of the volunteers and their John Rogers Pumper, the whole business might have been lost and maybe a good portion of Casper, as well. Young towns made of wood were easy prey for fast-moving fires.

The boys found Thirsty Joe raking out a stall.

"Mornin', Thirsty," called out Hugo as they approached. "How's the horse rentin' and sellin' business?"

"Business is booming," said Thirsty with a wide smile. Thirsty had quite a few teeth, but he could no longer boast of having them all.

Thirsty Joe Thorp was in his mid- to late twenties but looked a couple of decades older. He didn't come by the moniker of Thirsty due to a fondness for tea, sarsaparilla, or water. He was a drunkard in the first degree. Billy and Hugo had seen him earlier when they'd picked up the horses for their ride to the Reshaw, but they'd not taken time for convivialities.

"Boomin', eh. That's good to hear." Hugo had pre-rolled two or three smokes while they were at breakfast, and he pulled one from his tobacco pouch.

Before he could light up, Thirsty said, "Mr. Parker doesn't allow smoking on the premises anymore." Theo Parker owned the White Star.

"Is that so? Why ever not?"

"It's been that way since the big fire last year. He says one fire's enough for him."

Billy and Hugo had witnessed the fire themselves, and it had been quite the conflagration.

"Well," said Hugo, "I guess I can see his reasoning, sort-a. Though I'm sure that not once in my life have I ever set fire to anythin' with a shuck nor the match I used to light it with."

"That's the rule," said Thirsty in an authoritative tone. In the stables, Thirsty Joe was a stickler for the rules.

Competition for town drunk was stiff in Casper, but Thirsty was successfully moving up the ladder. Even so, he was a good employee. He would not drink during business hours, and Mr. Parker maintained that Thirsty had not once been late in the eight years he'd worked there. With a frown, Hugo returned the cigarette to his pouch but stuck the match he'd dug from a vest pocket into his mouth.

"We're lookin' for a fella, Thirsty, and we figure he might've stopped in here sometime this mornin'."

"Lots of fellas stop in here, Hugo."

"This fella would-a been wantin' a horse."

"Let me get this straight. You're looking for someone who came into the livery for a horse?"

"That's right."

"Well, sir, that sure narrows it down, doesn't it?" Though a likeable man, Thirsty was capable of showing a nasty streak.

Billy hiked up his gunbelt and lifted his watch from his watch pocket. Checking the time, he said, "We're guessing he came in here three, maybe even four hours ago. He would've been wanting to either rent or buy a horse."

Thirsty shrugged. "What's he look like?"

"He's a shifty-eyed fella," said Hugo.

"He's about your size," Billy said, before Hugo could elaborate. "He has blond hair and a mustache. I expect he'd be wearing a bowler, a dark-red shirt, and a corduroy vest."

"Sure, I saw him. He was in this morning a half hour, forty-five minutes before you boys came in the first time."

Hugo perked up. "Zat so?"

"Yes, sir, and, you know, it's strange. Yesterday was the first time I'd ever seen that man, yet he's been in three times now."

"How come?" asked Billy.

"Yesterday morning, he wanted to rent a horse. Said he'd arrived by train the night before, and he needed to meet a fella on the river somewhere out of town. He was nice enough, even if he was a stranger." Thirsty had lived in the area most of his life and was slow to warm to outsiders.

"Did he say who he was meetin'?"

"Nope. What he said was he needed to meet a fella, and he didn't want to walk to do it."

"Did he say where the meeting was supposed to be?" asked Billy. "Maybe out at the site of the old Reshaw Bridge, perchance?"

"The Reshaw? Nah, he didn't say where he was meeting him, just on the river somewhere out east."

"So he came in three times?"

"That's right. Three times." Thirsty's brow furrowed. "What's this about? You boys looking to arrest this man?"

"We're after 'im, Thirsty, for our own purposes," said Hugo. "We might arrest 'im, we might shoot 'im, we might buy 'im supper and a beer."

"Hell, if those're his choices, I expect he'll go for the supper and beer. I know I would."

The three shared a quick chuckle, and Billy asked, "So what did he want those times he's been in?"

"Like I said, he came in yesterday morning to rent a horse. Then later, he came back riding our horse, and he was leading two other horses as well. One was a real beauty. A sorrel with three white stockings decked out in a fine-looking saddle. The other horse looked to be one used for a spare or maybe for packing, though she wasn't carrying packs at the time."

"Where'd he get 'em?" asked Hugo. "Did

he say?"

"He did not. I assumed he'd struck a deal for them with whoever he met at the river. We settled up on the rental. He paid for two days in advance to board the spare. Then he rode off on that nice saddle horse."

"And," Billy said, "that was the last time you saw him before this morning?"

"Right. That was strange, too. Today he came in on foot. And you're right, Hugo. This morning he was a little shifty-eyed. He looked to be sick. I asked why he was walking and what happened to that handsome sorrel he'd ridden off on, but he didn't give me an answer. All he said was he wanted to apply the cost of the day's board that he'd already paid for but hadn't used to the price of tack for the horse he'd boarded. Then he walked to that pail over yonder" — Thirsty nodded toward a large galvanized bucket in the corner — "turned it over and plopped down on it. He waited for me to find a saddle that'd suit him. Once I did, I ran the numbers on what he owed, and he paid up. After that, I saddled the horse, and he left."

"Did he give you any hint where he might be headed?" asked Hugo.

"Nope. He just thanked me, gigged his mount, and headed out David Street here. But, I'm telling you, fellas, the man did not look good when he left. I had to give him a hand climbing onto his horse. You boys have any idea what's wrong with him?"

"He's been shot," answered Hugo.

"The hell you say."

"That's right. Shot in the back."

"I'll be. I guess considering he'd been shot, he didn't look so bad." Thirsty jammed his left little finger into his ear and dug around. Inspecting whatever it was he pulled out, he said, "If that's all you fellas need, I gotta get to work," and he turned and walked away.

The boys called out their thanks, but, if Thirsty heard them, he didn't let on.

Before the boys made it to their horses, Billy said, "I worry about ol' Thirsty."

"Why's that?"

"I expect the way he drinks, by-and-by, he'll come to poor health and a hard demise."

"I'm sure you're right, and it's too bad; he's a smart fella. Spent a couple-a years down in Laramie goin' to school."

"I heard that. Studied mathematics, of all things. Got himself kicked out, though, because, after getting drunk every night, he couldn't make it to his morning classes."

"That's all right. Gettin' kicked out taught 'im the painful but true lesson that, no matter how bad the hangover, come the harsh light of day, a fella's still got responsibilities. Which is good. I've known lots-a folks who've spent a full four years in that Laramie college without learnin' a thing."

Chapter Twelve: No Time to Dawdle

They left the White Star and decided to go on the hunt for Elijah Thorn before he could commit another heinous crime. On the way, they stopped at Hugo's room. He shoved a few things into a saddlebag and attached a sheath holding a knife with a sharp, six-inch blade onto the left side of his gunbelt.

"What're you going to do with that thing?" Billy asked.

"Hell, boy, we're goin' into the wilds of Wyomin'. It's impossible to know when you might have to stick a frog or skin a rabbit for your supper. It could be a matter of life or death. Eatin' or starvin'."

"God, I hope it doesn't come to that."

"I might even teach you how to play mumblety-peg just to pass the time."

"Speaking of eating, have you got any food in here?" Billy knew the answer before he asked the question.

"Now why would I keep food in my room as long as they got a pickle jar at the Half-Moon?"

"C'mon," said Billy. "Let's get to my place so we can stock up for the trip."

As they rode through the gate at the Young Ranch, Billy pointed to a strong black mare in the east pasture. "She's a solid one and makes for a fine pack horse. I've used her before. You fetch her while I gather the pack saddle and gear." Billy knew the mare was easy to catch, which was a good thing considering Hugo's poor skills as a wrangler.

Once the mare was saddled and loaded, they mounted to leave. "You got any whiskey?" asked Hugo. "I hate to start a journey without whiskey."

"Nope, Kradec took the last of it. Don't you have a bottle in your bag?" Billy could not remember a time when Hugo's right-side saddlebag was without a supply of Kentucky.

"I do, but she's mighty low." He dug into the bag and came out with a bottle that contained a couple of fingers of amber liquid. He pulled the cork and tossed the bottle back, finishing it off.

"You're not much for sharing, are you?"

"I would've, Billy-boy," Hugo said with a smile, "but I figure with your genteel upbringin' you'd rather not drink this early in the day." Leaning over in his saddle, he set the empty bottle on the front porch. "You can toss that dead soldier in your trash pit behind the barn after we get back." He jerked a thumb toward the south. "Now let's getta goin'. We gotta catch us a vile Nebraskan torturer. There ain't no time to dawdle."

Billy knew in Hugo's younger days he had often hunted game for survival. Things in the state now were bustling — off and on, anyhow — but when Hugo first pinned on his star the times were different. A half-dozen cities and towns had popped up in the south, along the Union Pacific line, but up here in the eastern, central, and western frontiers of Wyoming Territory there had been little more than an ocean of prairie grass and tall, foreboding mountains. There were, however, the large, open-range ranches, and a few of their owners over the years had gotten together and set up communities here and there. The more established of these small settlements were most often made up of nothing more than a church and a trading post. Maybe a school. And the few that survived had been separated by many days in the saddle. The dance halls, rowdy saloons, hotels, and cafes that

Hugo now enjoyed had been scarce back then, and the young deputy was often forced to live off what game he could kill.

These days Hugo was fond of saying, "Since we're surrounded by prime Wyomin' beef, it's a mystery to me why anybody'd wanna go on an antelope or deer hunt."

The idea of going on a *man* hunt, though, set Hugo's eyes to sparkling.

"It's a fine day, Billy," said Hugo as they rode along the western side of the North Platte River on what pretended to be a trail. The trail's markings were vague, but every now and then they could spot some wagon-wheel ruts from the thousands of prairie schooners that had passed this way after crossing John Baptiste Richard's excellent bridge. Looking up at the broad dome of clear, blue sky, Hugo repeated, "Yes, sir, she's a fine day, indeed." He brought his gaze down to Billy, who was riding on Hugo's left. "And," he added, "it also promises to be a warm night. Which is good news for two fellas who'll be sleepin' beneath the stars."

Billy felt good, too. Hugo was right. The day was fine, and Billy was glad to get out of town and on with the search for Elijah Thorn. A man who was capable of doing what had been done to the Pinkerton by the river needed to be shot or hanged as soon as possible. Any time that passed while that man continued to breathe was time poorly spent.

"What d'ya think, Hugo? Should we shoot that bastard as soon as we lay eyes on him, or should we haul him in for trial?"

Hugo made a couple of quick wraps of his reins around his saddle horn and shook some tobacco into the trough of a rolling paper. He put away his makings, folded the paper over, gave it a lick, and popped the cigarette into his mouth. "I've been ponderin' that problem myself, Billy," he said as he dug for a match. "The way things stand now" — he struck the match on the butt plate of the Winchester sticking from his scabbard — "I'm leaning toward shootin' 'im right off." He lit his smoke and unwrapped his reins. "What's your stand on it?"

Billy's usual thinking was, if possible, to take any outlaw they caught in for trial. This was America. And America was a nation of laws. In America men had rights. But Billy was not a fanatic about it, and his position was flexible. "With this one," he said, "maybe we should just go ahead and shoot him first thing."

"Problem solved," said Hugo.

■ ■ ■ ■

As they rode, Billy kept an eye peeled for any place Thorn might choose to hole up. Billy agreed with Thirsty. Thorn could not have gotten far, not on the first day or so, anyway.

"How well do you know this area, Hugo?"

"Not much. As a rule, the marshalin' profession requires dealin' with human bein's, and there ain't many of 'em out here. Now, if I ever have call to serve a writ or warrant on a raccoon or prairie dog, why, sir, this'll be the first place I look."

"I wonder if there's any old abandoned structures around. That would be the sort of thing Thorn would look for. He'd want to get out of this sun as soon as he could." Billy glanced at the greenish-gray flow of the Platte. "And he'd want to stay close to the water."

"There ain't much out here. I suppose it's possible we could run onto a picket shack or a soddy, but I doubt it. If you're thinkin' we're gonna catch up to that fella, it won't happen."

"How come?"

"If he's hurtin' as bad as we think he is, then you're right: he'll be goin' to ground.

But look around, Billy-boy. There's a damn lotta ground out here. The odds of us comin' across his hidey-hole are pretty slim. And if he ain't hurt as bad as we figure — which I doubt — but if he ain't, and he's able to ride much at all, then he's got enough of a head start on us that it's doubtful we could run 'im down."

Billy looked out at the thick stands of cottonwoods and tall green grass that grew along the banks of the river. Beyond this lushness was a vast stretch of yellow nothingness that reached to the faraway sky. He suspected Hugo was right.

"No," said Hugo, taking a draw on his cigarette and allowing the smoke to leak out as he spoke, "our best bet is to go on to Tom Sun's headquarters at Devil's Gate and see if Thorn did what we told 'im to. If he stopped there and checked on the location of the little shirttail spread belongin' to Kradec's sister, they'll let us know, and we can hope we get there before the killin' starts. If we beat Thorn to the Sun place, then that's good. We can get to the sister's and wait for the son of a bitch to come to us."

"True," agreed Billy. "And Ivan Kradec and Abraham should already be at his sister's. Once we get there, we can decide what we want to do with him."

"Now that we know what the back-shot fella is capable of, I'm not as offended as I was earlier by Kradec's poor behavior. And I don't see much need to take 'im in on a charge of attempted murder. Of course, it wouldn't hurt to beat the ever-lovin' dog shit outta the little weasel for bein' such a coward."

Billy smiled. Hugo had no patience when it came to cowards.

Chapter Thirteen: A Special Sort of Madman

They made camp an hour before dark at a fine spot along the river. Having a pack horse was a luxury. It allowed them to bring along items they otherwise could not.

"What do you want to do, Hugo, open some cans or build a fire? Your choice."

"It's my opinion the chore of wood gatherin' and fire buildin' should fall to the *junior* deputy."

"I figured as much," said Billy. He pointed to a spot next to a cottonwood where they had placed their saddles and stacked their gear. "There are some canned goods in the larger of those two gunnysacks."

"Canned goods? My, my. What'd you bring us, Billy?"

"I'm not sure. I grabbed some things real quick, but I expect there's a few cans of beans, corned beef, maybe some peas. In the smaller sack, there's some fresh tomatoes and two or three ears of corn. I pulled them from the garden while you were fetching Mabel." He nodded toward the large, black horse munching grass with the other two.

"Holy fire, boy. We'll be havin' us a feast. How 'bout dessert? Did you bake an apple pie or whip up a batch of butter cookies with yella icin'?"

"I did not."

"Damn," said Hugo, "what good are you?" He provided Billy with a smile.

"Take a look in the sack. You'll find a can or two of peaches." Billy knew the old coot was fond of peaches. Maybe not as fond as he was of apple pie or butter cookies, but he had a particular liking for the thick, sweet syrup the peaches were packed in. Billy had made sure to stick a couple of cans in the bag.

Dead fall in the cottonwoods was easy to locate, and Billy had a fire built and supper heated in short order. Once they'd finished their beans, corned beef, and sweet corn, they ate a couple of tomatoes — biting into them like they were apples. For their treat, they shared a can of peaches, although Hugo took more than his share. Each man rinsed his own tin plate and spoon and set them aside to be used again at breakfast, which would be two-day-old biscuits, honey, and jerky. Not a feast, but quick and easy.

While Hugo drank another cup of coffee and smoked a cigarette, Billy caught a few grasshoppers for bait and tied a piece of line and a hook to a stick. A boulder sat a few feet off the bank and rose above the waterline another couple of feet. The river's current lapped around on either side of it in gentle waves. Billy baited his hook with a squirming grasshopper and tossed the line into the calm water on the rock's downstream side. He leaned back in the grass and watched the grasshopper do a frantic dance on the water's surface.

"Maybe you should-a tried to catch us a fish before supper."

"Why? Are you still hungry, Hugo?"

"Nope not a bit. If I eat another bite, I might pop like a toy balloon."

Billy smiled. "A toy balloon, huh?" He doubted Hugo had ever seen a toy balloon. "Don't worry about popping. I'm fishing for sport, not eating. Should I happen to catch us a trout, even if he's a fat one, I'll toss him back."

The warmth of the summer day lingered, and, though they both sat near the fire, they had allowed the flames to burn down, and the gray embers produced little heat.

The grasshopper continued to kick, but

his movements had slowed, which was too bad. Billy had hoped the hopper's energetic water dance would attract a big fish.

They sat in silence — Hugo smoking and Billy watching his line. Their comfortable camp and full bellies had brought a lull to the conversation, but after a while Billy broke the silence. "Have you ever seen anything like we saw at Reshaw Bridge this morning?" He expected he knew the answer but asked the question anyway.

"I have." Hugo turned away and squinted across the prairie. He was either looking through the waning light at the climbing moon or through the distant years at horrors Billy cared not to imagine. "More than a few times," Hugo added.

Billy recalled the first time he'd gutted a deer. He was eight and was with his father and older brother. Many times, he had watched the butchering of cattle and hogs, though he had not done it himself. And he'd been on hunts and seen antelope, deer, elk, and one time an enormous moose being field dressed, but that small buck that lay at his feet was the first one he'd killed himself.

"You brought him down with a fine shot," his father had said. "It's as good a first kill as any boy ever made."

Billy didn't say anything. He was transfixed by the buck's glassy stare.

"Here." His father handed Billy a skinning knife. "He's your kill, son, and he's yours to tend to."

When Billy slit the deer's belly and watched the red, shiny viscera roll out, the only things that allowed him to stem his rising gorge were the scrutiny of his father and what he knew would be the endless taunting by his elder brother. Since then he'd cleaned untold numbers of animals of every sort, but the sight at the Reshaw of the gutted corpse of a human had brought back those queasy childhood memories.

"It'd take a special sort of madman to do what Thorn did to the Pinkerton," said Billy.

When Hugo didn't respond, Billy glanced up and noticed that the old deputy still stared out into the dusk.

After a bit, Hugo cleared his throat, and said in a hoarse voice, "Damn, I wish we'd brought some whiskey."

A trout rose and nudged the grasshopper. The fish considered it for a second, but then, without taking the bait, he turned and swam away. In one of those strange ways of judging luck, this could be counted as the hopper's lucky day. Even though he was not long for this world, at least he had avoided becoming supper for a fish.

■ ■ ■ ■

They came to the confluence of the North Platte and Sweetwater Rivers by late morning, and, following the Sweetwater, they arrived at Independence Rock a little after noon. Once they'd tended to the horses, they picketed them in the trees and walked over to the long, tall monolith.

"Frank and I climbed to the top of this thing when we were boys," said Billy. "Frank had a fondness for climbing rocks."

"What did you find up there?"

Billy ran his fingers over one of the hundreds of names and dates that had been chiseled into the granite surface by the many pioneers who'd passed this way. "About what you see down here. Folks's names and the dates they cut them in. Frank also put our names and the date on the rock up top." Billy thought about that and added, "He had a fondness for chiseling our names, too. We found one spot where some fella had put his name, and the date he did it was in the month of September. I can't remember the exact year, but it was in the early '50s, as I recall."

"September, eh? That's late in the season to be passin'. If them pilgrims hadn't got here by the Fourth of July, they ran the risk of hittin' snows in the mountains."

"That's what Pa said, too. He figured if they came through as late as September, they were guaranteed to have a hard go of it in the high passes. I've often wondered whatever became of the man who carved his name on the top of this thing that September so long ago."

"I expect what happened to 'im was he ended up freezin' his balls off on the side of some mountain while strivin' to stay alive by eatin' his oxen."

"You always see the dark side of things, don't you, Hugo?"

"The truth can be harsh, Billy-boy. Instead of wastin' time chiselin' his name on a rock, that fella shoulda been makin' tracks. Which is what we should be doin', too. Let's get movin'. Tom Sun's headquarters is right on the other side of Devil's Gate."

Chapter Fourteen: A Man Who Enjoyed His Work

As they rode the trail along the east side of Devil's Gate, Billy asked, "How long do you figure it took the Sweetwater to cut through that granite over yonder, Hugo?"

"Couldn't say, but I expect the dinosaurs watched it happen."

"Maybe," said Billy. "Though the dinosaurs might've been gone before the river even started chiseling those rocks."

"I doubt it. I figure those big lizards ruled the roost around here for a mighty long time."

"I'm not sure. It could go either way, I suppose."

"All I know is the whole thing was before my time."

Billy waited a few seconds and said, "Just barely."

They followed the trail into the headquarters of the four-thousand-some-odd-acre

Sun ranch. The ranch's main house was located up from the river fifty yards or so, and maybe a quarter mile south of the narrow, steep, three-hundred-foot gorge that was Devil's Gate.

There were barns, corrals, and various outbuildings scattered about. The place bustled with activity, but it appeared most everyone's attention was focused on a man in a corral who had that moment been thrown from a pitching horse.

The boys dismounted, tied their reins to the crossbar of a weathered buck-and-rail fence, and walked to where the action was.

"What've you buckaroos got goin' here?" Hugo asked a lanky cowhand who was about as weathered as the buck-and-rail. "An afternoon rodeo?"

The man glanced at Hugo and spit a stream of tobacco juice into the dust before he spoke. "Nah," he said, "just watching the boss trying to teach a swap-ending bronco some manners."

"The boss, eh? Is that Tom Sun brushin' corral dust off his pants?"

"It is."

They watched as the man who had been thrown crossed to where a couple of riders who had caught the angry bronc were doing their best to keep him controlled. The man grabbed the saddle and shoved his boot into one of its oxbow stirrups.

"Looks like he's 'bout to climb aboard again."

The cowboy nodded. "I know the boss to be a forked rider, but he's done been tossed off that fire-breather twice. He said he'd keep at it, though, 'til the animal got bored."

"He don't look bored yet. How old is he?"

"You asking 'bout the horse or the boss?"

"The boss."

The man shrugged. "I ain't sure. Middle to late forties, I reckon."

"I figured a cattleman with a spread like this would keep a few frisky teenagers on hand to break the critters with wild eyes. Once a fella's past a certain age, the ground comes up mighty hard."

"There's some pups around who'd rather mount a jumper than eat ice cream, but when the boss takes a liking to a horse, and he plans to use it hisself, the boss is the one who does the breaking."

The man took another look at Hugo and Billy. "Who are you boys?"

Hugo pushed back his vest and showed his badge. "Name's Hugo Dorlin'. This here's my young friend, Billy. We're a couple of deputy marshals from Casper, and we're down here lookin' for some folks."

"What folks might that be?"

"A man and a woman. They have a small operation somewhere along the river."

"They got a name?"

"I'm sure they do," said Hugo. " 'Cept I don't happen to know what it is — not the man's, anyhow. The woman's name is Marlene. Her last name is Glatt, though it's possible she ain't goin' by that name anymore. They were livin' over in Nebraska before they came here. The man has land somewhere around the area, and I hear they're runnin' a small herd of cattle — *very* small, I expect. You know anybody like that?"

"Nah, but I'm new to this country myself," said the cowboy. "Name's Hank Teeters. I was working on a farm on the Wheatland Flats 'til right before roundup."

"Workin' on a farm, eh? So, did you decide you'd rather sit a horse than walk behind a plow?"

"That's about right. I've been punching cows most of my life. Lost count of the number of outfits I've rode for over the years, but I took a break from it and followed a widow woman up from Colorado a couple of years ago. Turned out I didn't get along with her any better than I did the plow. Being a slow learner, it took me a while to figure that out. After I did, I aimed myself west, crossed the Laramies, and ended up here." He spit another shot of his chew into the dirt.

"Why here, Hank?"

The cowboy shrugged. "I always figured when a fella ain't getting along where he is, he can never go wrong by heading west."

"That makes sense," said Hugo.

"And," continued Hank, "this place is as good as most of the good ones and better than plenty that aren't."

Billy agreed with what the cowboy said about heading west, but he got lost somewhere in the middle of the second part of the man's comment. Before Billy could parse it out, though, his attention turned to Tom Sun, who, for the third time, took a deep seat atop the bronco and told the men holding it to let 'im buck.

"Once the boss is done getting bounced around over there," Hank said, "you can ask him 'bout the folks you're looking for. I doubt there's anybody with cows anywhere near the Sweetwater, no matter how few they're running, that the boss don't know about."

Hugo thumped the front-underside of his hat brim and said, "Thank ya, sir. We'll do that."

"Be careful, though. The boss ain't fond

of lawmen. And you'd be well-advised not to mention the unpleasantries of four years past."

Hugo nodded. "Wouldn't think of it. Has nothin' to do with why we're here."

Billy didn't know many of the details, but he was acquainted with what the cowboy referenced. Back in '89, Mr. Sun and five other ranchers had been arrested by the Carbon County sheriff and accused of hanging a couple of rustlers by the names of James Averell and Ella Watson. Miss Watson was also known as Cattle Kate; at least she was after her death, if not before. Billy expected little would've been made of it had Averell dangled alone. Jim Averell was a small-time businessman who dabbled in various enterprises and was considered by many around the neighborhood as a high-binding scoundrel. But, because a woman was also hanged, the incident received considerable attention. No indictments were issued, but the hangings became a topic of conversation in the territory and had remained so for the past four years.

Hugo looked across the yard. A half-dozen watering troughs were scattered about. "Is it okay if we water our mounts while we wait?"

"Sure, help yourself. I figure it won't be

long before either that surly crockhead or the man on his back decides to surrender."

Billy and Hugo were about to leave to fetch their horses when a yell exploded from the hands watching the show, and the boys looked up in time to see the bronco swallow his head and pitch the boss toward the clouds. The cattleman flew like a bird until gravity caught hold; then, in short order, he hit the ground with a thud that could be heard from one end of the large corral to the other. A collective groan burst from the onlookers, but the boss hopped to his feet laughing and called out, "Damn, he is a salty bugger." The words came out, "Hee eess a saltee boogare." Billy had heard that Mr. Sun was born to a couple of French Canadians who had migrated to Vermont before his birth, so Sun was an American, but he didn't sound like one. Not exactly. Billy doubted he sounded exactly like a French Canadian, either, but Billy couldn't be sure. To his knowledge, he'd never known a Canadian, French or otherwise.

The horse continued to buck even after his rider hit the dirt. Sun laughed harder as he watched the poor luck the two men trying to catch the animal had as they made fruitless grabs at the flying hack reins. Tom

Sun looked to be a man who enjoyed his work.

Still laughing, the boss walked through the corral gate and tugged his long kerchief from his neck. He lifted his hat, blotted beads of shiny sweat from his forehead, and crossed to a trough. He dunked the kerchief into the water, and, it being a hot day, after wringing it out, he tied it back around his neck. A dozen hands milled about, but the boss, speaking to no one in particular, came out with another hearty laugh, shook his fist at the sky, and shouted, "Back to it, boys. By God, it is him or me." *Eet eess heem or me* is what it sounded like. The hands gave out a cheer when the boss started toward the corral for another go at the bucker, who still did not appear bored.

Hank Teeters jerked his head and said, "Come on. I'll take you to him." He led the boys across the yard and called out to the boss before he made it to the corral gate. "Mr. Sun, 'scuse me, but I got two fellas here who'd like to have a visit, if you could spare a minute. They're a couple of deputy marshals out of Casper."

Sun's first reaction was a smile, but it melted away when the cowboy mentioned they were deputies.

Hugo moved fast and extended his hand to shake. "We won't take much of your time, Mr. Sun. I'm Hugo Dorlin', and this young fella's name's Billy Young."

The cattleman shook their hands, but with reluctance, and his shake was curt.

"We're lookin' for a couple-a folks, a man and a woman. We believe they have of late started a small cattle operation on a piece-a ground the man has owned for some while. I don't know the man's name, but the woman's name is —"

"Marlene."

"Yes, sir, that's right. You must know 'em."

"I know of them." *Uff zeem* — though Mr. Sun's accent was less pronounced when not mixed with good nature and peals of laughter.

"We'd appreciate help in findin' 'em."

"Why?"

"We know their lives to be in danger."

"How?"

It appeared Mr. Sun was not eager to provide information to a couple of marshals. Billy had witnessed Hugo's reaction to such behavior before. It seldom went well for the person with-holding the information, but this time it would be interesting. Billy doubted Sun was a man quick to be intimidated, especially not on his own property surrounded by a yard full of hired men.

"How do we know their lives're in danger? Is that what you're askin'?"

Sun said nothing.

Hugo waited for a response a couple of beats longer than his usual willingness to wait. When still no answer came, Hugo moved in a step closer, found Sun's eyes, and said in an even voice, "We know it because we saw what little remained of a dead man who had the bad luck to cross paths with the man who's now after Marlene and her beau."

After taking a moment to ponder the situation, Sun said, "They're at the old Garvey ranch. They called the place New Hope. It's a bit east of Split Rock on the north side of the river."

"New Hope, eh?" asked Hugo.

"Some folks like to give their spreads a name. The story was that in his younger years, old man Garvey had tried his hand at quite a few business enterprises, and they were all failures. But he came out here and homesteaded that spot of land by Split Rock with high hopes of success."

"So Marlene's fella's name is Garvey?"

"It is. Seth Garvey. The Garveys did pretty well, too. They eventually picked up a couple of more quarter sections and were doing fine."

"So Garvey's family is livin' out there?"

"Not anymore, no. Once Seth hit a certain age, I guess he wanted to see the world. He left quite a while ago. A couple of years after that, the old man and his wife both caught an influenza, or some damned thing, and died. The place fell into pretty bad shape over the years. Folks around here stopped calling it New Hope and took to calling it Lost Hope. That turned out to be a name that caught on. The Garveys had a big sign on their gate reading 'New Hope Land and Livestock.' A tad pretentious, if you ask me. Anyhow, after a while, someone painted a line through the word 'New' and wrote in the word 'Lost' over the top of it. Some folks around thought that was pretty funny and figured I was the one who done it. But that wasn't true. I do admit that it's likely one of my young, smart-alecky cowboys had a hand it. They're always doing mischief of one kind or another. But the Garvey place ain't like that anymore. Since Seth came back with his woman, they've fixed it up real nice."

The cattleman did not sound altogether happy about Seth Garvey's return. Billy guessed before Garvey and Marlene started the place up again, that Mr. Sun had his eye on the land or at least had been putting cattle on its grass.

"Thank ya, Mr. Sun. You've been a big help, and Billy and me appreciate it." Hugo started to leave but stopped and turned back. "Oh, another thing. Did by chance a man and a young boy also stop here and ask for directions to the Garvey ranch? I figure if they did, it would-a been yesterday sometime."

"They didn't ask me," said Sun. "Could be they talked to one of the boys. Which direction would they be coming from?"

"Comin' from Casper."

"I had some fellas working out north yesterday. I suppose the man and boy could've spoke to them. Most of my hands know Seth Garvey's come back."

"Well, thank ya again, sir." Hugo smiled. "We'll be lettin' you return to smoothin' the edges on that rough horse in the corral yonder."

"Another man did ask directions to the Garvey place, but he wasn't with a boy."

"When was that?" asked Billy.

"Ain't sure. I didn't see him. I wasn't told about it 'til this morning. But I guess the man showed up late yesterday afternoon."

"And you're sure he didn't have a boy with him?" Hugo asked.

"He was alone, according to what I was told."

"Did he give his name?" Billy asked.

"No, not a name. He said he was searching for some thief called Cratchet or Kreychek or something like that." Then, in what appeared to be an afterthought, Sun added, "You know, now that I think on it, he did mention to my hand that he was with the Pinkertons."

Chapter Fifteen: Always Assume Evil Intent

Billy considered what they'd learned from Sun, and Hugo must have been thinking on it, too. Neither of them spoke until they were out of the ranch yard and riding in a westerly direction on the Sweetwater's north bank.

"Thorn," Billy said after a bit, "left Casper yesterday quite a while before we did, but it's hard to believe he could've gotten clear out to Tom Sun's place by the afternoon. Even late afternoon."

"Nope," agreed Hugo, "not even if he was in perfect health and ridin' the fastest horse in the county."

"So, Sun's cowboy who gave directions for the Garvey homestead was talking to somebody who was not Elijah Thorn."

"I guess it'd have to be. But who?"

"He said he was a Pinkerton. Could it be the late Dub Warren had a partner?" Billy reached into a drawstring poke that hung from his saddle horn and pulled out a piece of elk jerky. He tore it into two pieces and handed one to Hugo.

Hugo took a bite, and, as he chewed, he said, "It's possible he did, though it's hard to believe. And, if that's true, this partner was lucky to get away with his innards left where the good Lord stuck 'em."

Billy rubbed the back of his neck. He felt a headache coming on. "I guess a partner explains it. If he's out here, he has not stopped looking to arrest Kradec for the theft of a violin." Billy felt a cringe at the idea that Dub Warren died his terrible death while chasing a violin thief, no matter how much the violin was worth. "But," Billy added, "there being a partner doesn't feel right to me."

"How come?"

"Kradec's sister told him that Elijah Thorn was a tough, vicious man, but do you figure he could be so tough as to handle two Pinkertons, take his time killing one, and get away unscathed? Thorn looked pretty healthy to me right up to the second Ivan Kradec put a bullet in him. So even if Thorn got a jump on Warren and his partner, don't you figure, if the partner got away, he would do something while Thorn took his time cutting on Warren? At least shoot him from behind a tree."

"You'd think so, wouldn't you? But if it wasn't another Pinkerton, who could-a been askin' questions at Sun's yesterday?"

"It's puzzling," said Billy. "And another thing is, too."

"What?"

"According to Thirsty, Thorn said he arrived in Casper by train the night before he rented a horse."

"That's right. So?"

"So how did Thorn know the Pinkerton — or Pinkertons — were camped at the Reshaw? He couldn't have asked around Casper about it, because Warren and his partner, if he had one, hadn't even gotten to town yet. No one in town knew anything about a Pinkerton being anywhere near Casper."

Hugo's response to Billy's question was some sort of guttural emission followed by a long stretch of silence.

"I'll take that grunt you made," said Billy, "to mean you have no thoughts on the matter."

"My thinkin' on all of this, boy, is I *damn* sure wish we'd brought some whiskey."

A mile or so east of Split Rock Mountain, the boys came across four head of cattle along the river and a few more in the grass up higher.

"I expect these animals belong to Seth Garvey and Marlene."

Billy nodded. "We should be hitting their place soon." As he said it, they came over a rise, and, far down in a narrow valley, fifty yards north of the river, they saw a pine-log cabin. There were also a couple of corrals, a medium-sized barn, a shed, a springhouse, and an outhouse. The place appeared well tended, with everything in good repair. A tiny stream ran from beneath the stone foundation of the springhouse and meandered its way to the river. A log gate stood over a trail that led into the yard. The gate was about fifteen feet high and built of two log poles topped by a crossbar. "Use your glass and see if anybody's moving around down there."

Hugo reached into his left saddlebag and came out with the eight-inch-long felt sack he used to hold his telescope. He removed the scope and extended it to its full length. Aiming it toward the buildings in the valley, he said, "Can't see any humans. There are a few chickens struttin' about. There's a couple-a hooks hangin' from the crossbar on the gate."

"I bet those hooks once held a sign," said Billy.

"Most likely. I guess Seth Garvey didn't like it that somebody had renamed his ranch."

"I can't blame him."

"They've got three horses in the large corral."

Even without a spyglass, Billy could make out the horses. "No white mule, though."

"Nope. Looks like Kradec and the boy haven't got here yet."

That was good. Billy didn't like the idea of riding into the place and Kradec taking shots at them with the Winchester he stole from Billy's gun case. And since Billy doubted the man who spoke to Sun's cowboy yesterday was a Pinkerton, Billy didn't like the idea of riding down if Thorn was there, either.

"If Thorn has gotten here as fast as he might have, it'd be nice if you could spot him. I'd like to know what we're dealing with."

"Agreed." Hugo jerked a thumb to their left. "Let's get back to the river and stay in the cover of them trees for as long as we can before approachin' the house."

"Lead on."

They continued upstream and stopped a

hundred feet to the west of the cabin. From there, they could see the place's rear and southern side. The barn, with its open double doors, was in view, as well.

Hugo said, "Dismount and tie off the pack horse and your gray. Then take that Marlin in your saddle scabbard and get behind a tree."

"Why? What are you planning, you ol' buzzard?"

"I'm plannin' on ridin' to that cabin up yonder."

"Why can't I ride with you?"

"What time is it, Billy?"

"I don't know." Billy looked skyward but the trees blocked the sun. "You have a watch in your pocket. Why don't you check it, if you want to know what time it is?"

" 'Cause I don't care what time it is." Billy was about to say something sharp when Hugo added, "I do know it is the mid-afternoon of a summer's day, and I would think there'd be lots-a work goin' on 'round here."

"Maybe they're off somewhere moving cattle."

"Could be," said Hugo without conviction. "But what we heard at Sun's and what we're lookin' at now, I find to be bafflin'."

Billy couldn't argue with that. Something

about this didn't ring true. Although, whatever was wrong was too fuzzy for Billy to get a fix on.

"And," continued Hugo, "it's so bafflin' that we'd be wise to use extra caution. It doesn't look like anybody's here, but the only way to be sure is to go up there, and there's no need for both of us to get in the open before we know who might be in that cabin."

"Okay," agreed Billy. "Go on and have a look."

"There's one window on this side of the house. And its shutters are open. If you see a rifle barrel poke out of it as I ride up, you put one-a them forty-five-seventy Governments from your big-ass Marlin right through the middle-a that window."

"Without even knowing who's holding the rifle or if they have evil intent?"

"Always assume evil intent until you know different, Billy-boy. That's my motto. Now pick a tree and get behind it."

Unlike Hugo, Billy wasn't sure that always assuming evil intent was a good idea, but he had to admit, if a gun barrel came out of the window, that might be a good time to make the assumption.

Billy drew his Marlin and did as he was

told. Once he settled in, Hugo gigged his bay.

"Approach at an angle," said Billy, "so you don't block my view. The thought of shooting you is appealing, but I don't suppose now is the time."

As Hugo trotted his horse to the rear of the cabin, Billy watched for movement in the window, but everything was quiet. He guessed Hugo was also watching for movement coming from the barn, but things must have been quiet in that direction, too.

When Hugo made it to the back of the house, he dropped from his bay and allowed the reins to fall. He gave the horse's neck a pat and edged his way around the corner of the cabin. As he crept to the window, he drew his forty-four and peeled back the hammer. Once at the window, he took off his hat and peeked inside. After he studied the cabin's interior, he turned toward the trees and waved Billy up. Billy took the pack horse's reins and climbed onto the gray. As he rode toward the cabin, Hugo walked his horse to the front and wrapped his reins around the porch rail.

"We'll tie up here," said Hugo, "and check the rest of the place."

"Anything of interest in the cabin?" asked Billy.

"Nah, it's bein' lived in, but nobody's inside."

Hugo led the way past the smaller of the two corrals and into the shed. It contained nothing out of the ordinary.

They moved on to the springhouse and stepped into its cool darkness. Once their eyes adjusted to the dim light, they saw it held nothing but a smoked ham, a crock of butter, a few slabs of waxed cheese, and an antelope haunch.

From there they headed toward the barn, passing the large corral with the horses.

When they came to the barn, Hugo stepped to one side of the wide door, and Billy moved in behind him.

Again, Hugo took off his hat and peeked in. Billy doubted Hugo would see anything that posed a danger. Though they were moving about the small homestead's yard and buildings with stealth, if anyone was around, Billy expected they would know he and Hugo were there.

"There's enough light comin' in from the hayloft doors up top that I can see across to the far wall," whispered Hugo, "but there's plenty-a shadows off to the sides."

"Let's go on in, Hugo. If Garvey, Marlene, or some Pinkerton were around, they'd have shown themselves. And, if Thorn was lying in wait, he'd've taken a shot at us by now."

Hugo gave that some thought and nodded. "It won't hurt to go easy and quiet, though." He stepped through the door, and Billy followed.

Hugo had been right. They could see the barn's far wall, but the light was dim everywhere else. Hugo motioned for Billy to check the area to their right. He then pointed to himself and jerked his head to the left. Billy mouthed an "Okay," but, before he turned to go, he leaned toward Hugo's ear and whispered, "Let me have a couple of matches." Hugo dug three from his pocket and handed them over. Billy stuck the wooden stems between his front teeth and moved off to the right.

A round was in the Marlin's chamber, but Billy had lowered its hammer when no one appeared in the cabin's window. Now he thumbed the hammer back.

The stone-quiet barn was filled with the usual smells. Its dim light grew even dimmer as Billy moved farther in, but he could make out a few shadows. There looked to be a buckboard between a couple of stalls farther down the line. Forty feet from the double doors, he pulled a match from his mouth and, lifting his leg, struck it alight on the back of his thigh. The match flared, and he saw that the stalls held no animals. Except for the horses, chickens, and hordes of black, summer flies, the Garvey place was without life.

He had not yet made it to the last of the stalls when Hugo shouted from the other end of the barn.

"Billy, get down here! Now!"

Billy reversed his path and followed Hugo's voice, moving as fast as he dared in the gloom. His match had gone out, and, after a dozen steps, he pulled another from his mouth and fired it up. Its light allowed him to move a little faster, but the faster he moved, the more the flame flickered. When it went out, he continued on without bothering to light another — hoping he would not trip over something and break his neck. His luck held. He made it to the wall on the far left and saw a bright light. It came from Billy's right and from the other side of a tall stack of hay that had yet to be hoisted into the loft.

Billy followed the light, and, as he rounded the haystack, he saw Hugo holding a lantern that he must have found somewhere in the barn. The lantern's harsh light bleached the color from Hugo's ruddy face.

"Hugo, what the hell is —" Before he

could ask his question, Hugo raised the lantern and turned its light onto the wall behind him. When he did, Billy knew the lantern's light was not what had stolen Hugo's color.

Staring down at them with cloudy, vacant eyes were the bodies of a man and a woman. They hung on the wall like grotesque decorations.

Chapter Sixteen: The Cottonwood Trees Sure Were Nice

"Good God," said Billy once he'd found his voice.

"It must be Garvey and Marlene."

"Let's get them down, fast."

"They're long past savin', Billy."

"I know that. Let's get them down, anyway. Right now." Billy found the obscenity of this tableau a gross affront to . . . everything.

A wooden barrel sat off to the side a few feet away. Billy lifted its lid, saw the barrel was empty, and moved it closer to the man. He climbed onto the barrel and, as best he could, turned the man's upper body away from the wall in order to see what he was dealing with. Two large nails had been driven into the wall's thick planks. They were parallel to each other and four or five inches apart. The wooden handle of a ten-inch hay hook had been placed between the nails with the working end extending outward. The man had been impaled, and his body weight had forced the hook deep into his back. His shirt, his pants, and the floor were drenched in thick, viscous blood.

Billy wrapped his right arm across the man's chest and took hold of the hook's shaft with his left hand. He lifted, but the angle was awkward. "Give me some help, Hugo."

Hugo took hold of the man's bloody legs and said, "On three." He counted, and the two, working together, hefted the man down. Once they had him on the floor, Hugo turned away and, raising his arms, examined the gore on his hands and the sleeves of his shirt. "Let's get the woman down, then I'm gonna go to the river or find a well around here someplace and wash this away."

They took the woman down, but, before Hugo left to wash, Billy said, "Let's see if we can figure out what happened."

"Pretty clear, ain't it? These poor folks've been hung like ornaments on a Christmas tree."

"Were they alive when it happened? If they were alive, I'd think it would take at least two or three men to do the job. I doubt anyone would go peaceable onto a hook."

"I don't see any other wounds on 'em. Unless —" Hugo rolled the man over. The back of the man's hair was matted in blood. "Looks like this fella got hit on the head." He took a closer look at the injury. "Not hard enough to kill 'im but hard enough, I'd say, to knock him out."

Hugo looked toward a stall ten feet away. "And judgin' by those ropes wrapped around them two lower slats on the stall gate, I'd say after the killer knocked out the man, he tied the woman over there."

Billy nodded. "And kept her tied while he dealt with the man."

"That's the way I see it."

Turning his attention back to the man, Billy said, "So you figure he was unconscious but alive when he went on the hook?"

"I do."

"Mr. Sun said one man asked for the whereabouts of the Garvey place."

"Yep."

"If one man did this, he must have been strong. It took both of us to get them down."

"That's true," said Hugo, "but figurin' the killer used the barrel the same as you, once he climbed on it and lifted them up to the hook, gravity would-a lent a hand with the impalin'."

"I wonder if Garvey regained consciousness before he bled to death."

"I'd say he did."

"How do you know?"

Hugo pointed to the man's back. "See how the wound's tore and jagged around the edges? This fella struggled on that hook. So it looks like he was out when he went up, but he didn't stay out 'til he died."

Billy gave a shudder. "My God," he whispered.

"And look here," said Hugo. He rolled the woman over. "The same with her. The wound's tore up. The one difference between 'em is she hasn't been hit over the head."

"No, and she's a small woman."

"Yes, she is."

"Small enough," Billy said, "that the killer could have controlled her fighting him when he lifted her up."

"That's right," agreed Hugo. "So this little gal watched what the killer did to her man, and she was wide awake when the killer did the same to her."

Billy and Hugo located a pitcher pump on the north side of the cabin. It sat on a three-foot cast iron stand and was attached to a lead pipe that ran between the stand's legs and disappeared into the ground. A five-gallon galvanized bucket was beneath the pump's spout. The bucket held about a gallon of water, which Billy used for priming. Once he had the water flowing, he filled the bucket and handed it to Hugo. "Here," he said, nodding to Hugo's bloody hands and shirt, "you got it worse than me."

"Thanks." Hugo took off his shirt, tossed it aside, and washed his hands and upper arms. While Hugo did that, Billy pumped more water and washed his own hands.

When he was finished, Hugo tossed the pink water into the dirt, refilled the bucket, and washed his shirt. Wringing the shirt out, he left the shade of the cabin and crossed to a two-foot-wide stump behind the house. He draped the shirt over the stump and looked up at the clear sky. "The sun's beatin' down pretty hard," he said. "It'll dry my shirt in short order." With that, he pulled his knife from its sheath, dropped to the ground, and, sitting Indian style, began to scrape out whatever blood remained beneath his fingernails.

"You got it right last night, Billy, when you said we're dealin' with a special sort of crazy. I've chased my share of killers, and, like I said, I have seen some real horrors. But I have not seen the likes of what we have with this man. He is different."

Billy walked to where Hugo sat and knelt beside the old deputy. He squatted with his right knee on the ground, and his left leg bent in front of him. Resting a forearm on his thigh, he took off his hat and pushed back his floppy hair. The thought crossed his mind that he needed a haircut. Then, with a snort, he chastised himself for such a trite thought at a time like this. Such a thought was selfish and stupid. But after a bit he admitted that any thought, no matter how foolish or insignificant, that held at bay the thoughts and images fighting to get into his head was a welcome thought, indeed.

"I guess we know now Elijah Thorn, not some Pinkerton partner, stopped at Tom Sun's headquarters. Whoever did this has to be the same man who did what we saw at the Reshaw."

"I can't believe there could be two of 'em," Hugo said. "That kinda lunatic is a rarity."

"A few years ago, a fella on the back streets of London, England, was cutting women open."

Hugo looked up from his nails. His brow furrowed. "You don't say. Cuttin' women?"

"It's true. He cut up lots of them. From what I read, he did to them what we saw was done to Dub Warren."

"Well, god*damn* it, I hope them Englishmen caught that butcher and hanged him," shouted Hugo. "I hope they hanged that bastard high."

Billy didn't say anything. He didn't want to give Hugo the bad news. Instead, he turned toward the river.

It might have been a meaningless and foolish thing to notice, but the green cottonwood trees sure were nice this time of year.

Chapter Seventeen: I Hope You Can Spare a Minute

Billy found a couple of shovels in the shed, and they buried Garvey and Marlene next to a copse of evergreens on a rise overlooking the river.

"You ought to say a few words," said Billy, as they patted the last mounds of dirt onto the graves.

"A hopeless sinner like me is a poor choice for talkin' over a grave. Some folks've even hinted that I might be a heathen."

Hugo was understating it. He must have forgotten that one night at the Half-Moon, Billy had heard one of the girls call Hugo the devil. "You are the *devil!*" she had shouted. "You are Beelzebub himself." Billy assumed she'd added that last part so everyone would know she was a girl who knew her devils.

"You're lots of things, Hugo, but you are not a heathen. Besides, you should do the speaking because, in a way, words are your specialty. Of course, with you, it's more a matter of quantity than quality."

Any other time, Hugo might have taken offense at that comment and provided a quick retort, but now he appeared tired and forlorn. "Okay, but I'm gonna make it short."

"I think short would be fine."

"I figure we should do somethin' religious, though. What's that thing them Catholics do?"

"What do you mean?"

"You know, they touch their forehead and then move their hand around over their chest. I like the way they do that. It looks real respectful and reverent. I bet God likes it, too."

"I've seen them do it, but I don't know what it's called. And since we don't know the first thing about it, we shouldn't try it ourselves. If we do it wrong, it might bring bad luck to the deceased and us as well."

Hugo pondered that possibility. He nodded his agreement and shoved his hands into his pockets. After a bit, he cleared his throat and said, "Well, Lord, Hugo Dorlin' here. It's doubtful you remember me. I'm Eugenia Dorlin's son. I expect you've run across her up there from time to time. She's hard to miss. When she was on this side, she was quite the feisty little thing, but she was always as pious as an angel. I don't know what your thoughts are on Presbyterians, or any of them other Calvinists, for that matter, but if it makes any difference, I'd like you to know that she was a good one all the way from her birth to her passin'.

"I know it's been a while since you and me've visited, but I hope you can spare a minute. I'd like to talk to you 'bout these two poor, murdered souls. My friend Billy Young and me just now put 'em in the ground, so I expect you'll be seein' 'em here directly.

"By the way, this is Billy standin' beside me. He's a good young man, though sometimes a smart-aleck.

"Anyhow, me and Billy didn't know these dearly departeds, but, from what we've been told, it sounds like they were nothin' more than a young woman and her man tryin' their best to make a go of it in this harsh old world. So even though, Lord, I can't vouch for their character with any specifics, I am sure that in the end they got much worse than they deserved. It's hard to believe that even the vilest of sinners would merit the sort of demise these two have suffered. So, I was thinkin', since things went so bad for 'em down here, you might give

’em a special break up yonder. I expect it’d mean a lot to ’em, if you did.”

Hugo paused. Billy thought he was finished, but before he could tell Hugo he’d done a fine job, Hugo started speaking again.

“One more thing, God. If you’ll give me ’n Billy a hand catchin’ the dirty son of a bitch who did this, we’ll send ’im your way *muy pronto,* and that’ll give you the chance to do with ’im whatever you think best. Amen.”

They picked up their shovels, and, as they headed back to the shed to put them away, Billy said, “That was good, Hugo, but I don’t think you should say things like ‘son of a bitch’ when you’re praying. It’s not commonly done.”

“Don’t worry, Billy. If God’s as smart as I bet he is, then just like any other reasonable man, he’s already got Thorn figured as one great big son of a bitch.”

As the boys washed again after digging the graves, Billy asked, “What do you suppose Thorn did once he’d finished his bloody business here?”

“Well, sir, he was sent by the fake prophet Martin Glatt to kill Glatt’s wife and the man she left the Community with. He was also sent to find Kradec and Abraham and do his worst there as well. Since half the job is all he's accomplished, I expect Thorn's out there somewhere huntin' for the fiddler and the boy."

"That's where we should be, too," said Billy. "Like Tom Sun said, it's possible Kradec got directions to the Garvey place from some cowhand working the north side of Sun's ranch. But he must not have, because, if he had, he and Abe would've been here by now. Since they aren't, do you have a guess where they might be?"

"Maybe they holed up somewhere. If they did, not comin' to this place was Kradec's smartest decision ever. There's no way that little man can protect himself and Abraham from the maniac. And, as sorry as I am to say it, it's clear poor Mr. Garvey would not've been able to protect 'em either."

"I hate to think of Thorn's getting his hands on Abraham."

Hugo stiffened when Billy said that.

"Thank goodness," Billy added, "Kradec had not yet brought the boy to his mother when Thorn arrived. Like you said, the way things turned out, he was smart not to."

Hugo said nothing. It looked as if Thorn's getting to the boy was a thing the deputy did not wish to discuss.

After Hugo washed, he looked toward the west. Most of the sun had slid below Split Rock, and the highest part of the sky had turned the color of a three-day-old bruise. "It'll be dark soon." He nodded toward the corral. "I'll put our horses in with them others. I'll also throw some more hay in the corral and take our saddles into the barn. You go to the springhouse and round up some chuck. We can figure our next step once we put somethin' in our bellies."

Billy finished washing, and the boys went their separate ways. Hugo left to retrieve the horses from in front of the cabin. Billy collected an armful of wood from the pile and carried it to the cook stove. After the firebox was loaded and lit, he went to the springhouse and cut a couple of slices off the ham. He started to take some of the antelope but decided against it. Instead, he cut more ham. *Who,* he wondered, *would ever eat antelope if ham was available?* He grabbed some waxed cheese and the small crock of butter and carried it all to the cabin.

The fire was going well when he returned, and he placed a skillet on the stove and tossed in the ham slices. He located some plates — ceramic, not tin — and took them to the table. He checked the bread box and was pleased to discover four biscuits that appeared to have been baked that very morning.

By the time Hugo returned, the plates were piled with fried ham, cheese, and buttered biscuits.

"Damn," said Hugo, "look at this."

"And there's one can of peaches left for dessert."

"The eatin' sure has been good on this trip, Billy-boy. One more of these fine meals fixed by you, and my ol' horse won't be willin' to tote me around anymore."

The events of the last two days lay heavy on Billy, and he guessed Hugo felt the same. Once they began to eat, they ate without conversation.

The sun had dropped all the way behind the mountain by the time they finished, and the room had become gloomy. Hugo popped a match, lit the lamp on the table, and handed the burning match to Billy. "Go fire up that lamp next to the rockin' chair over there. Let's get some light in this place." He nodded at the match in Billy's hand. "You better hurry before you burn yourself."

Billy had lit lots of lamps without burning himself, but he didn't bother to point that out. He had no mood for it. He was ready to put this day behind them.

He lifted the lamp's chimney, lit the wick, and a second before the flame bit his fingers, he shook the match out. He gave the wick's raiser knob a turn and brought up the light. Like frightened mice, the dark shadows scampered into the corners.

"That's better," said Hugo. "If there's one thing I hate, it's a dark room."

Billy replaced the lamp's chimney, and, as he was about to walk away, he spotted something tucked under the lamp's base. At first he doubted his eyes, but the moment he accepted what they told him, he felt the air seep from his lungs.

"Oh, God," he said.

"What's wrong?" asked Hugo.

Billy tilted the lamp and picked up what the light had allowed him to see.

Again Hugo asked, "What's wrong, Billy? What d'ya got there?"

Billy crossed back to where Hugo sat and opened his hand. Across his palm lay an empty tube of Hub Wafers.

Chapter Eighteen: Billy Lifted the Latch

"Let's get to the barn," said Hugo. He grabbed his hat and headed for the cabin door. "I don't think they're in there, but we need to check. Once we found Garvey and Marlene this afternoon, we stopped the search."

The sliver of moon over their shoulders provided little light, but, despite the dark, they sprinted across the yard. Remembering where he'd left the lantern, Hugo went to it and, in short order, had it going. "There's another one of these things," he said. "I'll show you where."

He led the way around the large haystack. When they arrived at a double row of shelves, he lifted his light and pointed to another lantern on the top shelf. Billy took it down, and Hugo struck a match and lit it.

"I'll climb the ladder and check the loft," said Hugo. "You finish lookin' down here."

Billy knew if Kradec's and the boy's bodies were around, they had to be located, but the thought of what he and Hugo might see when they were found shot an icy arrow into Billy's chest.

Billy had made it to the far end of the barn on the other side earlier. When he got to the far end on this side, all he saw that caught his eye was a six-foot-long sign with a couple of eye-hooks screwed in at the top. Written along the length of the sign were the words New Hope Land and Livestock. The word *New* had a line drawn through it, and above it had been written the word *Lost.*

Billy imagined that was the first thing Seth Garvey had seen when he brought Marlene home with him. And Billy expected it had not taken Seth long to get the sign off the gate and leaned against the barn's dark back wall. As it turned out, the augury of the vandalizing Sun ranch cowboy was true.

"Did you find anythin'?" asked Hugo as Billy came back.

"No."

"Me neither." He ran a hand over the stubble on his chin. "That Hub package tells us we had it wrong and that Kradec and Abraham were here for sure. But," he added with a note of thin optimism, "maybe they got away."

"Maybe," said Billy without confidence. If they were here when Thorn arrived, Billy doubted they could have escaped.

"We checked the other buildings earlier. No call to do it again. We need to walk the property. I'll start at the river and come up the west side. You look around past the shed and up the hill east of the small corral."

Billy nodded. As he turned to leave, he said, "Call out if you come across anything."

"Same with you."

Billy knew they hadn't needed to tell each other to call out. If either of them found a body out here in the dark, they'd be yelling with everything they had. *Especially,* Billy thought without forming the words, *if the body they found was the boy's.*

As Billy walked about the place, his light reached no farther than four or five feet before the dark night sucked up the lantern's glow. The going was slow, but he got the area on the east side covered, though without success — if success is what it's called when you find a dead and likely mutilated body.

He was about to give up when he lifted his lantern one last time and realized he was standing next to a root cellar that had been dug down into a small rise on the far side of the corral. He and Hugo hadn't noticed it earlier because its roof was thatched with prairie grass, and its river-rock front wall faced away from the cabin and other buildings.

Billy held his light out farther and spotted a few dozen potatoes, onions, carrots, and various other vegetables strewn about in front of the cellar's plank door, which was locked with a hasp and staple. The hasp engaged the staple and was held in place by a six-inch-long bent nail that had been dropped into the staple's round opening.

Swallowing hard, Billy removed the nail and tossed it aside. He pulled the hasp away from the staple and tugged at the heavy door. It swung open, and Billy was hit by the thick smell of cool, dry dirt. He released a breath and contorted his six foot two inches through the five-foot doorway. Once inside, he held the lantern in both hands and shone its light about the earthen-walled cellar. Squinting into the glare, Billy directed the light downward. When its glow struck the gray dirt floor, Billy saw, lying in a curled ball, what he first thought was a dead or sleeping coyote. He blinked, rubbed his eyes, and, when he looked again, he realized that the curled ball was the tiny violin player, Ivan Kradec.

■ ■ ■ ■

Billy left the cellar and lifted his lantern above his head. Waving the light from side to side, he called out, *"Huuuugo."* He could see the shine of Hugo's lantern as Hugo walked the property behind the springhouse. When Billy called, Hugo's light came to a stop. "Over here," Billy shouted, and Hugo's light turned and started in Billy's direction.

Leaving his lantern outside where Hugo could see it, Billy reentered the cellar. Without the lamp, the place was dungeon dark, but, groping about, he soon found Kradec's limp body. Billy was too tall to stand erect in the cramped space, so, rather than trying to pick Kradec up, he backed out, gently pulling the small man through the door, and placed him next to the light.

Kradec was close to unrecognizable. His face was as gray as rotten meat. Blood drenched the front of his white shirt. Cuts covered his face. His nose was smashed, both eyes were swollen shut, his lips were split, and it appeared he'd lost at least one tooth.

But he was alive.

Again Billy shouted, *"Hugo,"* and, as soon

as he did, the light from Hugo's lantern approached and joined the light from Billy's. The better the light, the worse Kradec looked.

"Is he breathin'?"

"He is, but it's shallow."

"Has he said anythin' about the boy?"

"No, he's out cold." Billy put his left arm under Kradec's shoulders and his right arm under Kradec's legs. "I'll carry him to the cabin."

"Go gentle."

Billy drew the small man close and stood. As he did, Kradec's face contorted, and he let out a soft groan. The groan wasn't much, but Billy sensed if Kradec was conscious, the groan would have been a scream.

Hugo carried both lanterns and lit their way down the hill. Once inside the cabin, Billy placed Kradec on the feather bed in the corner. "Let's get the bloody shirt off him and clean him up."

"He could use some drinkin' water, too," said Hugo.

"Get the water while I take off his shirt."

"Best cut it off." Hugo pulled his knife. "This fella's been beat bad, and I doubt the beatin' was confined to his face. If you twist 'im around takin' off the shirt, a busted rib might stab a lung." He handed Billy the knife. "I'll fetch the water."

By the time Hugo returned, Billy had cut away the shirt and was standing above the little man staring down.

"How's he doin'?" asked Hugo. He carried the same galvanized bucket they had used earlier. A bit of water sloshed onto the floor as Hugo placed the bucket at the head of the bed.

"He isn't dead."

"Is his breathin' any easier?"

"No, but he's still doing it." Billy crossed to a cabinet next to the cook stove. He looked inside and came out with a cup and a couple of cotton rags. He dipped the cup in the water, slipped his hand behind Kradec's neck, and lifted his head. Tilting the cup to Kradec's lips, he gave him a drink. Kradec sputtered and coughed most of it out, but at least a tablespoon's worth made it into him, and Billy gave him a little more.

"It wouldn't've taken 'im long to die if he'd stayed in that root cellar," said Hugo.

"I expect leaving him to die in the cellar was the idea."

"I wonder why Thorn didn't hang 'im on the barn wall like he did the other two."

Billy dipped himself a drink from the bucket and dipped it again for Hugo.

"There's no making sense of a crazy man's

behavior. It's useless to try. Did you check everywhere on the west side of the place?"

"I did," answered Hugo.

"And no sign of the boy?"

Hugo's lack of response was Billy's answer, which was all right. The question was stupid, anyway.

Billy dunked one of the rags into the water and, as gently as possible, blotted away the blood on Kradec's face. The little man didn't look quite so bad once the gore was gone, but his clean face did allow Billy and Hugo to get a better look at the extent of the damage, which was considerable.

Kradec's upper body was also covered with lumps and deep red splotches. Billy knew the splotches would soon darken to purple.

Hugo reached down and ran his hands over Kradec's jaw, shoulders, and chest. When Hugo's fingers moved across Kradec's rib cage, the little man wrenched and groaned. "Some busted ribs," said Hugo. "But," he added, "when you gave 'im the water and he coughed, there wasn't any blood mixed in, so it doesn't appear either of his lungs is flattened, which is good. We ain't hardly equipped to deal with such a thing. I sure would like to wake 'im and ask about the boy."

“I doubt we could get him awake. He looks to be down pretty deep.”

“I suppose so. And that’s all right. Maybe even good for ’im. It’s late, anyhow. We’ll give it a try in the mornin’.”

Billy wrung dirty water from the rags into the bucket. “I’ll take this out and dump it,” he said. “While I do that, you take a look in that cabinet where I got the rags.”

“Why?”

“Just do it.”

Billy stepped out the door and into the yard. As he dumped the water, he heard Hugo shout, “Hot *damn. Yahoo.*”

When Billy found the rags in the cabinet, he had also spotted the bottle of Scotland whisky that Kradec had stolen from Billy’s kitchen.

Chapter Nineteen: A Walking Dead Man

Billy and Hugo had brought their bedrolls in the night before and slept in the front part of the cabin — or tried to. After a couple of hours of struggling with the sweltering mid-summer heat, Billy moved onto the porch in search of a breeze. But, for once, the near constant Wyoming wind refused to stir, and it took another hour or so before Billy drifted off.

Not long after sunrise a scream from Ivan Kradec brought both boys to a quick awakening. By the time Billy made it into the house, Hugo was already at Kradec's side.

"Shush," said Hugo. "Shush, now. You're safe. It's all right." Billy was surprised by the compassion in Hugo's voice. Billy knew that compassion existed somewhere beneath Hugo's parchment of leathery skin, but it so seldom showed itself that, when it did, it came as a shocker.

Kradec continued to scream and flail his

arms, and Billy could tell the thrashing increased Kradec's pain. Hugo made a grab for the man's forearms, caught them in both hands, and held Kradec tight. After a bit, things settled down, and Hugo tucked the little man's arms beneath the sheets, where, to Billy's relief, they remained.

Kradec looked no better. If anything, he looked worse. The swelling of his face and torso had increased during the night and gave him the look of an overstuffed sausage. His left eye remained swollen shut, and a gooey matter had crusted the lashes. His right eye had opened into a tiny slit no wider than the nail on a baby's pinky, but it was wide enough for Billy to see that the white of the eye was now ripe-tomato red.

After Kradec's screams subsided, Billy knelt next to the bed. "Mr. Kradec, can you hear me?" The man didn't respond, but the one eye that wasn't swollen and crusted shut did blink, or tried to.

"You've been hurt, sir, but you're going to be fine." Billy said that with a confidence he did not feel. Kradec might recover from his visible wounds, but there was a possibility — maybe even a likelihood — of internal injuries. It would take someone with more skill than Billy and Hugo to figure that out.

"Abraham . . ." Kradec said. His voice was

soft and came out in a rusty-hinge creak.

"Yes," said Billy. "The boy. We can't find him. Where is he?"

"Thorn did . . ." It appeared difficult for Kradec to focus his thoughts. "Thorn was here."

"We guessed it was Thorn," Hugo said. "He killed your sister and her man."

Billy had refilled the bucket and replaced it beside the bed before turning in the night before. Now he dipped the cup and gave Kradec a drink.

Kradec winced when he swallowed but wanted more. Billy took that as a good sign and gave it to him.

"Who are . . . you?" Kradec asked.

"It's Billy Young. We met the other day when you were playing your violin on the street in Casper."

"The young marshal?"

"That's right, yes."

"Thorn . . . knows . . . who you are."

"Yes, I met him in Casper, too."

"He knew we . . . left town with you."

"Yep," said Hugo, "The large fella who tried to smash your fiddle told him."

"Who . . . is —"

"That's Hugo Dorling."

"Old marshal?"

"That's right," Billy said with a smile.

"Hummph," said Hugo.

"He said the old one might follow him."

Now Hugo smiled. "He got that right."

Kradec's words came it fits and starts, and, Billy assumed, so did the man's thoughts and recollections of what had happened. "Thorn said he will kill the old one. The old one is a dead man. A walking . . . dead man."

Hugo's smile vanished. "We'll see about that."

Kradec's hand came from beneath the sheet, and he groped at the air. "More water."

"Sure," said Billy. He tilted the cup to Kradec's lips.

"Made . . . me watch."

The talking took a toll. The little man's voice was now so soft Billy had to lean closer to hear. "What did you say, sir?"

"In the barn . . . Marlene, Seth."

Hugo dropped next to Billy. "He made you watch? Where was the boy when that was happenin'?"

"The springhouse. Thorn . . . put . . . him . . . springhouse."

"What?" asked Billy. Kradec's voice was so soft and his words so slurred, he was difficult to understand. "Thorn what? Put him in the springhouse?"

The man's head moved in what appeared to be a nod. Billy wondered if Thorn's putting Abraham in the springhouse rather than making him watch was an act of mercy or convenience. He answered his own question. He did not believe Thorn, the Enforcer, was any part mercy.

"With Marlene and Seth, he . . . in the barn . . ." Kradec's words trailed off as he struggled to complete his thought. Billy suspected the man's mind balked at the memory of what he'd watched.

"We know," said Billy. "We gave your sister and Garvey a decent burial, Mr. Kradec. They are in a nice spot above the river."

"We'll be killin' Thorn," Hugo said, "at the first opportunity."

"No," whispered Kradec. "Impossible. Pure evil. Thorn . . . cannot . . . be killed."

"Oh, he can be kilt, all right."

"No," Kradec insisted, and, as he spoke, he drifted into sleep or unconsciousness or, Billy feared, maybe even death. "The man," muttered Kradec in his rusty voice, "is . . . the devil."

Moving in closer, Hugo used his elbow to nudge Billy out of the way. The old deputy leaned in six inches from Kradec's left ear. "Devil or not, I am gonna kill Elijah Thorn," he whispered. "Prophet Glatt'll be dyin', too. That, Mr. Kradec, is a promise."

Earlier Billy had lit a fire in the cook stove's box, and he sat now and watched Hugo scoop coffee into a tin pot. Hugo set the pot on the stove and joined Billy at the table.

"I can see how he might figure Thorn to be impossible to kill."

"Why's that?" asked Hugo. He pulled his makings and rolled a shuck. "Ain't nobody impossible to kill."

"I don't know. Kradec put a bullet in the man less than three days ago, yet here we are. We have a missing boy, two folks dead and buried on a hill, and another beat to hell and close to death not ten feet from where we sit."

"A well-placed bullet'll kill any man. Ivan Kradec don't know how to place a bullet; that's all."

"I wish we could've gotten more from him before he went out again. If the boy's dead, I want to find him. If he's alive" — Billy released an exasperated breath — "I *sure* want to find him."

Hugo lit his smoke and looked toward the corner at the injured man. "Kradec's in bad shape, but how he is now ain't gonna stay the same."

"What do you mean?"

"If he wakes up, he'll either be a little better or a little worse. If he's better, he might even be hungry. Let's boil some of that meat stored in the larder and make some broth. We won't give 'im anythin' solid. We'll start 'im off eatin' a little bit at a time."

"And if he's worse?" asked Billy.

Hugo didn't answer.

"I don't think the boy's dead, Hugo. I think Thorn took him."

"You're right. Live or dead, we'd've found the kid if he was around."

"And if he is alive —" Billy looked at his watch. "It's after ten. If he is alive, we're wasting a hell of a lot of time sitting here." Frustrated, Billy stood and began to pace. "If Thorn did leave with the boy, where do you suppose he would take him?"

"Back to Glatt at the Community."

"So Kradec was wrong back in Casper when he told us Thorn would kill the boy."

"Looks like it. Since the wayward wife got her brother to steal the boy away, could be Glatt figured he made a mistake lettin' Marlene and the man she run off with live, so he sent Thorn here to fix that. But it looks like what Glatt wanted done with the boy was for Thorn to bring 'im back to Nebraska."

"Maybe," said Billy, continuing to pace. "But if Thorn and the boy were headed east to Nebraska, don't you think our paths would have crossed yesterday when we left Sun's place and headed here?"

"Only if Thorn stayed along the river."

"Which is likely."

"It is, assumin' Thorn's plan was to head back to the Community with him on horseback and the boy astride a mule."

Billy stopped pacing and looked at Hugo. "Thorn did tell Thirsty he came to Casper by rail. So maybe he wants to go back by rail."

"Once Glatt knows Thorn has the boy, Glatt'll wanna get the kid in his clutches as soon as possible. I doubt havin' Thorn travelin' back six hundred miles by horse and mule would appeal to him. Glatt likes to have things his way. Those kind-a folks seldom have much patience."

"But Thorn would have to get back to Casper to catch the train, and we should have seen him yesterday along the trail."

"He wouldn't have to go to Casper. He could've headed south to Rawlins and caught a train there. But anyway, all this is just us guessin'. You know that, don't you, Billy? There's a bunch-a things Thorn might've done when he left here with the boy."

Billy nodded. "And he's crazy. No predicting what he'd do." Billy began to pace again. "But I do like the idea about the train. No one's so crazy he'd choose riding six hundred miles on a horse rather than on a train."

Billy's pacing took him to the window, where he stopped and stared for a bit at something outside. Turning to Hugo, he said, "We got us company coming."

"What?"

"There's four men about a quarter of a mile out."

"Headed this way?"

Billy turned back to the window. "Looks like it."

They had brought their saddlebags in the night before. Hugo rose from the table and fetched his spyglass. "Here," he said, "let me take a look." He put the telescope to his eye and located the riders. "Well, sir, they ain't strangers. We know at least one-a them boys."

"We do?" Billy leaned forward and squinted through the window's wavy glass. The men were too far away for Billy to make out anything. "Who is it?"

"Hank Teeters. The Wheatland Flats cowboy who introduced us to Tom Sun."

"What could he want?"

"I expect we'll soon know." Hugo shoved his 'scope closed, crossed to the stove, and poured himself a cup of coffee.

Chapter Twenty: A Pious Group of Visitors

Billy checked Kradec again. The man slept, if what he was doing could be called sleep. He gleamed with sweat, and his breathing, though consistent, was shallow and ragged. Billy found another pillow and placed it on top of the pillow beneath Kradec's head, raising him higher. Billy couldn't tell if doing that helped Kradec's breathing, but it made Billy feel better to do something for the man, no matter how small.

The cloth he had used earlier had not yet dried. Billy folded it into a rectangle, bathed the man's face, and placed it across Kradec's clammy brow. Hugo had said when Kradec woke, he might be a little better and want to eat. Billy had brought in slices of the ham and antelope meat and set them to boiling on the stove, but as he stood at the bed now looking down at the injured man, the possibility of Kradec's wanting to eat did not appear likely.

Billy poured himself a cup of coffee and joined Hugo on the porch. They sipped their coffee and watched as Hank Teeters and his three companions rode into the yard.

"G'day, Mr. Teeters," Hugo called out. "What brings you and your friends this far from home?"

"Mr. Sun sent us to see what's going on here." Speaking to his fellow riders, he said, "Boys, these gents're Deputy Dorling and Deputy Young."

All three touched the brims of their hats.

Hank jerked a thumb toward the largest of his three companions. The man's full beard was as red as the lips on a Wheeligo girl. "That big galoot's name is Charlie. Them two look-alikes are the Larson twins, Matthew and Mark. Don't bother trying to tell them fellas apart. We never do." Hank smiled and swung a leg over his horse. "Rumor is they got a couple more brothers down in New Mexico named Luke and John." He shook Billy's and Hugo's hands.

"It's the truth," said either Mark or Matthew. "We also got us a first cousin named Timothy, but that's just a coincidence."

Not wanting to be left out, Charlie said, "Them twins've even got a dog back at the bunkhouse named Corinthians."

"She's the second dog with that name that

we've had," said the other one who was either Matthew or Mark. "She answers to Cory."

"Well, damn," said Hugo. "It's humblin' to be around such a pious group of visitors. Why don't you boys hop down and come in for coffee? Be warned, though. I like my java more full-bodied than the average man."

"Is it hot?" asked Hank.

"It is both hot and wet."

"Then it sounds fine, but first we'd like to water our horses and loosen their cinches."

"Sure thing. There's a couple-a troughs around." Hugo pointed toward the small corral. "The closest is right over yonder."

Charlie took Hank's reins. "You go on. We'll get this done, then come in."

Hank nodded his thanks and followed Billy and Hugo into the house.

"So Tom Sun sent you over, did he?" asked Hugo as he poured Hank a cup and topped off his and Billy's.

"He did." Hank took a sip of coffee, and, Billy noticed, to the man's credit, he did it without a grimace.

Hugo refilled the pot with water from the bucket and reloaded it with coffee. Either Marlene or Garvey had pre-ground some beans and kept the coffee in a can stored in the cupboard. Hugo placed the pot atop the stove next to the boiling meat and tossed another couple of sticks into the firebox.

He sat at the table with Billy and Hank and said, "So Sun likes to keep an eye on the happenin's 'round here, does he?"

"He does," said Hank. "He has a profound dislike for cattle rustlers and most other miscreants. The nearest law is in Rawlins. Jens Hansen don't make it up here to the northern reaches of the county too often."

Jens Hansen was the Carbon County sheriff.

"From what I hear," said Hugo, "Ol' Jens spends most've his time tossing miners in jail."

Hank smiled. "If that's true, then it's time well spent."

"Why didn't Mr. Sun ride here with you?" Billy asked.

"Mr. Sun don't do much policing of the neighborhood anymore. I reckon he's learned his lesson and leaves that work to others." Hank looked toward the bed in the corner. "So what's the story with that fella?"

"He had the sad misfortune of gettin' the dog shit beat out of 'im by a killer named Elijah Thorn."

"A killer?"

"That's right. He murdered Marlene and Seth Garvey, plus at least one more that we know about, a Pinkerton by the name of Warren."

Hank's thin eyebrows moved a tad closer together. "I hear it was a Pinkerton who stopped by the ranch asking how to find this place."

"That was Thorn," said Billy. "He pretends to be a Pinkerton."

Hugo agreed. "That's the truth. I expect he figures if folks think he's a Pinkerton, they'll be more willin' to help 'im track his quarry."

"So Seth Garvey and that little lady staying here with him are dead?"

"They are," Hugo said.

"I never met them, but . . ."

Billy stared into the darkness of his thick coffee. "Thorn hung them with hay hooks on a wall in the barn."

"Damn," said Hank, "that's bad." He looked into the corner again. "That fella don't look killed. Maybe close to it, but not all the way. How'd he escape?"

"He didn't," said Hugo. "When Billy found 'im, he had all but the last drop of life beat plumb out of 'im, and then he was thrown into a root cellar without food or water. Thorn locked 'im in the dark to die a long and lonely death."

"Lucky for him you boys came along. So

where's this Elijah Thorn now?"

"Me and Billy were ponderin' that very question when you and your friends rode in."

"Did you come up with an answer?"

"No, sir, we did not."

"Too bad," said Hank. "Sounds like somebody ought to kill that son of a bitch."

Chapter Twenty-One: Ivan Kradec Began to Stir

The cowboys came into the cabin after tending to their horses. They were eager for coffee, and, as with Hank, and to their credit, they made no complaint once it was served. There was a good deal of boisterous chitchat around the table, and, after a bit, Ivan Kradec began to stir. Hugo gave him water. And — though Billy considered it ridiculous since Kradec's eyes were beaten shut and he was more unconscious than awake — Hugo introduced him to Hank, Charlie, and the Larson twins. Kradec showed no interest, and Billy guessed the fiddle player was more concerned with getting from one breath to the next than he was with making new friends.

After tending to Kradec and visiting for a couple of hours, Billy caught three of the chickens that wandered around the yard and fried them up. He, Hugo, and the Sun Ranch cowboys made short work of the birds, and Billy agreed to fry another if someone would catch it, but no one volunteered.

After they'd eaten, the fire in the cook stove burned down enough that the meat was no longer boiling. Though greasy, the broth smelled good. Billy hoped to get some of it into Kradec while it was hot, but, when he looked into the corner, he saw that Kradec was out again.

"That little fella needs doctoring," said Charlie.

"He does for sure," agreed Hugo, "but I figure the closest doctor is all the way down in Rawlins."

"That's true," Hank said. "They got them a new doc down there, and it's a female."

"You don't say? A female?"

"Yes, sir. Dr. Lillian Heath's her name."

"Well," said Hugo with a shrug. "I expect a female doc could handle a bad beatin' or dig a bullet out of a fella as good as a man. And I bet down in them rough places along the UP, she gets lots of practice doin' both." He shook his head. "But Rawlins is too far off. I doubt Mr. Kradec could make it."

"As it turns out, females doing the doctoring around Carbon County ain't rare," said Hank.

"How's that?"

"We got us a lady up here by the name of Sally Barker. She lives with her husband and a couple of grown kids. They got a place on the north side of Whiskey Peak. Missus Barker was a nurse during the war and has considerable skill when it comes to sickness and even more skill when it comes to injury."

"She's also a fine midwife," said Charlie, for no apparent reason. "She's delivered every baby that's come along in the last five years."

"That's true," Hank agreed. "Though I'm guessing her midwiferying skills were acquired after Appomattox."

"How far away is Whiskey Peak?" asked Billy. He knew it was in the Green Mountain Range, which he didn't think was far. If she was close, Mrs. Barker sounded like the first piece of good news in an otherwise grim few days.

"It ain't too far, I don't think. What would you say, Charlie?"

"It's due south of here fifteen miles or less." He looked toward the man on the bed. "The problem is how could we get that fella down there? I doubt he can sit a horse."

"There's a buckboard in the barn," said Billy. "And horses in the corral to pull it with."

Hugo snapped his fingers. "There you go," he said. "If you boys wouldn't mind haulin' Kradec to the nurse, then that'd free up Billy and me to hunt Killer Thorn."

"Except," said Billy, "we have no ideas on where to begin the hunt."

Hugo gave a dismissive snort. "That don't matter. If we have to, we'll go all the way to Albion, Nebraska, and to the Community beyond."

From the corner came a weak, close to inaudible voice. "Thorn . . . Thorn took Abraham . . . to Deer . . . Creek."

Billy saw Hugo's eyes bulge wide, and he expected his did the same. All six men rushed to the corner. Billy dropped to a knee at the head of the bed. "What did you say?"

"Thorn . . . thought I was unconscious, but I heard . . ."

Kradec continued to drift in an out, and Billy gave him a drink.

Hugo asked, "What were you sayin' about Thorn and Abraham?"

Kradec didn't answer. Billy placed a hand on the man's shoulder and gave it a gentle squeeze. Kradec's swollen right eye opened a bit. Perhaps the lid rose a little higher than it had earlier, but not much.

Hugo repeated his question.

"Told Abraham had to . . . reach Deer Creek . . . by dark. Important . . ." They waited for him to say more, but Kradec had drifted off yet again.

Billy stood and looked at the other men. "Deer Creek? How many Deer Creeks do you figure there are in Wyoming? I'm guessing there's plenty."

"Could be," said Hugo. "There's sure plenty-a deer and a whole bunch-a cricks."

"There's a Deer Creek in the Laramie Mountains," said Hank. "It flows down and meets up with the North Platte where that old stage station used to be."

"Nah, can't be that one. It's too far away," said Hugo.

Billy agreed. "I know that creek. It wouldn't be possible to leave here and reach anywhere on that stream by dark, no matter what time of day they headed out."

"There's a Deer Creek that runs along the bottom of the Rattlesnake Range," said Charlie.

"How far from here?" Hugo asked.

"To where it starts up, probably twenty miles. A few miles on, another stream runs into it. I think that one's called Canyon Creek, but I'm not sure on that. That's the only Deer Creek I've heard of around these parts."

"That has to be it," said Billy.

Hugo took off his hat and scratched the top of his head. "We might as well try it. We got nothin' else."

Billy couldn't argue with that. "I guess we don't."

"But," Hugo said in a flat voice, "I can't figure why Thorn'd have any interest in goin' up there."

"Or," said Billy, "how he'd even be able to."

"What do you mean?" Hank asked.

"The way we figure it, Thorn made it all the way from Casper to the Sun Ranch in one long day. He then left the ranch and rode here and did the many things he did at this place. Now we're thinking, after that, he made it from here to the Rattlesnake Hills." Billy looked down at Kradec. "And he did all this with a bullet hole in him."

"A bullet hole?" asked Hank.

"That's right. A couple of days ago, this little man right here shot Elijah Thorn in the back."

When Billy said that, Kradec stirred again. "No," he said. To Billy's amazement, Kradec wasn't out and had been listening to their conversation.

"What?" Billy knelt again. Kradec might have been more aware than Billy had thought, but the man looked even worse than before, and his voice was growing weaker.

"I didn't shoot him."

"What the hell do you mean, you didn't shoot him?" Billy couldn't believe the audacity. Beat to hell or not . . . *Dying* or not, the fury Billy felt for Kradec when he watched him step from the darkness and shoot another man in cold blood returned and hit him like a fist to the gut. "Don't you dare tell us you didn't shoot him, *goddamn* it. I watched you do it with my very own eyes."

"No, I didn't. It wasn't Thorn . . . the man I shot . . . was Martin . . . Glatt."

Chapter Twenty-Two: A Hard One to Figure

Matthew and Mark rounded up Billy's black mare and the three horses that had been left in the large corral. They led them into the barn and hitched them to the buckboard. Luckily, the animals all took to their traces.

While the twins did that, Billy and Hugo went about shutting the place down. Theirs was an easy chore. Except for the few cattle grazing by the river, which they didn't intend to move, the only animals left on the place were the chickens. Billy located where the chicken feed was stored, and he and Hugo spread it around the yard. There wasn't much, but it didn't matter. Billy expected the foxes would feed on the chickens before the chickens finished the feed.

They closed up all the buildings except the cabin. Once Matthew and Mark had brought the buckboard around to the front porch, and they loaded Kradec onto the wagon bed, Billy closed up the cabin, as well.

The pain of moving from the house to the wagon was enough to waken Kradec. When Billy saw he was conscious, he explained to the little man that he was being taken to a skilled nurse who would patch him up.

Kradec reached out and took a handful of Billy's shirt. Pulling Billy closer, he said in his weak voice, "Help Abraham." When he said it, a single tear leaked from the corner of his swollen right eye, and he added, "I couldn't protect him."

"We will find him, sir," Billy said.

Kradec gave a nod. "Thank . . . you."

"And we'll exact justice."

Seeing into Kradec's eyes was not possible, but his puffy face, bruised and beat to hell, showed no confidence they would exact much justice.

It had been decided that either Matthew or Mark would take Kradec to Sally Barker's place below Whiskey Peak, and that either Matthew or Mark would ride back to the Sun Ranch and let Mr. Sun know that Hank and Charlie were tagging along with the deputies.

"You don't have to," said Hugo to Hank when Hank told him he and Charlie wanted to help put an end to Elijah Thorn. "Me 'n

Billy get paid for this sort-a work. We gotta do it. You don't."

Billy smiled when he heard that. He'd seen Hugo in his current frame of mind before, and Billy knew that Hugo was not hunting Thorn for his deputy's pay. Billy expected that to get his hands on Thorn, Hugo would gladly donate all his pay to the charity of Thorn's choice, and, he'd also be willing to toss into the donation whatever funds he had on deposit in the First National Bank down on Wolcott Street in Casper — which, considering Hugo's parsimonious nature, said plenty.

"Mr. Sun don't like scoundrels coming into this country and killing folks," Hank said. "Even though I'm a newcomer 'round here, I don't like it myself."

"Me neither," said Charlie.

Everyone bid their farewells, and the twins went their separate ways. One headed south to the nurse's place — his horse tied to the back of the buckboard — and the other headed east toward the ranch.

The four who remained saddled up and, before leaving, drew water from the pump.

"Wish we had some whiskey to take along," said Hugo as he jammed the cork into his canteen.

The Scotch Hugo had found in the cupboard the night before had lived a short and selfless life.

There was no trail to the valley below the Rattlesnake Hills where Deer Creek ran, but the weather was fine, and the ground's rise was gentle — so far, anyway — and they made good time.

Their start was late, and it had taken so long to get ready to leave the Garvey place, all Billy and Hugo had voiced regarding Kradec's revelation about shooting Glatt was their surprise. But Billy had been working it over in his mind, and he expected Hugo had, too.

They were a mile or so north of the Sweetwater when Billy said to Hugo, "Looks like there's two men pretending to be Dub Warren."

"Like I said before, pretending to be with the Pinkertons probably smooths the way."

Billy rubbed the back of his neck. "We've been wrong about this from the beginning, Hugo."

"We've been wrong about a few things, Billy-boy."

"First, we thought that the fella I saw shot and who you and I talked to at Doc Waters's clinic was Elijah Thorn."

"Yep, we did, all right. Then he convinced

us he was Dub Warren, but, after findin' Warren opened up and layin' dead next to the North Platte River, we again took the man we'd been talkin' with to be Thorn." Hugo smiled as he laid it all out, but Billy gave a derisive and embarrassed snort.

"Even shot up and cockeyed with smiley juice, the bastard was a smooth-talkin' poser," said Hugo, "and me 'n you fell for it; that's for sure. But it don't change much, Billy. As it happened, we *were* on Elijah Thorn's trail, even if we did have it figured a bit sideways. Only thing that's changed, really, is now it looks like Glatt is here in Wyomin', which means we won't have to suffer the inconvenience of goin' all the way to Nebraska to kill 'im."

"I guess this new information explains how Thorn got to Sun's place from Casper as fast as he did."

"How? I guess I ain't come to that part just yet."

"One reason Thorn got to Sun's faster than we expected is he isn't the one with the bullet hole in him. Another reason is we also thought he left Casper not too long before we did. But it's likely he left the afternoon before, once he'd finished torturing poor Dub Warren by the river."

"So you're thinkin' Warren told Thorn,

and I guess Glatt, too, what he knew about Marlene and the man she run off with being on the Sweetwater?"

"He must have."

"Yes, sir, now that you say it, I guess it'd have to be, but we're the ones who told Glatt at the clinic that Tom Sun's place was where he should go to find out where on the Sweetwater Marlene was. And Glatt would've had to've relayed that information to Thorn before Thorn left Casper."

"Right," said Billy, "but Glatt couldn't have done that until after he left the clinic, could he?"

"Nope, he could not."

"Maybe Glatt already knew about the Sun Ranch, too. Maybe he knew even before he came to my place the night Kradec shot him."

Hugo considered that for a moment. "Only way he could've known is if they got that information outta Dub Warren, too."

"But how would Warren know about Tom Sun?"

"Could be he found out about the Sweetwater and the Sun Ranch when he was at the Community."

"That possibility has crossed my mind," said Billy. "Maybe Warren found out from those talkative women Glatt himself told us about, and those women happened to be the ones Marlene had been corresponding with."

"Sure, and Marlene also told those women about the big ranch that was on the way to hers and Garvey's place."

"But if the Pinkerton was told at the Community that Kradec, the boy, *and* what he was most interested in, the costly violin, were all headed to Wyoming and a homestead on the Sweetwater River, why didn't he hop a train at Albion and head straight to Casper?"

"I'm thinkin' not everythin' Glatt told us when he was pretendin' to be Dub Warren was a lie. Could be Warren did go to the train station and was told by the ticket master that Kradec and the boy took the train to Kearney, and he figured if he did the same, he could catch 'em before they got out of Nebraska; but, as it turned out, when he got there, Kradec and the boy had already left."

"So Warren got a horse in Kearney and followed, eventually crossing paths with another fella who was also after Kradec and the boy."

Hugo nodded. "Elijah Thorn. But neither one of 'em admitted to the other the truth about what they were doin' out on the trail."

"Probably not, but Thorn was likely shooting off telegrams to Glatt from every place they stopped along the way that had a telegraph office. I imagine Glatt told Thorn that a Pinkerton had been at the Community looking for Kradec, and the man he was riding with was likely that Pinkerton."

"And," said Hugo, "Glatt, bein' the brains of the outfit, decided *he* would take the train from Albion to Casper and meet up with Thorn and Warren when they arrived."

"At which time, they'd use Elijah Thorn's skills at persuasion to convince Warren to tell them everything he knew about where Kradec and Abraham were headed."

"They convinced him all right," said Hugo.

"Warren told them everything in hopes of saving himself," Billy said, "but, being the cold-blooded killers they are, even after getting what they wanted, they granted the man no mercy."

"So after they finished with Warren, they came back to Casper."

"And, like Glatt said, they ran into Earl Whitson —"

"And his trusty bootlicker, Evelyn."

Billy allowed his imagination to roam a bit. "And the four of them get to talking, and Whitson and his pal tell Glatt and

Thorn about Kradec and the boy being with us at supper and going to my place after."

"So Glatt sends Thorn on ahead to the Sweetwater to murder the wayward wife and her paramour —"

"And Glatt stays in Casper to head off Kradec, kill him, and take the boy before Kradec and Abraham even leave town."

"Not just kill Kradec," said Hugo, "but kill you, too. He would've had to so he could take the boy."

"I expect so."

"That was his plan, but he didn't allow for gettin' plugged in the back."

"It all makes sense, except for why Thorn is going to Deer Creek."

"That is a puzzler, all right. Another puzzler, though, is if them Community women knew about Wyomin' and the Sweetwater, and the Sun Ranch, and they were willin' to tell all this to Dub Warren, why didn't they give that same information to their leader and prophet, Martin Glatt?"

"That," said Billy, "is a hard one to figure."

Chapter Twenty-Three: What Do We Have Here

The ground grew harder and steeper as they continued north, but when they came to Sage Hen Creek, they trotted along its meandering, grassy banks, and the going wasn't bad.

They made camp that evening at the confluence of Sage Hen's western and eastern forks. The small, lush oasis was surrounded by a rough terrain of sandy, yellowish-brown alkali loam that was barren, sunbaked, and suited for nothing unless it crawled or slithered. Billy looked around before he dropped his bedroll, hoping that the things that crawled and slithered stayed where they belonged.

Before they left the homestead that afternoon, Billy had sliced and divided more of the smoked ham. Everyone received enough to make a meal, if not a feast. They all carried jerky, and Hank had a burlap poke filled with tasty dried apricots. The meal was a thrown-together thing, but filling, and they washed it all down with what Charlie described as a big chunk of Hugo's coffee.

They bedded down not long after dark. Again, the night was warm, and Billy struggled for sleep. After a while, he surrendered to his insomnia. He lay on his back with his fingers laced behind his head and stared at the gray river of Milky Way that flowed across the night sky. Though the creek-bank grass made a poor mattress and the aggressive mosquitoes were pesky, Billy enjoyed lying beneath the stars on a summer's night. The Youngs had done this many times when he and Frank were kids.

Billy had worn a badge only eight months, and going after Elijah Thorn — and now Martin Glatt — was his first real manhunt. He had been hesitant to become a deputy because he feared it would require he do and see things he did not wish to see and do. Now he was in the midst of doing and seeing those very things, and he realized that it was as unpleasant as he had known it would be. But, he also realized, as he lay there watching a million stars sparkle, that because of what he had witnessed in the last few days, deciding to become a lawman had been the right decision. A quick end needed to be brought to both Elijah Thorn and the man pulling his strings.

As Billy allowed those thoughts to swirl, he felt himself sink into slumber.

With the Rattlesnake Hills to their right and the broad-shouldered Garfield Peak rising on their left, they made Deer Creek by early afternoon. After allowing their horses to take a breather, they followed the creek as it flowed toward the northwest.

A mile farther on, Billy said, "Look yonder." He could hear the surprise in his voice, and he assumed the others could, too. They all reined in when he lifted his arm and pointed to the creek's left bank. Two hundred yards ahead, a brown and white steer strolled along the stream bank, munching on the damp green grass.

"My God," said Hank. "What's that critter doing out here? I can't believe anybody'd be fool enough to try ranching in this rough place."

He was right. Since the only grass was along the creek bottoms, it meant there wasn't enough available to support a herd of sufficient size for a man to make a living. But the steer was there. It had to have come from somewhere.

They nudged their horses and started off but pulled up when Hugo, who was in the lead, turned and brought a finger to his lips. He cocked an ear and then jerked his head toward the trees. They made it into cover seconds before a lone rider came around a bend in the creek. He was a small man on a dun-colored horse. He carried a coiled rope and wore a pair of black, fringed chinks. His hat's extra-tall crown was of the sort that appealed to short men.

"Hey, stray," the man said to the steer, "what're you doing way up here?"

The rider went to the steer and swatted it on the hindquarters with the coiled rope. "Get along there," he said. He got it heading back downstream.

"What d'ya figure that's all about?" asked Charlie.

Hank answered. "Can't say, except it's damned peculiar."

"Let's let 'im put a little distance between us and then follow and see what he's up to," said Hugo.

Hugo had them wait long enough that Billy became antsy. When he complained about it, Hugo said, "All right, let's go."

They moved along the creek single file, with Hugo in front. When they came to the spot where they'd seen the cowboy emerge, Hugo held up his hand, stopping the others. With his right spur, he gave a gentle tap to his bay and edged up to the bend. He looked out ahead, and, after a bit, he turned and motioned for the others to come up.

Billy stopped next to him. Not seeing anything, he stood in his stirrups and asked, "Have you still got an eye on the fella, Hugo?"

Hugo nodded downstream. "The slope gets steeper."

That was a poor answer, but Billy noticed Deer Creek's otherwise gentle flow bubbled into white water as it spilled over rocks and continued below their line of sight.

"He disappeared down the hill just as I came around," Hugo said. "I'd like to know where he's takin' that steer, but the trees're so thick along the crick bank as it heads into the valley that, from this angle, a fella can't see a thing. If we go down any farther, we run the risk of that cowboy lookin' around and spottin' us." He turned toward an embankment on their left. "Let's get up there. Maybe that hilltop'll give us a view."

The climb was too steep for the horses. They handed their reins to Hank and Charlie and dismounted. Hugo glanced up at the rise as he dug out his spyglass.

Like a waiter in a fancy Denver restaurant, Billy made a shallow bow and gestured with his left arm for Hugo to proceed. "Lead the way, Deputy Dorling." Billy wasn't being gracious. In case Hugo's aging legs couldn't get him up the sharp incline, Billy wanted to bring up the rear so he could catch the old coot before he tumbled backwards and broke his neck.

Hugo nodded and stepped out first, but, as he did, he provided Billy a nasty look that suggested he was suspicious of his young partner's sudden courtesy.

Hugo began the climb and made it to the top thirty seconds before Billy. He was waiting with folded arms and a smug smile as his young partner scrambled up the last few feet. Once he was on top, Billy gave Hugo a nod and returned the smile. Billy allowed the deputy to make his point and chose not to mention the older man's huffing and puffing.

Turning to the west, they crossed to the pine- and spruce-covered hilltop's far edge. On their right, they could see Deer Creek roll down to the valley floor, where it was met by another, smaller creek and continued to the north.

Where the two streams came together, like with the confluence of Sage Hen Creek's east and west forks, there was a lush and verdant park.

But, unlike with the Sage Hen, this confluence was larger, and its broad green fields were spotted with upwards of two hundred head of cattle.

"Well," said Billy "what do we have here?" The question was not one he expected answered.

The cowboy they'd seen earlier was moving the stray down the hill. Six or seven other men were riding in and out of the herd or performing various chores at their well-established camp.

There were three wagons. Two were buckboards. The third was a covered chuck wagon. One of the buckboards was empty. The other's bed was half full with supplies. A shirtless fat man stirred something in a black pot that hung over a fire.

A large canvas tent was set in from a stand of rabbitbrush and cottonwoods. The rabbitbrush's bright-yellow flowers had not yet blossomed. They would come along in another month or two. The tough plant did well in the dry, alkaline soil but seldom grew taller than two to four feet. The seeds that had produced this healthy six-foot thicket had likely blown in from the harsh country beyond the streams.

A second, smaller tent was set up on the far bank of the creek that flowed in from the narrow canyon that ran between the tall hill they were now on and the next one to the south. Billy had noticed the canyon when they rode in. It began on the south side of Garfield Peak and ran to the north and west. That stream left the canyon down below where they now were and ran on for a quarter of a mile before it merged with Deer Creek.

Hugo shook his telescope from its felt bag, extended its drawtubes, and raised it to his right eye.

"Do you recognize anybody down there, Hugo?"

"No, I do not." He turned his glass toward the herd, moving it around as he looked at the cattle. "That's interestin'," he said.

"What is?"

"I count at least four different brands on them cows. Here." He handed the telescope to Billy. "You take a look. You're a cattleman, or were. See if you recognize any of them markin's."

"I don't know the brands of the outfits way out here, Hugo." Part of the reason for that was because there were no outfits way out here.

"Take a look, anyhow," Hugo said, as he turned and squinted into the valley. Billy knew, without his spyglass, all the myopic

Hugo could see was a smudged blur of activity.

Billy lifted the telescope to his eye and aimed it toward the herd.

"Wait," said Hugo. "What's goin' on at the big tent?"

Billy moved the 'scope away from the herd, across the camp, and onto the bony face of a fence-post-thin man. The skinny man tied open the tent's front flap. Once the tent was open, another man, whose back was to Billy, came out carrying one end of a cot. This man was followed by another man carrying the cot's opposite end. Like the first man, this fella's face was visible, but he was no one Billy recognized. As they emerged from the tent, Billy could see there was a man with his arms at his sides lying face up on the cot. He wore a dark-red shirt, but it was impossible to see him well enough to tell anything more about him. The two cot carriers edged their way into the heavy shade of a cottonwood tree, where they set the cot down.

Hugo, showing no patience with his own poor eyesight, spewed a couple of obscenities and asked, "What the devil's goin' on down there?" Hugo refused to wear specs. He defended that bit of illogic by saying if something was so far away that he couldn't see it, then it was too far away to worry about. Apparently, that rule didn't apply at times like this. Billy knew the actual reason the old buzzard would not wear spectacles was his bone-deep vanity.

"A couple of men are hauling a fella on a cot out of the tent. They put him down in the shadows."

"Do you recognize any of 'em?"

The others had walked away, but the man on the cot could be seen, although the shade made it difficult to make out much about him. Billy pushed the spyglass's first draw-tube in a little, and, with that, the tableau slid into better view. As it did, an amazed Billy watched as the image in the spyglass's lens focused onto the sharp, angular features of the man Billy had first seen peeking into his parlor window.

Chapter Twenty-Four: A Slow One to Learn

"That fella on the cot," said Billy, "is Martin Glatt." Billy lowered the telescope and looked at Hugo. With a smile and a shrug, he added, "Also known as the late Dub Warren. And he's been thought by some — and when I say 'some,' I mean only you and me — to be the Enforcer, Elijah Thorn."

Hugo's brow furrowed as he jutted his head forward, trying to get his eyeballs a little closer to the man in the shade. "You're sayin' that cot rider down there is Glatt?"

Cot Rider. Hugo could make even innocent words sound obscene.

"It is," Billy said. "His bullet wound must not be doing too good. Why he ended up here at the foot of the Rattlesnake Hills is a mystery, but it must've been a thing he and Thorn arranged before Thorn left Casper."

Hugo's lips peeled back in a wide smile. "The reason he's here don't matter to me. Whatever it is, it's good news for us. Mr.

Glatt is not only in Wyomin' instead-a Nebraska, he's right down there *waitin'* for us. Damn, boy, this chore's gettin' easier and easier."

Billy, who, as Hugo talked, had once again turned the spyglass toward the scene below, told himself that there was nothing about any of this that was easy, nor did things appear to be getting easier. But, to avoid stepping into the maze of one of Hugo's labyrinthine debates, Billy stayed silent.

"Killer Thorn's likely down there, too. I wonder what the bastard looks like."

Billy lowered the glass again and turned to Hugo. "Mean and ugly is my guess."

"You didn't happen to spot little Abraham, did you?"

"No."

Hugo huffed a sigh. "How many men?"

"Looks like maybe six cowboys, counting the fella moving the stray down the hill. Plus, the cook would make it seven. There's another fella strutting around not doing much. I couldn't get a good look at him, but he'd make it eight."

"The struttin' fella's runnin' the outfit, no doubt," said Hugo.

"There could be more in those tents."

"I doubt it."

"Why do you say that?"

"It's too hot to be in a tent. I bet Prophet Glatt thought so, too. That's why he's layin' in the shade. Now, it is possible there could be other men roamin' about lookin' for more strays." He aimed four fingers at the herd. "Did you know any of them brands?"

"I can't see them all, of course, but I did recognize Ben Henshaw's Lazy S."

Hugo chuckled. "Ol' Ben registered that brand when his no-account wife, Shirley, ran off with that copper-pot salesman. Ben said Shirley leavin' was fine by him. He could never get that slothful woman to do a lick-a work 'round the place anyhow. All she'd do was sit on the porch sippin' tea and readin' *The Ladies Home Journal.* I thought him registerin' that brand as the Lazy S was a pretty good joke."

That old story was a saw that had been passed around for the last six or seven years, but Hugo never tired of repeating it.

"Also" added Billy, "I spotted Cal Brewster's Open B Bar brand."

"So these are the cattle that've been rustled from the Casper ranches. Why in the world would they bring these animals to this God-forsaken place?"

Billy used the heel of his hand to collapse the telescope's three drawtubes. "How far do you figure it is from Casper out here?"

"As the crow flies, I'd say thirty, thirty-five miles."

Billy jerked a thumb toward the herd. "For the sake of this conversation, let's agree none of those brown and white four-legged critters can fly."

Hugo's eyes turned to slits, and his lips pursed beneath his bushy mustache, but, despite this mild burst of pique, Hugo provided an answer. "Comin' around the northwest end of the Rattlesnakes would make it forty-five, fifty miles, I suppose."

"It must have taken a couple of days to trail all those cattle out here."

"If they were movin' this whole bunch at once, probably at least two days. Though some of these animals might've been out here since the rustling first started, and those that had been stole that Skip Garner told us about at the Reshaw could-a got here yesterday or even the day before. If they were movin' 'em out a few at a time as they stole 'em, they could get here lots quicker than two days. The ground's pretty flat north of the Rattlesnakes, and it appears they have plenty of hands. Though one thing's for sure."

"What's that?"

"Prophet Glatt is in league with whoever these cattle thieves are."

Billy thought about that for a bit. "Sure. He wouldn't be here if he wasn't with them in some way. And they must be the ones that brought him. He doesn't look like he could've gotten here on his own."

"He's a curious fella, that Glatt is."

"What's real curious," said Billy, "is why are they way out here? We know this bunch of thieves wants to sell these cows."

" 'Course they do. Why bother to steal 'em if it ain't to sell 'em? You sure can't eat that many. How much do you figure all them steers're worth?"

"Oh, I don't know. I'd put them at about 850 pounds each, more or less. Selling them legally, they might go for four-seventy-five, maybe five dollars a hundred weight."

"I would-a guessed more than that."

"Nah, the market's not been the same since the winter of '86-'87. So figuring them at 850 pounds at five bucks per hundred, that would be . . . Give me a second here. Forty-two-fifty, times — let's go with two hundred head to make it easy. I'd put it at about eighty-five hundred dollars."

Hugo let out a soft whistle.

"Of course, on the rustled-cattle market they'd sell for quite a bit less than that. The question is: who do they plan to sell them to? There's no chance any of the other ranchers around the area would buy stolen cattle — not ones with local brands, anyway. So the rustlers are going to have to cattle-car these beeves at least out of the central part of Wyoming and probably, to be safe, all the way out of state. What would be the closest railhead from here? Rawlins or Rock Springs?"

"Not Rock Springs. Maybe Wamsutter, though I expect Rawlins is a little closer than Wamsutter. But if they were plannin' to transport stolen Natrona County cattle by rail, they'd've trailed 'em down to Rawlins in the first place."

Billy nodded. "They'd have to take them somewhere. They sure couldn't ship them from Casper. And probably, Hugo, not out of Rawlins, either. It'd be a risky thing to try anywhere."

"True," said Hugo, "but what else're they gonna do?" Then, answering his own question, he said, "I guess they could get themselves a bunch-a runnin' irons and start changin' brands."

"Big job," said Billy. "So big it wouldn't make sense to even try."

"So if they aren't able to railroad 'em out of the state or change the brands, what the hell're they to do with 'em? 'Specially way out here." He lifted his arms, palms up, indicating everything around: the hill where they stood, the valley below, and the desolate country beyond. "This is as close as a man could get to the middle of nowhere."

Hugo's question was a good one, one Billy could not answer. "Here," he said, handing Hugo the telescope. "Let's get back to Hank and Charlie and tell them what we've seen."

They crossed to the spot where they had scaled up. It looked even steeper going down. Before they started, Billy said, "We need to find out where Abraham is before we move in on these men."

"Yes, we do. We wouldn't want the boy to fall into any crossfire."

"Should it happen to come to shooting," said Billy.

"It'll come to shootin', all right," Hugo said, without elaboration.

He didn't need to elaborate. Billy nodded, admitting the obvious.

The rocky descent slanted away at more than a sixty-degree angle. Billy released a breath and said, "I'll go first." He dropped onto the ridge's edge, turned around, and started down backwards. Billy wanted to lead the way down for the same reason he had followed going up. He could tell Hugo didn't like Billy's taking over this way, but so what? He suspected the old man had not been much of a climber even in his younger days. However, Billy, not being stupid, kept that opinion to himself.

When he was three feet from the bottom, Billy called out, "Okay, Hugo, come on." If, on his way down, Hugo began to slide, Billy would be in a position to break the fall, and they would be close enough to the ground that, when they hit, there wouldn't be much damage.

Billy's idea was a sound one, but, to his surprise, ol' Hugo made his descent like a monkey scampering off an organ grinder's shoulder. Watching that, Billy smiled and told himself — not for the first time — that Deputy Geezer should not be underestimated. And that Deputy Still-Wet-Behind-the-Ears was a slow one to learn.

Chapter Twenty-Five: Eight Ain't Near Enough to Save 'Em

At the bottom, despite descending with efficiency — even grace — Hugo was again huffing and puffing. He dealt with that annoyance by rolling a smoke and firing it up. "Let's visit for a bit, boys," he said, taking his reins and leading the way upstream to a wider spot on the creek bank where they could all have a seat. He opened a saddlebag and tucked in the spyglass. Stepping around to the other bag, he said, "All this up 'n down climbin's enough to give even a vigorous man like myself a parchin' thirst." He reached into the bag and took out his cup. He dipped the cup into the creek and, sitting on his haunches, took a long drink. "Me 'n Billy got a look at what's in the valley."

Hank's and Charlie's ears perked up. "Whadja see?" asked Hank.

"A couple-a hundred cows, for one thing."

"Nah," said Charlie with a look of disbelief. "Can't be. Who'd be fool enough to trail even one bovine into this place, much less two hundred?"

"We saw 'em, Charlie. They're munchin' grass between where this stream here and another one down the way come together. It's not a bad spot considerin' what a damned piece-a misery the rest-a this country around here is." Hugo took another sip.

"We also spotted one of the men we're after," Billy said.

Hank, who was perched on a more or less flat boulder, asked, "Elijah Thorn?"

"No," said Hugo, "but we figure he's there, too."

Billy allowed his reins to drop and removed Badger's bit and bridle. He then took a feed bag and a small sack of oats from his drawstring poke. He poured some oats into the feed bag, put the bag onto Badger's muzzle, and snugged the bag's strap over the horse's poll. The big gray nickered his thanks, blowing oat dust through the air holes, and started chomping away.

As Billy did all this, he explained, "The man we saw is the other one. Glatt. He's the fella who's telling Thorn who to kill." He straightened the feed bag, gave Badger a pat on the shoulder, and crossed the open space to join Charlie where he sat on the white trunk of a fallen aspen.

"Lord, who *are* these men?" Hank's innocence with this sort of thing was apparent and something that a large part of Billy envied.

"They are a couple-a not-long-for-this-world sons-a-bitches; that's who they are."

"There are at least eight men down there," said Billy, "who I suspect will be unwilling to see that happen, Hugo."

"So," Hank asked, "you're saying there are eight men in that outfit working for this fella Glatt, and they'd be willing to spill blood?"

Billy shook his head, "Nah, Hank, I don't suppose they work for Glatt; they didn't at first, anyway, though he may be paying them now to protect him from Hugo and me and maybe the sheriff in Casper, as well. But those eight men have a pretty lucrative business of their own that they'd also like to protect."

"Plus," added Hugo, "since that lucrative business happens to be cattle rustlin', you can bet they'd gladly fight to avoid bein' jailed."

"Jailed or hanged," said Billy. "They've already murdered one fella during the course of their thievery."

Hank and Charlie did not appear pleased with how things were shaping up.

Billy knew Thorn wouldn't go down easy, and, to whatever extent he was able, Glatt would fight, too. They'd have to. If they were taken back to Casper alive, they'd be tried and hanged within a month for the murders of Dub Warren, Garvey, and Marlene. The rustlers might fight for the same reason. No one could prove which of them had killed the hired man back on the Poison Spider, and the law wouldn't hang them for cattle thievery alone. But there was the real possibility these thieving culprits would be dragged from jail and lynched by a bunch of rampaging Natrona County ranchers.

"They'll fight," Billy said. "But, again, Hank — you, too, Charlie — you don't have to be a part of this. We'd not think one bad thought if you boys turned around right now and headed back to Devil's Gate."

Hank and Charlie looked at each other and did some sort of non-talking communication that only they could understand. "No, sir," said Hank, after a bit. "We signed on for it, and we'll see 'er out."

Billy found both men's eyes and gave them a smile. Billy knew cowboys looked at the world in a special way, and these two were cowboys through and through.

Charlie laughed. "Hell, they's only eight of 'em. How bad can it be?"

Hugo joined in Charlie's laughter. "You're right about that, Charlie." He took the last pull on his shuck. With his thumb and middle finger, he flicked the butt into Deer Creek. "And," he said, "eight ain't near enough to save 'em."

"What is it we want to do here, exactly?" Hank asked.

Hank had directed the question to Billy, but it was Hugo who answered. "What we wanna do is kill us a couple-a bad men and retrieve a little boy who has fallen into their clutches."

"You fellas are the law. Shouldn't you try to arrest them without killing them?"

Hank was a good citizen.

"Sure," Billy said, noticing he was thinking more and more like Hugo all the time, which he doubted was a good thing. "We'll arrest them. If they ask us to *real* nice."

"*Maybe* we will," corrected Hugo. He gave Charlie a wink, and they shared another laugh. Even Hank joined in with a soft chuckle.

"You got a plan?" Hank was willing to do his part, but it was clear he expected some leadership along the way.

"Nah, me 'n Billy just make stuff up as we go along."

"That's not true," said Billy. "Of course, we have a plan."

Hugo stood and slung his cup back and forth a couple of times to fling out its few drops of remaining water, then he crossed to his horse and dropped the cup into his bag. "We do?" he asked. "We really *do* have us a plan?" His incredulity sounded sincere.

Billy didn't blame him. Though at times like this they did try to make plans, Billy had to admit, their plans were rarely very good. And, more often than not, they fell apart fast, which, as Hugo said, led to making stuff up as they went along.

"What's the plan, Billy?" asked Hank.

"When it gets dark, I'm going to sneak down into that camp, snoop around, and see if I can figure out what's what."

"That's it?" asked Charlie. "That's the plan?"

Billy answered with a shrug.

Hugo, Hank, and Charlie all shared a disbelieving look, but Hugo was the only one who laughed.

They made a cold camp there at the creek and shared what food they had left. Once they'd shaken out their bedrolls, Hank said something Billy figured had been on the cowboy's mind since before they settled in. "Your plan don't sound so good to me, Billy."

"He hears that about most-a his plans," offered Hugo.

"There's a boy down there," Billy said. "We need to know more about what his situation is before we make any move against his captors or the rustlers who are with them."

Hugo lifted his eyes to the sky. "Well, moonlight is scant, so this is a good night to be skulkin'. But I'll not be lettin' you go down there by yourself."

"The job requires stealth, Hugo. And one man makes half as much noise as two men do. Less than half as much if one of those two men happens to be you."

"I can sneak as good as the next fella." He put his hands in front of him, palms down, and waggled his fingers and shoulders in a scary sort of way. "I can be as quiet as the ghost of a painted Sioux."

"I do not agree with that," Billy said. "And I won't argue with you. I expect there'll be plenty of time before this chore is done for you to make your always surly presence known."

Billy walked over to where they had placed

their saddles and lifted his Marlin from its scabbard.

"If bein' quiet is what you're goin' for," said Hugo, "firin' off a rifle ain't smart."

"Let's hope it doesn't come to that, but, if it does, then *that* would be the time for you to make your surly presence known." Billy jacked a round into the Marlin's chamber.

Chapter Twenty-Six: The Darkness Behind the Tent

Billy agreed for the others to follow him halfway down the hill, where they could hunker behind rocks with their rifles. They were beyond the thick growth of trees and from here could look out over the park-like space below. Though the night was dark, the camp was lit by the orangish glow of three large fires on the flat, grassy meadow between the two streams and a fourth, smaller fire, on the far side of the creek that merged with Deer Creek. There was not enough light to provide many details, but the dark shapes of men could be seen sitting around the fires and milling about the camp. The men appeared to be drinking coffee and whiskey and chatting about whatever it was thieves and murderers chatted about in their free time.

"Are you gonna be careful, now, Billy?" asked Hugo.

"Sure, I will."

Hugo looked skeptical.

"You know me, Hugo."

"Yes, I do." Hugo dropped behind a boulder.

Hank and Charlie were behind their own boulders, and, as best as the sparse light would allow, they also appeared skeptical.

"Don't worry, boys," Billy said. "I'll be back, but, if you hear gunfire, you start picking off as many of those bastards as you can."

"You stay hid down there, Billy," Hugo said. "Don't let anybody see you. We don't want them to know we're here yet." He jerked his head toward the camp, telling Billy to get going. "And hurry back."

Billy gave his partner a two-fingered salute and started down.

Glatt and his cot had been moved to the campfire closest to the large tent, and, though the others around this fire visited with animated gestures and barks of laughter, the cot rider, as Hugo called him, did not join in.

Billy couldn't see Glatt's face, but he suspected the false prophet and Pinkerton imposter was acting less chipper now than he had a few days earlier, because, as Glatt had said himself, gunshot wounds, if they don't kill outright, have a way of coming back on you. Even from this distance, it looked to Billy as though Ivan Kradec's cheap and poorly made pocket gun was at last taking its toll, and Doc Waters's concerns about infection had come to be.

Hugo would be disappointed if he lost his chance to kill Martin Glatt because an infected bullet wound beat him to it.

Billy wanted to get close enough to the men around the campfire by Glatt to hear what was being said. He doubted it would be anything more than the usual whiskey-fueled blatherskite that passed for conversation around most cowboy campfires. Billy had participated in plenty of those himself and had enjoyed every one. But he hoped for more. Little Abe being at the mercy of Elijah Thorn was a situation that needed correcting.

No guards were posted. These fellas must have doubted they'd ever be bothered out here in this lonesome place. They couldn't be blamed for thinking such a thing.

Deer Creek flowed down the hill from where they were camped and then turned to the west for a couple of hundred yards, where it widened and shallowed before it met the creek coming out of the canyon. Billy crept down the hill and onto the grassy bottom ground. Even though the stream was shallower here, he found a spot where there were enough rocks sticking up that he could cross without getting wet.

The large tent was six or eight feet inside the line of rabbitbrush. As he approached the bushes, their pungent aroma filled his nostrils, and he hoped he could avoid falling into a fit of noisy sneezes.

The voices were more understandable now, but the men's conversations were no more than Billy had expected.

He guessed Abraham would be kept in one of the two tents. Probably the big one where his father had been before being brought outside. It looked as though the bottom of the tent wall could be lifted high enough for Billy to bend down and peer in. He stepped from the bushes and crossed the narrow space between the rabbitbrush and the tent. He dropped to his knees and lifted the canvas. Peering underneath, he saw a lamp atop a small table in the center of the tent. The lamp provided enough light to see that, except for a couple of bedrolls, the place was empty. A water bucket with the handle of a ladle sticking above the bucket's rim was next to the table.

The lamp's light was unable to reach into the big tent's dark corners, but it was clear Abraham was not inside. Billy decided to crawl in to take a closer look, anyway. But before he could slip beneath the canvas, he saw two men leave the fire and heft both ends of the cot. As they carried it and its cargo toward the tent, a third man at the fire stood and headed in Billy's direction.

Damn, Billy thought to himself and hoped he hadn't said it out loud. As quietly as he could, he scuttled back into the bushes.

The man heading toward Billy's hiding place appeared a little drunk. He staggered, but it wasn't too bad — just enough to put a sway in his gait. He crossed the camp the way a sailor might cross the deck of a ship rolling in a moderate sea. With the fire to the man's back, nothing could be made of his face.

Humming some ditty — maybe *Little Brown Jug;* it was hard to tell from his squeaky, off-key rendition — the man lurched his way into the camp's deeper darkness beyond the large tent. Once he reached whatever spot he was aiming for, he lifted his gunbelt higher on his waist and unbuttoned his trousers. The man took out his dingus, and, as he continued his humming, began to water the shrubbery.

Billy was glad he was back in the bushes as far as he was.

The two men who had carried the cot into

the tent came outside. One mumbled something to the other, and he, too, turned toward the darkness behind the tent.

The first man was in mid-flow when the mumbler approached. This fella was larger than the one doing his business. Though the larger man also walked with a wobble, he was no drunker than the first.

When the mumbler saw the first man, he coughed out a loud, boisterous laugh. His voice was raspy and so wet-sounding, it gave Billy the urge to clear his throat.

This man slapped the first on the back, causing the first man's stream to shoot dangerously close to Billy's right boot.

"So," said the larger man, nodding toward the first man's crotch, "you were able to find that little rascal in the dark, were you?" He dug his paw into the fly of his jeans. "I bet it weren't easy." He burst into another laugh as he drew his own weapon and opened fire.

The first man voiced some feeble comeback to the larger man's gibes, but he showed even less wit than the giber. Billy's attention, though, was more focused on the sound of their voices than their snappy repartee.

The squeaky tones of the first and the hoarse rasp of the second were familiar. At first Billy couldn't place them, but he was certain he'd heard those voices within the last few days.

He rubbed the tip of his chin as he thought back, and, after a bit, he recalled. The raspy sounds came from the bully, Earl Whitson, and the squeaker was Whitson's toady, Evelyn Jones.

Billy now understood how these two always-unemployed ne'er-do-wells made their spending money: they stole other men's cattle. Although, how those cattle were turned into cash remained a mystery.

"Did you hear any more 'bout what the hell's going on?" asked Evelyn. "I'd like to get outta this mosquito plantation and back to Casper before I'm chewed to death." He swatted something on his cheek.

"The deal's s'posed to get done first thing tomorrow morning."

"That sounds good to me." Finishing up, Evelyn gave his pecker a couple of hearty shakes and tucked it away. "It'll be a hard ride, but with luck we can be back in our own beds late tomorrow night."

"Maybe."

"Maybe? What d'ya mean 'maybe'?"

"Sounds like the deputy ain't bringing enough boys to trail these animals away when he shows up tomorrow with the cash. It might fall to us to do it for him."

"Why the hell wouldn't he bring enough men? He knows what we've got here."

"I ain't saying he won't. I'm saying *maybe* he won't. I'm just telling you what Jarrod said."

Whitson dribbled to a stop, holstered his shooter, and he and Evelyn returned to the fire.

Chapter Twenty-Seven: Lucky You

Billy left the bushes, lifted the canvas, and rolled into the tent.

Martin Glatt lay on his back. The night was hot, but, despite the tributaries of sweat that streamed from his forehead, the man shivered as though the tent held freezing drifts of blowing snow. A woolen blanket was pulled to his chin, but a single blanket was not enough.

Lamp light washed over Glatt's ashen face, and Billy could see what he had expected. This man was not well. He was skeletal and looked even closer to death than Kradec had looked when Matthew or Mark hauled him off to the nurse's place on the north side of Whiskey Peak. It appeared a toss-up as to whether either man would survive.

That thought had only half formed when Billy did a quick amendment. Kradec's chances of survival were much better than the man lying on this cot. Even if Glatt's infection eased off and his fever broke, Hugo or Billy would surely kill him.

Billy realized killing Glatt right now would be easy. He could pull the blanket over Glatt's mouth and nose, and in minutes the chore would be done.

What would it feel like to have the cadaverous face squirming beneath his hand? The only thing separating them would be the thin wool of a tattered blanket.

As Billy pondered that idea, Glatt's eyelids fluttered open, and, wide eyed, he gaped up at Billy. Seeing a man in his tent staring down at him with a rifle in his hands did not appear to startle Glatt or even cause surprise. Billy guessed Glatt had expected company from the law sooner or later. Billy, though, was startled by those rheumy eyes popping open and locking onto him. He tensed, prepared to muffle any scream or call for help that Glatt dared to make.

But Glatt lay silent. He even smiled. The smile was weak and crooked and . . . Billy searched for a word to name it, but he came up empty handed.

"It looks like . . ." Glatt sounded as rough as emery, and he stopped and averted his eyes toward the bucket below the lamp. "Water?"

Billy's first impulse was to tell him to die and spend eternity witching for water in hell, but he didn't. Instead, he leaned the Marlin against the table and, with the ladle, dipped some out.

Glatt nodded his thanks and sipped.

He cleared his throat, found his voice, and began again. "It looks like every time we run across each other, Deputy Young, I am flat on my back. The first time I was in the dirt in front of your ranch house. Then, in a bed at good Doc Waters's clinic. And now here we are with me atop this wobbly camp cot. I'm always at a disadvantage when we meet."

Glatt was able to communicate better than Kradec had, but, depending on the abilities of his nurse, Billy didn't believe Kradec's injuries would prove fatal. Billy was not so sure with Mr. Glatt.

"I expect lying on your back does not affect your skills at lying."

Glatt smiled as though Billy had made a joke, which Billy had not. Billy didn't realize how it would sound until he heard himself say it.

"You're right, of course. I have lubricated my way through this world with lies. Lying is the only thing I was ever good at." He lifted a hand from beneath the blanket and, for emphasis, aimed a bony finger heavenward. "Prevarication was not a learned skill, Deputy. My lies were a gift. A talent endowed at birth."

"Lucky you."

"I fear not so lucky at the final count." He put his hand back beneath his cover and pulled the blanket tighter. With a shudder, he said, "It feels like July has turned to December."

"You think you're cold now, just wait."

Glatt nodded. "Once again, you're right. I should've stayed at the clinic."

He spoke as though he had a good sense of his situation, though Billy refused to believe a word that left the man's mouth.

"At least there, even if I got infected, I would have had a good supply of Abigail Waters's benumbing laudanum. That stuff does hit the spot. I went through all I took much too quickly."

Glatt continued to shiver, but it wasn't as bad as it had been before he started speaking. Billy guessed the man was so fond of his own glib voice that putting it to work warmed him up.

"You couldn't stay at the clinic, though, or even in Casper, could you, Agent Warren?"

Glatt's left eyebrow went up a notch.

Then, shaking his head, he said, "It made sense to use Warren's name, and for Elijah to use it, too. I knew it would make things easier for us, and it did. Folks respect the Pinkertons — well, maybe not union men nor your pal Deputy Dorling, but most folks do. Where is Deputy Dorling?"

"Close."

"I bet he's not very close, or I wouldn't have to wait for my infection to do its worst."

"Hard to argue with that. Tell me, since we're talking like old chums here, what did you have to gain by murdering the Pinkerton?"

"Information, of course. And getting it wasn't easy, according to Elijah."

"You saw what was done to him."

"I didn't see the *coupe day grass,* as they say, if there was one. Could be Elijah whittled on the poor soul bit by bit 'til Mr. Warren at last gave up the ghost. My man Elijah is peculiar, if you haven't noticed."

The thought of pulling the blanket over this smug son of a bitch's face crossed Billy's mind once again.

"When Warren told us what I needed to know, I took his horses and went back to town. Exactly what Elijah did once I was gone, I do not know. Warren was a tough one. And, you need to understand, Elijah had been trying in more subtle ways to get information from him as they rode together all the way from Kearney to Casper. Elijah kept me apprised. He wired me at every stop along the way. I did not tell Elijah to kill the Pinkerton. I only told him to get the information. Elijah always employs his own unique skills when it comes to following orders. I have chastised him for it many times." Glatt turned away and said more to himself than Billy, "I fear what little control I've had over Elijah in the past is slipping away."

"So you're saying that makes you innocent?"

Glatt appeared to ponder the notion of innocence for a moment. But, without answering the question, he asked, "Could I have a bit more water, please?"

"No."

"Talk of Mr. Thorn has soured your mood, Billy." Glatt's puffy eyes narrowed. "Now, do both of us a favor and dip me some water from that bucket yonder before I give a shout, and a half-dozen guns are in this tent putting bullet holes in you."

The man's mouth coiled into a grin. When it did, Billy knew the word he had searched for earlier to describe this demon's smile.

The give-away was the curl of his thin lip. Martin Glatt didn't smile; he sneered.

Billy pulled his Colt and touched its muzzle to a spot between Glatt's red eyes.

The man shrugged. "There is a distinct possibility that I'm going to be dead in the very near future, Young. Do you think your pistol frightens me?"

Billy responded by pulling back the short-barrel's hammer.

The sound of the triple click caused Glatt's waxen features to lose what little color they had. He waited a full thirty seconds before speaking and said, "Now, now, let's both settle down, here, Billy. No reason we can't get along."

Billy left the muzzle where it was.

"Do you know why they send young men to war?"

Billy stared without speaking.

"They send young men to war because, when it gets right down to it, young men have no concept of death. They have so many years spread out before them, they cannot imagine an end to it all. But humans are funny creatures. The older and closer to that end we get, the more precious those remaining years become. I'm now learning the hard lesson that when life is no longer measured in years, but is likely measured in days or even hours, it is even more precious. Put your gun away. You've convinced me that calling the others would be a bad idea."

Billy, too, waited at least a full thirty seconds before he responded by lowering the hammer. After holstering his piece, he bent to the ladle and gave Glatt another drink.

Chapter Twenty-Eight: He Has Talents

"Thank you, Deputy," said Glatt. He sipped the water. "Your gun in my face was not the only reason I didn't call for help. The other was that I pay my debts, and I owe you. You could've let me die in front of your house, but you didn't. You took me into town."

Billy dropped the ladle back into the bucket.

"Now we're even," Glatt added.

"Considering one of the reasons you didn't call out was you would've been dead before help arrived, I'd say we are not even."

"You're right. I can't argue with that. Anyway, threatening to call that scraggy bunch of cattle thieves in to gun you down was a bluff, and you called it. You'd make a good poker player."

"Except for penny-a-point cribbage, I rarely gamble. I dislike leaving things to chance." Billy shrugged. "Though avoiding random chance is not so easy."

Glatt used the sleeve of his red shirt to blot sweat from his forehead. "That is God's truth."

"Though you've brought plenty of death to others, I see you're eager to avoid it yourself."

"Being dead doesn't bother me; it's the hard act of dying that causes concern. The most a man can hope for at my current stage of life — or any stage of life, I suppose — is to pass quietly in his sleep — to drift away without knowing it has happened. What a blessing an easeful death would be." He'd been speaking with his eyes closed. He opened them now and looked toward Billy. "Much more pleasant than a bullet betwixt my eyeballs as I'm lying on my sick bed."

Billy scoffed. "Dying in your sleep, huh? I expect those you've ordered to their gruesome demise would agree."

"As I said, I pay my debts. And I expect those who owe me to pay theirs." He turned his gaze upward. The lamplight flickered across the tent's low ceiling.

"Seth Garvey was my friend — my best friend — yet he stole my wife."

"One of your wives, anyway."

Glatt turned back to Billy. "She was *my* wife. And Marlene. Marlene stole my trust."

Again, his hand came from under the blanket. This time it was clenched into a fist. "She stole my heart." He used the fist to strike himself on the chest.

"Your heart?" Billy shook his head and chuckled. "You are shameless."

Glatt ignored the comment. "Ivan Kradec is the very worst of these debtors. The coward shot me in the *back*." Then with ice in his voice, he added, "Kradec stole my son."

"You'll not be getting sympathy from me, Glatt. Never."

"None of them had to die. I allowed Garvey and Marlene to leave the Community untouched. Elijah was ready — eager — before they were ever exiled to put an end to them; but, as long as Marlene left Abraham with me, I wouldn't allow it. Then she had Abraham kidnapped by her brother. Until Kradec did that, I had not given a thought to that little weasel in years."

"From what I hear, Abraham was glad to leave with Mr. Kradec." Billy expected Glatt to respond to that with some denial, some reasonable explanation, some twist of the truth, but this time the slick-tongued bastard said nothing. "Abraham doesn't want to be with you," Billy said. "Your wife didn't want to be with you. And it looks to me like your little Nebraska Community is coming apart."

Glatt's silence continued.

"You say you needed information from Warren, but, except for Warren's hunting Kradec because Kradec made off with some rich man's expensive fiddle, Warren got all his information from your own people — women in your tribe. Why couldn't you get the same information from the same women? Are things at the Community not running so smooth these days?"

"Get out."

"Or what? Are you going to call for help?" Billy patted his holster. "I promise you will not die in your sleep, if you do. You're a fraud, Glatt. I know it. You know it. And the folks under your charlatan's spell are figuring it out, too. Think how disappointed they're going to be once they realize you're not the voice of God after all. And, since you say it's getting harder to control your insane but loyal Enforcer, it sounds like even Elijah Thorn's realizing the truth about you."

Billy allowed a moment for his accusation to lie there. When Glatt didn't deny it, Billy asked, "What are you doing out here in this wilderness, anyway? What are you even doing in Wyoming? You sent Thorn after Kradec to bring Abraham back and murder all of those who were close to the boy, but Thorn didn't need you around to do that. Looks to me like all you've accomplished by coming here is to be in the way and get yourself shot."

"I wanted Abraham."

"Once Thorn butchered everyone in sight, I expect he'd been on the next train to Nebraska with little Abe in tow."

"He would have, but I decided to come to Wyoming so I could get Abraham myself. After dealing with Dub Warren, Elijah and I heard of Whitson and Jones's confrontation with a violin player. We found them and made their acquaintance. They told us you had taken Kradec and the boy to your place. I assumed Warren's body would soon be found, and that we should make ourselves scarce; so, after a few drinks and a few dollars, Whitson told us about a hideout where he and his business partners would be moving their stolen cattle the next morning. I threw in a few more dollars and hired Whitson to bring Abraham and me along. I sent Elijah to the Sweetwater to collect my debts from Marlene and Seth. Then, once I had dealt with Kradec, the plan was that Abraham and I would leave with Whitson and meet Elijah at this hideout."

"Getting shot altered those plans some."

"True." He looked toward the bucket again, and this time, without confrontation, Billy ladled him a drink.

"I came for Abraham," repeated Glatt. "He is special. He has talents."

"I've heard him play the violin."

"Yes, he's a wonder. But it's more than that. At first we thought he was dim-witted, but that's not true. He's the opposite of that, but he needs to be where he can flourish. I've decided to leave the Community. It's the right thing to do for lots of reasons." He let out a breath. "Many of those reasons you have guessed. Things there are not" — he paused — "going well with my flock. The sheep are becoming doubtful. But there's more. I wanted to take Abraham back East. New York, Boston, Philadelphia. Someplace where his potential could —"

"Be exploited by you?" Billy didn't say it as a question, and Glatt didn't deny this, either. Billy wondered if the dance Glatt had been doing with death the last few days had given him a new perspective on his many sins. Probably not. In any case, it no longer mattered.

"Where's Abraham now?" asked Billy.

"Here in this camp . . . with Elijah."

That bit of information must have put a

distressed look on Billy's face.

"Don't worry. Elijah wouldn't hurt Abraham. He worships the boy." With a shrug he added, "And that is no exaggeration."

"Where are they exactly?"

"They say the two creeks that come in here are Deer Creek and Canyon Creek. I've only seen Elijah and the boy once since they arrived, but I hear they're camped on the west side of Canyon Creek. My guess is that's upwind and away from the cattle. Elijah's not fond of the smell of cow shit."

Billy, the ex-cattleman, said, "It smells like money to me."

"Elijah says it makes him queasy."

Chapter Twenty-Nine: The Biggest Unknown

"What can you tell me about Mr. Thorn?"

"As I said, he's peculiar."

"He's more than peculiar. But you know that. Did you tell him to use hay hooks to hang your best friend and your wife to a barn wall?"

Glatt didn't answer.

"If your future is now measured in hours, as you fear it is, maybe you should unburden yourself and confess your sins. Could be you'll knock a few million years off your time spent roasting in the fires of Hell. Why don't you ask your good friend God about that in one of your chats?"

"Are you a religious man, Billy? Do you believe in God?"

Billy paused, unsure of where this was going. "Yes," he answered after a bit. "I do have some questions, though, I suppose. Sometimes."

"Let me answer one of those questions for

you. Are you ready? Here it comes: God did not create us, Billy."

"He didn't, huh?"

"No."

"I thought you were a man of the cloth. A prophet, even."

Glatt provided Billy with a wide version of his unpleasant smile. "Nah," he said. "I admit that's nothing more than a convenience. What I'm saying to you now, though, is the truth as I am convinced it to be. God did not create us; we created Him."

Billy stood silent.

"Do you know why we created Him, Billy?"

When Billy didn't answer, Glatt told him anyway. "One word." He paused a beat and said, "Death. We invented God because we fear the unknown. Always have. Primitives, at night, would huddle in their caves and stare into the darkness, terrified of what might be lurking. And they were right to be afraid because there *was* something out there lurking. Death. The biggest unknown of them all."

Billy tried to think of a response but came up blank.

"Once we created God to protect us from the unknown, we had to think of some way to keep Him happy. So we created religion."

"You're saying there would be no God and no religion, if there was no such thing as death?"

"That's right." What little energy that had seeped into him earlier in their conversation was now gone. "Of course, if there was no such thing as death, plenty of other things also would be different."

"Like what?"

"For one, there'd be no need for diversions such as novels. No need for drama. It would be lost on us. Tales of derring-do would never have existed, because they would be meaningless. How interesting would *Hamlet* be if there were no such thing as death?" With a sad, wistful expression, he looked again toward the shadows dancing on the canvas above their heads. "If there were no death, what use would there be for poetry?"

Nothing more was said for a moment. When the silence was broken, it was Billy who broke it. "Well, sir. You may be right or you may be wrong. But I'm one of those young men you were talking about earlier. I figure I have lots of time to try to figure it out. But time's a thing you're running low on."

Glatt tried to force a laugh, but it caught on something before it could form. Then, answering the question Billy had asked before Glatt's digression on death, he said, "I didn't tell him to use hay hooks. I didn't tell him how to kill any of them. Except for Kradec."

"And with Kradec?"

"I told him I wanted Kradec to have a long, painful, lonely death in some dark, dirty dungeon."

"Well, sir, you'll be sorry to know that it didn't work out that way. It came close, but not quite."

"You're right. I am sorry to hear that. I wished the worst for that cowardly child thief. How did he manage to escape?"

"He didn't escape. Thorn did to Kradec all you asked, but Hugo and I got to him in time. I hope by telling you that, I don't get poor Mr. Thorn in trouble." Billy smiled. "He did do his best."

"You have an odd sense of humor, Billy. I wonder if your friend Dorling ever finds you tiresome."

"Why, yes, I do believe he does. Speaking of odd, how did Thorn get so crazy?"

Billy could see Glatt's thin shoulders shrug beneath the blanket. "Until he joined the Community back in St, Louis, he'd had a rough life, if that makes any difference."

"Lots of folks live rough lives and they

don't field-dress a human like they would an elk or hook people onto barn walls."

"He was an orphan, deposited in a home for boys there in St. Louis when he was an infant. When he was ten, he ran away and lived on the streets for another ten or so years. One day he wandered into our tabernacle. I visited with him, and within an hour he had seen the holy light, and, at that very moment, he became a soldier for our righteous cause."

"Considering your thoughts on God, I don't find that story inspirational."

"I have to admit, what drew me to Elijah was that the things that bother others did not bother him."

"I'm guessing that's what he liked about you, too. I hope you're not too attached to him, because he's not long for this world. Maybe we can work it out so the two of you can travel together to collect your just rewards, whatever they may be."

"I doubt Elijah would like that. We're not as close as we were."

"Too bad. You'll be finding out real soon if your theories on God are right. So, since you won't be around, if Hugo and I don't stop him, it'll be Thorn who raises your son."

Glatt's throat clenched as he attempted to

swallow. "There could be no one worse."

"You have made a mess of things, Glatt."

"You're right," he whispered. "But, despite my own lack of belief, I've never told anyone I have ever encountered anything they didn't want to hear." It sounded practiced, like an assurance he'd given himself a few thousand times before.

He smiled. This smile was weak, but it appeared genuine. And, though slight and humorless, this one was more a smile than a sneer.

"I told them nothing," he repeated, "that they didn't want to hear." He faced Billy and added, "Which, I suppose, makes for a poor epitaph." He released another long breath. "Go on now, Deputy. Please. I won't call out. I don't owe these outlaws anything. I've paid them well for their services."

The prophet's eyes slid up; his lids shuttered down, and he slipped into the ragged, but even, breathing of sleep.

Once again, Billy considered pulling the blanket over Glatt's face; but, though it wasn't easy, he again forced himself to resist that sweet temptation. This sweating trembler had ordered the murders of four people that Billy knew about: Dub Warren, a man Glatt didn't even know; Ivan Kradec; his friend, Seth Garvey; and Marlene, the mother of his child. Any man who would order such things deserved the same hard fate that would soon befall the mad man who had followed those brutal orders.

But there would be time for that tomorrow.

Billy would not allow Glatt the luxury of dying an easeful death in his sleep.

Chapter Thirty: Pretty Stupid

Billy met the others where he had left them, and they all returned to the wide spot next to the creek where they had made their camp.

"You're sayin' that the bully Whitson and his partner with the girl's name are down there?" Hugo sounded surprised but pleased. "Are you sure it was them?"

"I'm sure all right. No mistake. I was closer to them than I wanted to be."

"Well, sir, that's dandy." Hugo rubbed his hands together with excitement.

"Who are you fellas talking about?" asked Hank.

"A couple of men," Billy said, "who've taken a strong disliking to Hugo."

"And versy-vicey," said Hugo, with a smile.

"Also, like we figured, the man who's flat of his back in the big tent is Martin Glatt."

"You got close enough to see his face?"

"I did. We had a conversation." Billy knew what Hugo's reaction would be to that.

"A *conversation*? I told you not to let anyone get a look at you."

"I know you did, but it didn't work out that way."

"So we lost the chance to surprise them," said Hank.

"We sure have," agreed Hugo, with a scowl.

"I don't think he'll say anything to anybody," Billy said. "He doesn't give a damn about that bunch of saddle-trash rustlers. He's using them; that's all. Plus, he's got other things on his mind."

"Like what?"

"For one, he's infected, and his fevers are such he expects it'll soon be over. My guess is there's a good chance he'll be dead by this time tomorrow."

"Ha," said Hugo. "I expect there's a *real* good chance he'll be dead by this time tomorrow."

Charlie laughed. It appeared ol' Charlie thought Hugo was funny.

Billy snugged his Marlin into its scabbard, unbuckled his gunbelt, and draped it across his saddlebags, which he'd placed next to his opened-out bedroll. "There's more," he said as he stepped to the bedroll and dropped onto his back. He laced his fingers behind his head and, looking toward the stars, said, "Those cattle thieves aren't planning to ship the animals by rail."

"What d'ya figure they'll do with them, then?" asked Hank. He also sat on his bedroll and, using no hands, shook off his boots.

"Damn, Hank," said Hugo. "Them boots are too big for you, aren't they?"

"I got bunions. I like my boots loose."

"Did you get them bunions walkin' behind a plow?"

"Nah, hell, I think I was born with the damned things. 'Course, the life of a farmer did not make them better."

"So bunions on your feet and a surly woman in your house is what drove you from the flatlands all the way over here to this splendid place?"

Hank smiled but gave a snort that communicated more a scoff than amusement.

It amazed Billy how easy it was for Hugo to get sidetracked. "If you boys are done talking about feet, I have more to tell you."

"Tell away," said Hugo. "Nobody's stoppin' you."

"According to Whitson, it sounds like they're selling these cattle to some man Whitson called 'the deputy.' "

"Deputy? You mean like a deputy sheriff?"

"He didn't elaborate, Hugo."

"What else could it be but a deputy sheriff?" Charlie asked. "How many kinds of deputies are there?"

"Lots," said Hugo. "You're looking at a couple of deputy U.S. marshals right now."

"So, you think it's a deputy marshal?"

"Doubtful since me 'n Billy's 'bout the only two around."

"Most public officials have a deputy or two," Billy said. "Not only sheriffs, but there's deputy prosecutors. There's a bunch of deputy clerks of different sorts working at all the county offices in every county courthouse. So there's a bunch of them."

Hugo shook out his bedroll and sat down. "Deputies," he pointed out, "are the ones who do most of the work in this world. That's sure the way it's always been with marshalin'."

"Maybe this deputy that's coming is some lawman playing a trick on them," said Hank, "and he'll show up tomorrow with a posse." When no one commented on that, he added, "It could be a deputy with the sheriff outta Casper, couldn't it?"

"Nope," said Hugo. "The Natrona County Commissioners wouldn't let 'im have a deputy. He told us that himself just a few days ago."

"And whoever it is," Billy said, "the man's in on the rustling, so there sure won't be a posse."

Charlie asked Billy, "It is strange that it's some kind of deputy, though, ain't it?"

"Not necessarily. Whitson saying it was a deputy doesn't tell us much. It could be a deputy sheriff from some other county, or a deputy assessor or treasurer, a deputy county or town clerk. Who knows? Even a deputy dogcatcher, for that matter."

"Dogcatcher, eh? Boy, I'd sure hate that job," said Charlie. "How do they catch 'em, anyhow? Do they rope 'em? That wouldn't be easy. Dogs are fast. And they can turn real quick."

Charlie was as easily sidetracked as Hugo.

"This deputy is coming for those critters sometime tomorrow morning. But Whitson's worried that whoever the deputy is might not bring enough hands to trail the cattle wherever it is he plans to take them. Whitson figures if that happens, the job'll fall to him and Evelyn and their fellow cattle thieves."

"Damn, Billy," Hugo said. "You're a pretty good spy. You learned a bunch considerin' you weren't gone very long."

"Earl and Evelyn like to chat while they pee."

None of the others requested the details of that bit of information.

"And there's more."

"What's that?"

"It sounded like the fella who's running things for the rustlers is a man by the name of Jarrod."

"Jarrod?"

Billy looked toward Hugo. After hearing Jarrod's name, Billy could see the surprise in Hugo's bulging eyeballs even in the low light.

"Who's Jarrod?" Hank asked.

"The only Jarrod we've heard of around this country is Dale Jarrod."

"That's right," agreed Hugo. "Dale Jarrod, the no good, poor excuse for a sheriff who was voted outta office this past November."

Hank said, "Well, if there is a crooked sheriff hooked up in this, I guess it's possible that there's a crooked deputy in it, too."

"Tell us about your visit with Glatt," said Hugo in a flat tone of voice.

"I saw a couple of men tote him into the big tent, and, when they left, I snuck in for a look."

"Pretty stupid."

"Maybe," said Billy. And, as he spoke of it now, going into that tent and talking to Glatt did sound stupid; but, even so, he doubted it would make any difference. And he felt what he'd learned made the risk worthwhile.

"So what did you and the prophet talk about?" Hugo took off his hat, set it on the ground, and, using both hands, gave his scalp a vigorous scratching. "Did he tell you anythin' 'bout little Abe?"

"Abe's with Thorn at a camp by themselves away from the cattle on the west side of Canyon Creek."

"We spotted a small fire over there," Charlie said. "That must've been them."

"Do you figure Abe to be okay?" asked Hugo.

"Well, he's alive, but, like I say, he's with Thorn."

"Did you tell Glatt if the fevers don't kill 'im me or you'd be glad to do it ourselves?"

"I'm not sure I said those words, but he understands our intentions."

"You should-a kilt 'im when you had the chance."

"I considered it."

"Considered it? Hell, Billy."

"I gave it some thought but decided it wasn't the right time." After saying that,

Billy didn't bother to squint through the darkness to check Hugo's expression. He was confident that Hugo, wearing a look of disgust, was squinting through the dark at him.

"There ain't no wrong time to kill Martin Glatt."

Hugo pulled off his boots and lay back on his bedroll. Tossing his blanket over his legs, he said, "Let's get some sleep."

Chapter Thirty-One: Die Just as Dead

Breakfast the next morning was skimpy. All they had left were a few of Hank's dried apricots. Even in the daylight, they were hesitant to build a fire for fear of giving themselves away. So, no fire meant no coffee. Hugo said it was the first morning since he was eight years old that he had begun a day without coffee. "It ain't a good omen," he added.

Hugo often said that something or another was not a good omen, but Billy knew the old codger put no faith in omens and had snippy words for anyone who did.

"Yesterday," said Hugo, "I spotted some wild raspberries growin' along the edge of the crick about a mile upstream. I'm gonna pick us some."

"I'll do it, Hugo. I saw them, too."

"Nah, boy, you stay here and think up a plan on how we're gonna accomplish gettin' little Abe outta that camp and killin' Glatt and Thorn when we do. I won't be long." He buckled on his forty-four, saddled his bay, and climbed aboard.

"Why don't you come up with a plan yourself? After all, you are the chief deputy."

"I am, and I'm assignin' the plan-makin' task to you. It is part of your intensive law enforcement trainin'. And make it a good one, boy. I was not impressed with the one you had last night."

"Get going, Hugo. And don't eat all those raspberries before you get back."

"I might. Why d'ya think I wanted to be the one to fetch 'em?" Laughing, he gigged his horse and trotted off.

Billy knew what needed to be done in the rustlers' camp would not be easy. And he had no ideas, good ones or bad.

As usual, he hadn't slept the night before. The creek bank was a little softer than it had been at the Sage Hen, and the sound of flowing water was relaxing, but, while the others farted and snored, Billy spent the night, without success, trying to worry a plan into life.

He pulled his suspenders up and threw his gunbelt and holster over his shoulder. To Hank and Charlie he said, "I'm going for a stroll, boys." He reached into a saddlebag and dug out his bone-handled toothbrush and a bottle of Sozodont. He dipped the business end of the brush into the creek and sprinkled its boar bristles with a few drops of the dentifrice. "I'll be back," he said, as he re-corked the small bottle and tossed it onto his bedroll.

"Would you care for some company?" asked Charlie.

"Nope," Billy said without explanation.

Many fruitless hours of lying awake helped to convince Billy that his brain worked better when he was on his feet. At least it didn't work any worse.

He brushed his teeth as he walked along the creek bank. Not far before the thick trees ended, he bent and used his hand to cup water into his mouth. He swished it around and spit into the grass. Smacking his lips, he blotted them with the back of his hand. He liked the feeling the Sozodont left in his mouth. His favorite flavor was star anise, which was much tastier than any of the chalky fruit flavors of Hugo's Hub Wafers. He swirled the brush in the water, gave it a couple of shakes, and tucked it into a back pocket.

As he edged his way toward the spot where the copse of trees thinned, he lifted his gunbelt from his shoulder and strapped it on. The large boulders that Hugo and the boys had hid behind the night before were down the hill a-ways. He would have been able to see better from there, but it was now daylight, and, not wanting to risk being spotted, he stayed where he was. The best and safest place to view the camp was from the crest of the hill where he and Hugo climbed the day before. He was not eager to make that climb again; besides, he didn't have the spyglass, anyway, so here would have to do.

The camp below bustled with activity. Billy guessed the outlaws were excited. The deputy, whoever he may be, should be arriving anytime, and today would be their payday.

Hank's hope last night about a posse showing up this morning was appealing, but impossible. If there had been some way to have gotten word to Sheriff Garner about what was going on, he could have easily rounded up plenty of ranchers willing to join a posse and ride out here to deal with these cattle thieves. There would have been a gunfight, no doubt, but, with that distraction, Billy and Hugo, along with their Sun Ranch cowboy pals, could have made short work of Martin Glatt and Elijah Thorn.

But there was no way to contact Skip Garner and no time now for him and his posse to get here even if there was.

Billy turned his gaze toward the cattle. There was plenty of grass, and the water in the two creeks flowed nicely. The animals bunched up in the area between the streams appeared restless, and a few would occasionally wander into one of the creeks. There were two men riding the herd's perimeter, and, when any of the cattle moved into the water, these men would chase them back between the streams. Billy knew they did this to both keep them from straying and from fouling the water that was being used downstream to cook with and to drink. Like most everyone else in the camp, when the men riding herd weren't chasing a cow, their attention was focused toward the west. The deputy and his cowboys, if he brought any along, would likely ride in from that direction.

The men in the camp scurried about, doing one chore or another, or pretending to. The fat cook Billy and Hugo had seen yesterday now flipped flapjacks in a large cast-iron skillet that sat on a grate over a fire. Next to that skillet was another filled with frying bacon. Billy was too far away to smell the grub, but his stomach rumbled anyway.

He did another quick count of the men

and got the same number he and Hugo got the day before. Eight. Eight guns against their four. And that eight was not counting Thorn and possibly Glatt, if he was alive. The odds were even worse considering two of Billy and Hugo's four guns were in the hands of cowboys who had never shot at anything more than a snake or a prairie dog.

As Billy watched, two men entered the big tent. Judging by their size and the way they moved, they might be Whitson and Jones, but from this far away it was hard to tell. A minute later, the smaller of the two men came out carrying something. He crossed from the tent to a shady spot and levered open a folding camp chair. He set the chair down and went back into the tent.

Two minutes later, he and the larger man emerged with a third man between them. The third man's features could not be made out, but he appeared emaciated, and Billy could see that he wore a dark-red shirt. To Billy's shock, he realized Martin Glatt was the man in the middle. Glatt's gait was an old man's wobbly shuffle, but, even though the two men at his sides were helping, Billy could see that the back-shot, infected prophet, who the night before looked to be so close to death, was now able to move under his own steam.

■ ■ ■ ■

"It don't matter," said Hugo. "The son of a bitch can die just as dead sittin' in a chair as he can layin' on a cot."

"If he's going to die sitting in that chair anytime soon, we're going to have to go down there in broad daylight in the presence of eight rustlers and shoot him."

Hank suggested, "Maybe we could get him with a rifle."

Billy shook his head and made a noise like he was sucking something out of a tooth. The noise told more about his frustration than he had intended. "It's doable, I suppose, but it'd be a mighty long shot. I doubt I could make it. And Hugo, here, sure couldn't with his poor vision."

Hugo grumbled, but he didn't deny the truth.

"How's your aim with a long gun, Hank?" Billy asked.

"Never was nothing to brag about."

Hank turned toward Charlie, but, before he could say anything, Charlie said, "Whoa, don't look at me. Even the broad side of a barn is safe with me around."

"We're not going to try to shoot him from up here. I'm not sure Annie Oakley could make that shot. Besides, if we tried, we'd be giving ourselves away. At the very least, it would provide Thorn the chance to make a run for it. Maybe Glatt, too, from the looks of it."

"Could be Mr. Glatt, the smooth-talkin' confidence man, was not as sick as he made you believe."

Billy hated to admit it, but Hugo could be right. Glatt was sick. Even a smooth talker can't make himself sweat, but it was possible Glatt's wishful musings about the blessing of dying in his sleep had been a ruse. Glatt could tell Billy was pondering whether he should kill him then or later. Thinking later would be better than now, Glatt might have voiced those wishes and then feigned sleep knowing Billy would never grant his wish to go the easy way.

The moment Billy had that thought, he knew it was true. Glatt had played him for a fool.

"If they had-a left Glatt in the tent," said Hugo, "it's possible we could get in and out of there without being seen. We could-a kilt him quiet-like and got across Canyon Crick to the small tent and taken care of Thorn."

"But they didn't leave him in the tent," Billy said, putting a stop to Hugo's pointless rumination.

"That's right, but *goddamn* it," snapped Hugo. "There's gotta be a way. I ain't believin' we came this far and got this close and can't get the job done."

Billy picked up a rock and threw it into the stream. "We can get it done. It's risky, and maybe farfetched, but I'm thinking we can get it done." And, despite the odds, he heard in his voice a cold determination.

When Billy said that, Hugo, who was lifting a raspberry toward his mouth, stopped his hand midway. "What're you gettin' at, boy?"

"Well, Hugo, I believe I've got a plan."

Chapter Thirty-Two: Surprise, Surprise

Billy and Hugo took the risk and, with rifles in hand, slinked their way to the boulders. It turned out not to be as difficult as they had feared. The only vigilance anyone in the camp exhibited was directed toward the west.

Hugo said, "Those rustlers must plan to sell the cattle to some rancher in the Wind River country. I can't guess who it might be. I know most-a them fellas over there, and they're honest men. It's hard to imagine any of 'em buyin' animals they know to be stole."

"Don't count on it, Hugo," said Billy, who, after being duped by Glatt the night before, now realized he'd spent too much of his naive life trusting people who didn't deserve it. "Greed is a common commodity in this world."

"Every one of them boys along the Wind is doin' fine. None of 'em needs to be buyin' stole cows."

"Just because a man's rich, doesn't mean he wouldn't like to be richer."

"You're not as trustin' of your fellow man as you were this time yesterday, Billy-boy." Hugo laughed and jabbed Billy with an elbow. "Whatever could-a happened since then to make you such a cynic?"

"Be quiet, you ol' coot." Hugo could usually tell when something was eating at Billy, and most of the time he could tell what it was. This appeared to be one of those times. Billy looked toward the camp, the cattle between the streams, and the narrow canyon behind the cattle. "You don't even know what the word 'cynic' means."

"Sure, I do. What it means is you have already, in your short life, turned into a sad, pitiful, bitter misanthrope."

Billy felt his eyebrows shoot toward his hairline. "Missing *wha—* "

Before he could finish, Hugo said, "I heard a fancy fella call another fancy fella that in a fancy saloon down in Cheyenne. It got a reaction from all the fancy fellas around, so I made sure I remembered it so I could use it on you when the time presented itself." Before elaborating more, he raised his arm and jabbed four fingers toward the far side of the camp. "Looks like the murderers and thieves've got company."

A rider was coming in from the west. The others spotted him, too, and a man who had been drinking coffee behind one of the wagons stepped into view. He mounted a horse that he'd had tied to the back of the wagon and rode out to meet the visitor.

"That fella who's ridin' out to greet the newcomer must be Dale Jarrod," said Hugo.

"You're right; he is. But how can you tell with your poor eyes?"

"I recognize his brindle horse. Though I find brindles to be homely, I know that horse to be a fine animal. Much too good for his owner, in my opinion."

"I don't know the other man," said Billy, "but he must be the deputy. It doesn't look like he's bringing any hands along."

"That's good news for us," Hugo said. "What we don't need is more gun-totin' cowboys takin' potshots at us."

The two men on horseback continued to mind the herd, but three other men, including the cook, left whatever they were doing and walked out to meet Dale Jarrod and the deputy as they rode into camp. Martin Glatt stayed in his chair.

"Let's get down to the bottom while they ain't lookin'," said Hugo. "We don't have much time."

In a crouching run, the two left the safety of the rocks and sprinted down the hill toward where Deer Creek veered to the west. Billy led the way to the crossing spot he'd found the night before. Once across, they continued their sprint to the rabbit-brush behind the big tent. The exposure caused Billy's nerves to jangle, but they were lucky and made it without being seen.

From their hiding place in the bushes, Hugo whispered, "There the blond-haired bastard is, Billy. Sittin' in that chair like a duck on a pond. We *could* wait 'til it gets noisy and shoot 'im where he sits. But that's too easy for 'im," said Hugo with a wicked smile.

"I agree. He needs to know what's happening." Billy suspected that Glatt was sleeping in his chair, and Billy had already decided that killing Glatt while he slept would not do.

"Let's jerk 'im outta that chair and drag 'im behind the tent." Hugo pulled his knife. "We can get 'im kilt quick and quiet."

Any debate, serious or otherwise, they'd had since this all began about killing Glatt or Thorn on sight had been forgotten.

Until now.

No matter how bad Glatt was, Billy was hesitant to watch Hugo stab him or cut his throat. Billy forced himself to recall the images of Dub Warren and Garvey and Marlene after Thorn had followed this man's orders and done his worst. But even that wasn't enough. Though Billy had considered it the night before and had decided against it for a different reason, killing any man in cold blood was not what Billy and Hugo did. He was about to remind Hugo of that, but, before he could get it said, Hugo had stepped from the brush and was headed in Glatt's direction.

In an instant, Hugo crossed the twenty-five feet that separated them and jammed the fingers of his left hand down into the space between the back of Glatt's neck and the collar of his red shirt. With a twist of his wrist, Hugo wrenched the collar as tight as a tourniquet. Glatt's hands flew to his throat, and he made a choking gasp, but that was the only sound he could produce. When Hugo pulled him from the chair, the prophet kicked and sputtered as he was dragged all the way to the back of the tent, where Hugo dropped him facedown into the dirt.

"Surprise, surprise, son of a bitch," taunted Hugo, as he drove a knee into the small of Glatt's back. "Let's see if you can smooth talk Jesus outta tossin' you into a boilin' lake-a fire."

Hugo let go of Glatt's collar and grabbed a handful of hair. He pulled the prophet's head back and put the blade against the front of Glatt's neck. The man squirmed and made noises that were likely supplications, but it was hard to tell.

Billy stepped from the bushes, and, as he was about to give voice to his thoughts on killing anyone, even this bastard, in cold blood, Hugo turned and found Billy's eyes. As soon as he did, Billy knew Hugo, even with his knife at Glatt's throat, was also having second thoughts. The deputy had killed any number of men over the years, and Billy didn't know the details of all those killings. But he did know Hugo. And he knew not one of those men had been murdered in cold blood.

As Hugo looked up at him, Billy gave a quick shake of his head. In answer, Hugo nodded. He then shrugged his shoulders with displeased resignation. Billy knew the old deputy wanted to do it, but he could not give himself permission.

Instead, Hugo raised his knee, grabbed Glatt's shoulder, and flipped him over.

Glatt yelped as he landed hard on his back. "Please, no. Please don't kill me," he begged and came out with another yelp as

Hugo again came down hard with his knee, this time into the center of the prophet's gut.

With Glatt pinned to the dirt, Hugo's knife was no longer at his throat, but its six-inch blade was at the end of Glatt's nose.

Things had happened fast, and only now did Billy and Hugo stare down into the squirming man's face. When they did, at first, neither of them spoke. But after a moment of staring, Hugo looked again to Billy, and, with a confused expression, he blinked and poked the point of his knife a couple of times in the man's direction. "Who in the hell," he asked, "is *this*?"

Chapter Thirty-Three: He Don't Look Friendly

Billy was confident that his own expression showed no less confusion than Hugo's. The man who lay there, his eyes wide with terror, was not Martin Glatt. He was as blond as Glatt. He was Glatt's height. He looked as thin and as emaciated as Glatt had looked the night before. But the man pinned and wriggling beneath the pressure of Hugo's knee was not Martin Glatt.

In a hard, deliberate voice, Billy said, "Hugo, put that knife underneath this bastard's chin."

In less than a second, Hugo nodded a quick half-dozen times. "You bet. You *bet,*" he said, and, in one smooth motion, he had the blade's sharp edge an inch above the skinny man's tremulous Adam's apple. Hugo gave the knife a little flick. Not enough to do much damage. Just enough to draw blood.

The man, whoever the hell he was, cringed

and whimpered even more than he had before. With his eyes now clenched, he began to make mumbling noises. He might have been praying, or pleading, or both. The sounds might have been addressed to Hugo, God, or to the man's mother; there was no way to know, because the words were indecipherable.

Billy knelt next to Hugo and his wriggling victim. "We thought you were somebody else, Mister," said Billy softly into the man's right ear. "Someone we plan to kill." The man's eyes popped open and bulged to the size of a hen's egg. He didn't dare move his head with Hugo's knife where it was, but he did lock his egg-eyes, as best he could, onto Billy.

Billy locked his eyes onto the man as well. "I'm going to tell you something," he said. "You not being who we hoped you were doesn't mean we won't kill you, if we have to." Billy wasn't sure he meant that, but he could tell the man with Hugo's knife at his throat was convinced. "Do you understand me?"

The large eyes moved down in an effort to see Hugo's hand.

"Lift your knife a bit, Hugo, so this fella can see for sure what he's dealing with."

Hugo did, but not by much.

"I'll ask again. Do you understand what I said?" Then to emphasize his point, he added, "If you are hiding the man who was in this tent last night, and you don't tell us where he is, we will gladly slit your throat. So, answer me. Do you understand what I am saying?"

The man's head bounced up and down the way a Jack doll's head bounces when he pops out of a box. "I understand. Yes, sir, I sure do."

"Good," Billy said. "You may survive this after all."

"I don't think so," corrected Hugo, and in a blink the blade was back at the skinny man's throat. Hugo flicked his knife again. This time the cut was a little deeper.

"You are wearing a shirt that belongs to the man we're after. The way I see it, you were pretending to be that man. Start talking."

"Jarrod. Dale Jarrod told me to do it." This man was not only frightened, he appeared to be none too bright.

"Why?" asked Hugo in a tone so chilly, it even sent a shiver into Billy.

The man whined, "I don't *know.*"

Another flick of the knife. A little more blood.

"Please. *Please.* I'll tell you everything I

know, but Jarrod didn't tell me *why* he wanted me to do it. He just handed me this red shirt and told me to put it on. He called them two fellas Whitson and Jones over, and he told us that he wanted us to do some play-acting."

He paused. "I sure wish you'd get that cutter away from my gullet, Mister. I got no reason to lie to you. I *swear.*"

Hugo gave it some consideration and pulled the knife away. "I'm gonna let you up, but if you call out to any of your fella rustlers 'round here, it'll be the last thing you do in this life."

Billy knew that was true, cold blooded or not.

"Don't you worry 'bout that," said the skinny man. "I got me a wife and a couple-a kids. We got a place on the river not far from Bessemer." He swallowed. "I hope to see them again real soon."

Hugo lifted his knee and stood. As the skinny man moved to a sitting position, Billy reached down and took the man's gun out of its holster.

"You can have that ol' thing, if you like," said the man. "I ain't no good with it, anyhow." He reached toward his pocket, and Billy cocked the shooter's hammer. "Whoa, there." The man's hands shot straight up, palms forward. "I'm getting my kerchief; that's all." Billy stared without speaking, and, with a tentative move, the man lowered a hand to his pocket and tugged out a grimy looking handkerchief. He used it to blot blood from his neck and sweat from his brow. "I don't mind admitting it; you boys scared the bejesus outta me just now." With a glance to Hugo's knife, he added, "You still are, Mister." Then, in what appeared an effort to show he was harmless, the man's mouth stretched into an awkward grin. He had large gums that hung over his tiny, beige teeth like a pink awning.

"What's your name?" asked Billy.

"Woodrow Bayliss. Like I said, I'm from over on the North Platte —"

Hugo gave the man an open-handed swat across the temple.

"Damn, that *hurt.*"

"We don't give a shit where you're from, you featherbrain. What did Jarrod mean when he told you and the other two he wanted you to do some play-acting?"

"Well, sir, there was a fella in that tent there. You're right about that. I never got a good look at him, myself, but I heard he was sick. We hauled him here to the Rattlesnakes all the way from Casper. Some of the boys're saying the fella's got lots of spondulicks." He rubbed his thumb and index finger together. "And he don't mind spreading it around. He paid Whitson and Jones to get him here, and it looks like he paid Dale Jarrod to let him stay." He lifted the kerchief from his neck and peered at the splotches of red.

"So," said Billy, "you knew you were pretending to be the sick man when Whitson and Jones led you out of the tent this morning and sat you in that chair?"

"I did, but I didn't know why. Jarrod just told me to do it. He said from a distance nobody'd be able to tell me from that sick fella. He paid me a silver dollar, so I didn't ask any questions." He again smiled that idiot smile. "Jarrod didn't give Whitson and Jones nothing. Only me. He said he wanted me to come outta that tent gimping along, and them other two to act like they was helping me."

"Why do you suppose Jarrod would do that?" Billy asked.

"Couldn't help you on that one. But I seen Jarrod talking to that other fella before he come over to get me to do it."

"What other fella?"

"I don't know him. He don't ride with us. I wouldn't've thought nothing of it, 'cept while him and Jarrod was talking, this man looks over in my direction and points right at me. Then he give Jarrod this here shirt."

"What does he look like?" asked Hugo.

"Oh, he's a big one. Real big. I'd say he's at least half a foot over six feet tall. Hell, maybe more than that. And another thing I noticed about him is that he's got the biggest hands I ever saw." Bayliss lifted his own hands and made fists. "His fists're like a couple-a hams."

"What else can you tell us about him?" Billy asked.

"He don't look friendly; that's for sure. And he sure ain't what you'd call handsome."

"What do you mean?"

"He's got a scar — a nasty one." With his index finger, Bayliss drew an invisible line from his left eye, down his cheek, and past his chin. "It runs all the way from here to here."

"Is there anything more you know about him?"

"No, not really. I ain't never talked to him. I had no reason to, nor desire to, neither one. He ain't sociable. All I know is he rode into camp a day or so ago."

Billy asked, "Was he with anyone?"

"Why, yes, sir, he was. A kid come in with him."

Hugo stiffened. "A kid?"

"Yep, a little boy riding a white mule. He had a beat-up looking case strapped to his saddle. That case was a strange sort-a thing. Kinda shaped like a geetar only lots littler."

CHAPTER THIRTY-FOUR: WHAT'S A THESPIAN?

Billy jerked a thumb in the skinny man's direction. "What d'ya figure we should do with this thespian, Hugo?" Woodrow Bayliss remained at Billy's and Hugo's feet blotting away the small spots of blood leaking from his neck.

"What's a thespian?" asked Bayliss.

"It's a play actor."

"A play actor?" asked Hugo. "Are you sure?"

Billy could tell Hugo thought it had another meaning, but Billy didn't ask what he thought it might be. "I'm sure," Billy said. He gave Bayliss's shooter a flip, caught it by the barrel, and threw it end over end into the rabbitbrush.

Hugo, with a twinkle in his eye, looked down at Bayliss. When he did, Billy knew what was coming. "I s'pose," Hugo said, "we should go ahead and kill 'im. It don't make sense not to."

Bayliss's sweaty forehead wrinkled like a blanket on an unmade bed.

Billy doubted this was the time for gibing, but Hugo's twinkle and Bayliss's furrowed brow made it too tempting to resist. "Well, Hugo, you make a good point. No need to take unnecessary risks."

The moment Billy said it, they heard someone coming in their direction.

The approaching man called out. "Damn it, Woodrow, why're you outta that chair? You know what Jarrod said. And where the hell are you, anyhow?"

As the speaker came around the tent, Billy saw it was the short man with the tall-crowned hat that they had seen round up the stray the afternoon before. The second the cowboy saw Billy and Hugo, his jaw hardened, and, lightning fast, his gun was in his fist and aimed right at Hugo. Billy filled his own fist, but, before he or the man could pull their triggers, Hugo's right hand jerked. Half an instant later there was a knife protruding from a spot a half inch below and to the left of the short man's chest bone. The way Hugo threw it, the blade came in at a slight upward angle.

When the knife hit, the man's gun dropped and so did the man. He lay on his back with Hugo's knife sticking up from the center of him. A surprising amount of blood spurted around the blade. It spewed like water from an artesian spring.

Hugo stepped to the man and squatted down. The man stared straight up at the sky. His lips moved, but no sounds came out. Hugo retrieved his knife and wiped the blade on the man's denims. Once the knife was out, the blood spouted faster and with even more force. By the time Hugo rose and sheathed his blade, the short man looked to be close to unconscious.

Billy guessed Hugo's knife must have sliced through something important.

Once Hugo was back with Billy and Bayliss, the artesian spring had bubbled to a stop — not because the short man had run out of blood, but because he had run out of heartbeats.

Watching all this, Bayliss had sunk into a stupor and turned as white as winter. Billy felt little sympathy for the rustler lying dead or dying. He was about to put a bullet into Hugo, and getting some steel into the bottom of his heart was what he deserved. But there was something about the expression on the simple face of Woodrow Bayliss that struck Billy hard. Bayless was not a man made for what he got when he'd agreed to ride with this outfit.

As Billy pondered all these swirling thoughts, the first shots were fired.

Hugo aimed an index finger at Bayliss and said, "Mr. Bayliss, you get away from this tent right now and hide behind them rocks up the hill. And stay there. If you do, you should be safe. You got that?"

Bayliss appeared no less stunned than he had ten seconds before; even so, he nodded that he understood, but he didn't move.

Though he made no contact, Hugo kicked at the man. "Get, goddamn it."

Bayliss leapt to his feet and took off without looking back.

Hugo turned to Billy. "Let's go."

Billy fell in behind Hugo, stopping only to grab the short man's gun and tuck it into the small of his back.

They ran to the far side of the tent and looked out over the camp. A grouping of five horses were galloping out of the narrow canyon. Behind the horses came Hank and Charlie, yelping and firing their pistols into the air.

"There they are," shouted Hugo. "Them rustlers must-a kept their horses picketed in that canyon."

The horses and the men behind them charged into the herd of already restless and spooky cattle. When they did, the bellowing bovines took off, stampeding through the middle of the camp and leveling everything in their path.

"Looks like Hank and Charlie are putting the horses to good use," Billy said. Earlier that morning, Billy had sent Hank and Charlie back the way they had come, around the base of Garfield Peak, and into the canyon on the other side of the mountain. Once they made it to the northwest end of the canyon, they'd be right behind the pasturing herd. The boys needed a distraction if they were going to locate Glatt, Thorn, and Abraham. A couple of hundred cattle rampaging through the camp should do the trick. Throwing the rustlers' own horses into the chaos and leaving most of the thieves afoot was a lucky bonus.

"Let's get across Canyon Crick," said Hugo, "but keep an eye on the little tent as we go. If Thorn's in there, he'll likely poke his head out to watch the ruckus."

Hugo dashed through the rabbitbrush and, using it for cover, headed for the creek.

As Hugo did that, Billy threw back the big tent's door flap and peered in. He hoped Glatt was there, but he was not. Billy let out a curse and took off after Hugo.

Dale Jarrod and the deputy were atop

their horses watching all that was happening. The two cowboys and the cook who had come over to meet Jarrod and the deputy ran to cover behind a stand of rocks and began shooting at Hank and Charlie. All they had were their sidearms, so, at this distance, they weren't much of a threat. All their gunfire accomplished was to make the stampeding cattle even more frantic.

Billy and Hugo sprinted to the creek, barely slowing as they hit the water. Canyon Creek, like Deer Creek, had widened as it came out of the higher ground. Where they crossed, the depth was short of their boot tops, and they were lucky enough to avoid stepping into any holes. Billy hated getting his socks wet.

Once across, they moved upstream through the cover of tall grass that grew along a line of cottonwoods.

Glatt had said that Thorn and Abe were in the smaller tent. Now that Glatt was nowhere to be found, it could be that he was in there, too. Of course, Glatt may have lied about that along with all his other lies, but Billy and Hugo had to check to be sure.

The front of the tent faced upstream, which would have required whoever was inside to step out and walk to the back if they wanted to see across the creek toward the pandemonium beyond. But there was no one about.

Maybe it was empty.

They moved up from the grass and edged their way through the cottonwoods, stopping twenty feet from the small tent's camp.

"If Thorn's in there," said Hugo, "he's waitin' for us. He ain't seen us comin', though, or we'd be takin' fire."

"Which means we have surprise on our side. How do you propose we do this?"

Hugo didn't answer the question, which was annoying. Billy was eager to get this chore done.

Billy made an exasperated groan, and Hugo said, "I'm think- in' on it."

Billy wished Hugo had started *thinkin'* on it sooner.

Hugo looked toward the mayhem taking place between the two creeks. "Your plan is workin' fine, Billy."

Hugo was right. The chaos caused by the stampeding cattle had allowed them to make it across the creek and to where they now were without being spotted. It could be, Billy thought, that his skills were better suited for making broad-scale plans. But when it came to planning things up close, he was glad to turn to Hugo.

Things were getting wilder across the

creek. The two cowboys who had been riding perimeter were attempting, without success, to turn the herd. One of them gave up on that idea. He reined his horse to a stop and drew his rifle. He jacked in a round and started firing at Hank and Charlie. Despite all the noise one of the cowboy's bullets must have whizzed past Charlie close enough to get his attention. He turned toward the shooter and, at a gallop, leveled his pistol and fired, hitting his target high in the left shoulder. The man jerked from the impact. When he did, his horse reared, and the cowboy tumbled backward and rolled off the horse's rump.

"Ooh, Lordy," said Hugo with a wince as he watched a tidal wave of hooves trample over the man.

Charlie and the man he shot had not been far apart, but Billy leaned toward Hugo and said, "Looks like ol' Charlie's a better shot than he let on."

The fat cook grabbed a blanket from his chuck wagon and ran toward the running cattle, waving it in an effort to turn them before they crashed into the wagon and the buckboard. It didn't take long before he realized that he was doing nothing but putting himself in harm's way, and he tossed the blanket to the ground and ran for his life. He made it back to the two shooters behind the rocks and dropped to the ground, his big chest heaving as he gulped for air.

Not counting Hank and Charlie, the only men now on horseback were the one cowboy who was trying to turn the herd, Dale Jarrod, and the deputy.

For the first time, Billy and Hugo were close enough to get a look at the deputy. He was a mid-sized man, in his later thirties, with thick side whiskers. He wore a business suit and gold-rimmed spectacles. After staring at him for a bit, Hugo said, "Well, I'll be."

"What's wrong?" asked Billy.

"I believe I know that man."

Chapter Thirty-Five: Toe-to-Goddamned-Toe

Before Billy could ask what Hugo meant, Jarrod pulled his rifle, gigged his horse, and started toward the herd. As he did, he shouted something to the deputy. Billy couldn't hear what it was through the din of pounding hooves, bellowing cattle, and gunfire, but the deputy's response was to shake his head, spin his mount, and take off in the opposite direction. Jarrod made a quick turn and charged after him. When he caught the fleeing man, Jarrod swung his rifle like a baseball bat and cracked its barrel into the back of the deputy's skull. The deputy went limp, fell forward, and hit the ground. Once he stopped bouncing, he lay motionless.

For a second it appeared Jarrod was going to put a bullet into him, but he didn't. Instead, giving his horse plenty of spur, he returned to the camp.

Billy had told Hank and Charlie that, once

they had the cattle running, they should take cover. And he watched now as Hank pulled his rifle from its scabbard and dropped from his saddle. He gave his horse a swat, and the animal continued on, following the other horses as they ran with the herd.

Hank rolled behind a boulder, but Charlie continued to ride, whooping it up and having what looked to be a hell of a good time.

Jarrod teamed up with the one rustler on horseback, and, together, they tried to get to the front of the herd. On the way, Jarrod spotted Charlie and reined in. He lifted his rifle and took a bead.

Billy brought his Marlin to his shoulder and laid its sights onto Jarrod's back, but, before he could pull the trigger, Jarrod fired, and Charlie flinched. He was hit, but he grabbed his saddle horn and held on.

Hank sprang from behind his boulder, shouted, and waved his arms for Charlie to head Hank's way.

Charlie veered, and, as he rode toward Hank's cover, Hank opened fire on both Jarrod and the cowboy who'd been riding the perimeter. Hank's first shot hit the cowboy's thigh, knocking out a chunk of meat the size of a turkey's egg. The man screamed, and his scream was loud enough that, even through the noise, it could be heard.

While Hank was in the open, the rustlers behind the rocks opened fire. The cook, who had regained his breath, was also up and shooting.

Charlie made it to within fifteen feet of Hank before he fell. Bullets blasted pieces of granite from the rocks behind Hank's head and kicked up gouts of dirt at his feet. Even with the gunfire coming his way, Hank grabbed Charlie's left leg and dragged him to safety.

"I'd like to walk up there and call Thorn out," said Hugo in response to Billy's second attempt to get some idea of what Hugo had in mind regarding the problem at hand. "You could stay here, and me and Thorn could go at it guns a-blazin'."

Billy was skeptical. "You think he'd come out and face you instead of shooting you dead from inside the damned tent?"

"Abe'll likely be in there, too. If what Glatt told you about Thorn worshiping the boy is true, I doubt Thorn, even as bad as he is, would want to risk return fire hittin' Abe."

Billy gave Hugo's foolhardy plan some thought. "If you go, I go." Billy figured they could approach the tent from the front without being seen by Jarrod or the shooters who were firing at Hank and Charlie. So all they would have to worry about would be Thorn and maybe Glatt. Which to Billy's thinking was a damned big worry.

"What d'ya say?" asked Hugo. "Should we call the son of a bitch out and have us an old-fashioned, dime-novel, toe-to-goddamned-toe-shoot-'em-up gunfight?"

Hugo was smiling that wild-eyed, demented smile he wore when bullets were about to fly. For reasons Billy could not understand, this sort of thing stoked Hugo's boiler.

Billy shook his head in wonderment. "That may be the dumbest idea I've ever heard. You have one helluva nerve ever saying bad things about any of my plans."

"I told you I liked the cattle stampedin' idea."

"You said that only after it worked."

"Well, then, you can congratulate me after this one works."

Billy knew Hugo's mind was made up. "If we're going to be doing close-up fighting, I might as well leave my Marlin here." He propped the rifle against a tree trunk and lifted his short-barreled from its leather.

Hugo's smile grew wilder. "All right. Now,

don't you be gettin' yourself kilt, Billy-boy. I'd feel awful if you did."

The cowboy who had taken Hank's bullet to the thigh had dropped from his horse and now leaned against a rock. It looked like he'd tried to use his suspenders to make a tourniquet, but, for whatever reason, he couldn't get it done and had given up. He wasn't dead yet, but, judging by the blood in the sand around his leg, that would soon change.

Jarrod was now on his own trying to turn the herd, and he was having no success.

Hank continued firing at the rustlers hidden by the rocks, and, from the corner of his eye, Billy saw one of them go down. He looked to be dead on the spot, but, at this distance, it was hard to tell. Since Hank had begun shooting again, Billy assumed he had Charlie settled in safely, or, a darker part of Billy suggested, maybe Charlie was dead.

Hugo placed his rifle next to Billy's and said, "C'mon." He turned and led the way upstream through the trees. When they were ten yards or so past the front of the tent, Hugo stopped. "That door flap's closed," he said.

"It is, but it's not tied shut."

"Keep an eye on it. If it moves, be ready.

He may come out shootin'."

Hugo stepped with caution from the trees. Billy followed. They stopped thirty-five feet away from the front of the tent and spaced themselves ten feet apart. Hugo pushed his hat up a notch with the muzzle of his shooter. "Thorn, you murderin', torturin' son of a bitch, come outta that tent and get your due. While you're at it, drag False Prophet Glatt out with you, if he happens to be there, too, and has the misfortune to still be breathin'."

They braced themselves and waited for something to happen, but neither movement nor sound came from the tent.

The boys gave each other a questioning look.

"Goddamn it, Thorn. Are you a coward as well as a killer? Come out here, and let's get this done."

Nothing.

"The hell with it," said Billy. He trotted to the tent, and, with his Colt cocked and ready, he threw open the flap.

The tall cottonwoods to the left and a pair of boulders the size of houses fifteen feet to the rear allowed very little light to find its way through the door flap. But there was enough for Billy to see that the small space did not contain a six-and-a-half-foot crazy killer or a four-and-a-half-foot eleven-year-old boy.

Billy had to blink a couple of times to figure out what it did contain. After a moment, he holstered his pistol and made a quarter turn toward Hugo. "Come take a look at this, Hugo."

"What?"

"Just come here."

Hugo holstered his own piece and crossed over.

Billy tied off the flap, and they both ducked inside.

"What's this all about, Bil—" Hugo's question was cut short because, once they were in the tent, he saw what it was about.

Covered with a blanket pulled to his chin lay Martin Glatt on his back in the dirt. His clouded, vacant eyes were open, and they stared straight up at nothing.

"I'll be damned," said Hugo, squinting into the dim light. "Looks like that little fiddle player got this bastard kilt at last."

"With the help of a raging infection," Billy said.

"I like 'er better that way. Sufferin' a few extra days is what this man deserved."

"I agree." Billy stepped in farther. As he did, he felt something soft beneath his boot. He lifted his foot to get a better look, but there was too little light to make anything out. "Strike a match, Hugo."

Hugo pulled one from his vest pocket and ran it across the back of his thigh. When it flared, he extended it toward the dead man's face. Glatt had been right. Every time his and Billy's paths crossed, Glatt was lying flat.

But the corpse before them did not wear the expression that might be expected of a man who had succumbed to the slow-moving death of infection. Nor was it the expression of a man who had gone peacefully in his sleep. Glatt's twisted features held the look of terror.

"Shine that light over here," said Billy.

"Where?"

"Down here at my feet."

Hugo moved the match to where Billy stood next to Glatt's body. "Damn, boy. What is that?"

Billy bent for a closer look. What he had stepped in was mud. He touched his index finger to it and lifted his hand toward the light. On his fingertip was a thick muck the dull, reddish color of copper.

"Blood," whispered Hugo.

Billy didn't respond, but he didn't disagree. He leaned forward and pulled back the blanket. When he did, they saw that an infection had not been Glatt's killer. As with the Pinkerton back at the Reshaw, Glatt had been eviscerated. His intestines lay in a neat pile at his side.

Chapter Thirty-Six: This Don't Look So Good

"Thorn?" asked Hugo. A tone of disbelief was rare in Hugo's voice. He had seen everything. But there was disbelief now in that one-word question, *Thorn?* And also in his next question, "Why?"

"The insane have their own reasons, I suppose."

"But I figured Elijah Thorn looked to Glatt like he was a god."

"Could be Thorn learned the truth and didn't like it. I know something was going on. Glatt said he and Thorn were not as close as they once had been."

"Hell," said Hugo, taking another look at the neatly stacked gut pile and the gaping wound in Glatt's abdomen, "he sure got that right." Hugo shook out the match. "So where could Thorn be now?"

When Billy offered no answer, Hugo said, "We can think on that later. Let's get out there and help Hank and Charlie."

"We'll need to get back to where we left the rifles," said Billy. "And those trees'll be a good spot to shoot from. There's lots of cover, and from there we can see the whole camp."

Billy stepped through the tent flap. Hugo followed and stopped on Billy's left.

Once outside, they saw that Earl Whitson stood in front of one of the house-sized boulders. He'd been waiting for them. In his hands was a doubled-barreled shotgun leveled in their direction.

"Morning, deputies. Mr. Jarrod said that once you figured out my friend Mr. Glatt wasn't in the big tent, that you two'd be coming over here. Looks like he got 'er right." Whitson wore a wide, not-so-friendly smile. "He said he wanted you two caught and brought to him so's all you gents could have a little chit-chat."

Whitson tilted an ear in the direction of Canyon Creek. "It's hard to see, but from the sounds of it, Mr. Jarrod's awful busy right now." He waggled his shotgun. "He said it was all right to kill you, if we must, though he really *does* wanna talk to you. So, one at a time, you boys unbuckle them gunbelts and let 'em fall to the dirt." He looked to Billy. "You go first, young fella."

Neither Billy nor Hugo moved.

"I admit, I'm for killing you right now" — he jabbed his gun in Hugo's direction — " 'specially you — but I suspect Mr. Jarrod'll let us do that anyhow once you've had your talk."

Without moving his eyes, he leaned a couple of inches to his left and called out, "What do you think, Evelyn? Should we take 'em to Jarrod or go ahead and kill 'em now? I could go either way on it m'self."

Evelyn Jones stepped from the trees and stopped at a spot on Billy and Hugo's right.

Evelyn did not answer Whitson's question, but it appeared that if he was forced to vote right then, he would go with killing them. The Winchester he held at his hip and had pointed at Billy was already cocked.

Billy had counted these two for a couple of imbeciles, and it's likely that they were. But these imbeciles had the boys in an uncomfortable crossfire, if the situation came to shooting.

"This don't look so good," said Hugo in a soft voice from the corner of his mouth.

"What was that?" snapped Whitson, cupping a hand to his ear.

"I said it's only been a few days since we last saw you, Earl, but in that short time you have grown even uglier, which I did not think was possible. How in the world do you do it?"

The smile Whitson wore dissolved, and he turned his attention again to Billy. "I want you to unbuckle that belt and let it fall. Once it's on the ground, take your foot and kick the whole thing out away from you — belt, holster, gun, and all."

In a voice even softer than Hugo had used a moment before, Billy said, "I'm going to do as he says, Hugo."

"Horse shit to that."

"No. As soon as I give it a kick, you drop to a knee and kill Whitson."

Hugo snorted. And keeping his eyes locked onto the large man and his large shotgun, he said, "Pretty tall order."

Whitson's lips thinned, and, through a tight jaw, he shouted, "Shut the hell up, goddamn it. You let that belt fall, boy, and do it now or die because you didn't."

"All right, Earl," said Billy, "don't get excited. I'm doing it. Relax." His hand went to his buckle. "You fellas could've just asked us nice to go see Jarrod. We'd been glad to do it. We want to have a little visit with him ourselves. Isn't that right, Hugo?"

"It sure is. I got a bone or two I wanna pick with that man." Hugo's hand eased to his side.

Billy unbuckled his belt and held it out. "I

gotta tell you, Earl, I don't like doing this. Instead of dropping everything on the ground, can't I come over and hand it to you? This belt and holster's not yet six months old, and my nickel-plated Colt cost my pa a pretty penny."

Staring at Billy, Whitson said nothing.

"All right, Earl, damn it. We'll do it your way."

In two quick moves, Billy let go of the gunbelt, and, the moment it hit the ground, he slipped a toe beneath the holster and kicked with everything he had. The rig rose six feet in the air, and, as it spun, both ends of the belt flapped like the wings of a bird.

Before it returned to earth, the boys dropped, and, as they did, Whitson fired off one of the barrels of his shotgun. In a tight group, the pellets *whooshed* over Billy's and Hugo's heads and tore through the canvas behind them, leaving a hole the size of a fat man's fist.

As Whitson was about to pull the second trigger, Hugo drew and fired. He didn't need to aim. His bullet hit an inch below Whitson's left eye. As the big man fell backwards, his gun went off again, propelling buckshot into the morning sky.

Evelyn's eyes were as big as pie tins. And, like a fool, instead of shooting from his hip, he brought the rifle to his shoulder, which allowed Billy time to reach to the small of his back and retrieve the shooter he'd taken from the body of the short man with the big hat.

Billy cocked and fired.

His skill at shooting without taking aim was not as refined as Hugo's. Billy's bullet struck Evelyn's left hand, blasted through the hand and the Winchester's fore stock, ricocheted off the barrel, and, together with pieces of bone and shards of wood, smashed into the center of Evelyn Jones's chest.

Evelyn hit the ground screaming, but before Billy and Hugo had made it back to their rifles the screams had stopped.

When they returned to the cottonwood where they'd leaned their long guns, they saw that most of the cattle were gone, and the ones that remained had settled down. There was much less chaos than earlier, but shots were being fired.

The fat cook and the last rustler had Hank pinned down. Billy and Hugo grabbed their rifles and returned the outlaws' fire.

On their second volley, one of Hugo's forty-four-forties caught the shirtless cook an inch above the belly button. Surprised, the fat man fell onto his butt and dropped his eyes to the bullet hole. He stared at it for a moment, then brought both pudgy hands up and rested them on the sides of his massive stomach the way women do who are eight months gone with child. Holding his hands there, he lifted his head and began to wail. The eerie banshee sound appeared to come less from the pain of his bullet wound than from a sudden, hopeless realization. He was about to die, and he knew it. His cries continued, piercing and mournful, until Hugo raised his rifle and sent another round across the creek.

Billy, Hugo, and now Hank, too, had the last rustler outgunned. Realizing his situation, he turned and ran toward the safety behind the buckboard, but he didn't make it. Hank stood, stepped from his hiding place, and fired. Hugo could not have possibly seen where Hank's bullet hit the rustler, but, the second the man dropped, Hugo said, "That fella's dead."

At last the shooting had stopped, and Billy and Hugo left the trees.

"Tell me, Hugo, how is it from this distance you could tell that man was dead?"

"I know it by the way he fell." Without saying more, Hugo turned his attention to Dale Jarrod.

From the far side of the camp, Jarrod

pulled his six-gun and galloped in Hank's direction. Hank faced him, lifted his rifle, and pulled the trigger. Nothing. He'd sent his last round into the fleeing rustler. He then turned and sprinted for the rocks, but Jarrod was closing in, and it was clear Hank was not going to make it.

Hugo jacked a round into his own rifle, aimed, and fired. The forelegs of Jarrod's brindle folded beneath him, and the animal went down, sending its rider sailing over the top of the horse's head.

"Good *God,*" shouted Billy. "Why did you kill his horse?"

Hugo didn't answer.

"It's a goddamned sorry thing, Hugo, when we stoop to killing horses."

Chapter Thirty-Seven: Plenty of Dead Horses

Canyon Creek was a little deeper on this end, but Billy, still wanting to keep his socks dry, made it to the other side by leaping from rock to rock. Hugo waded across. Wet socks were no bother to Hugo.

Over here, they had a mess.

The cattle were scattered well beyond the confluence, but, since this is where the grass and water were, given time, most would wander back.

Not only were the cattle scattered, so were the dead. And they were plentiful. Billy pointed to Dale Jarrod, who was face down fifty yards away. "Looks like we can count Jarrod among the goners. Flying off that horse the way he did must've broken his neck."

"He ain't dead," said Hugo.

"Now, how in the hell can you know that from way over here?"

"I could tell by the way he fell."

Hugo was fond of that answer.

As they walked toward Jarrod, they passed the cowboy who'd been thrown from his horse and trampled. There was no question whether he was dead.

The other man who'd been tending the herd — the one Hank had shot in the leg — sat propped against a boulder. He, too, was dead. The suspenders he'd been too slow to use as a tourniquet dangled from his limp left hand. The ground around his wound was puddled red.

The deputy was stirring beyond the wagons where he'd fallen after Jarrod knocked him from his horse. "Hey, you out there," shouted Hugo. The man turned in Hugo's direction but didn't say anything. "Get yourself back into camp here." When he didn't move, Hugo chambered a round, aimed his rifle, and fired. The ground next to the man's left foot exploded, and, like a startled bunny, he made an awkward hop to his right, lost his balance, and went tumbling. With what appeared to be some effort, he pushed himself to his feet, mumbled what was probably a curse, and started for camp.

"Falling off his horse kind of gimped that fella up."

"He'll be all right," said Hugo. "It wasn't

a tall horse."

Hugo raised a cupped hand to the side of his mouth. "Mr. Bayliss, do you remain hunkered behind them rocks up there on the hill?" There was no response. "Now, Woodrow, goddamn it, I'm callin' you. Don't you make me come up there."

A few seconds later, the thin man's blond head poked above a rock.

"Get down here. I gotta job-a work for you."

Once Bayliss started down the hill, Billy said, "Let's check on Charlie." Hank and Charlie were in the cover they'd used during the shooting. Charlie was moving and talking to Hank, who was bent over him tending his wound. The wound was in the upper arm, and it appeared Hank had staunched the bleeding.

On the way to Hank and Charlie, Billy and Hugo stopped to have a look at Jarrod. Hugo used his boot to roll the ex-sheriff onto his back. Leaning down with both hands on his knees, Hugo shouted into Jarrod's face, "Are you awake yet, you son of a bitch?"

Jarrod didn't stir, but he was breathing. Hugo had called it right when he said Jarrod wasn't dead.

Jarrod's pistol lay next to him in the dirt.

Hugo picked it up and examined it. Turning to Billy, he asked, "It ain't much, but do you want it?"

Billy said no, and Hugo tossed it as far as he could into a stand of rocks. He stepped to where Jarrod's horse lay and, looking down at the dead beast, said, "I apologize for killin' you, horse. I would-a rather kilt your rider, but I needed to talk to the man, and I had to stop 'im before he hurt my friend. I'm sorry it had to be you that took the bullet."

Billy guessed Hugo shared his distaste for killing the horse, after all. Many in this world would find it odd that they both showed more concern over the death of an animal than the death of all these men. But, in their defense, Billy reminded himself that the horse had not been shooting at them.

Billy tried to remember if he'd ever heard anyone apologize to a dead horse before, and he could not think of a time; though, he suspected there had been plenty of dead horses over the last few thousand years who had deserved an apology.

Hugo jerked Jarrod's rifle out of the saddle scabbard and held it up to Billy with a questioning look.

"No thanks."

Hugo moved to his left, took the gun by

its barrel, and smashed it onto a rock.

He scanned the camp, and, deciding there was nothing more to be done right then, he looked to the west and then up the hill. Satisfied that the deputy and Woodrow Bayliss were both doing as they were told, he said to Billy, "All right, boy, let's take a look at Charlie."

Hank had torn off the tail from his own shirt and wrapped it around Charlie's wound. The bullet had missed the bone, but it had dug a straight groove across the top of Charlie's arm.

"He'll live," said Hank. "Though I expect he'll be hurting for a while."

Charlie looked up at the boys with a smile and a shrug. "It don't hardly hurt at all right now."

"That'll change," said Billy. "We'll look for some whiskey. I saw the rustlers drinking last night. There might be some around."

"Some whiskey'd sure hit the spot," allowed Charlie, "even if my arm don't start hurting."

Hugo rubbed his hands together. "Sure would."

"If we find any," Billy said, "it'll be for medicinal purposes only."

Hugo glanced at Charlie, and Charlie gave

him a wink.

Hank stood and looked out around the camp. "Man, that was something, wasn't it? I don't mind saying, I was scared stiff, but, now that it's over, I feel sort of . . ." Hank fumbled in his effort to pin a name onto something he'd never felt before.

Hugo laughed and slapped him on the back. "I know what you mean, Hank. I get that same feelin' myself. It's somethin' you can grow fond of as long as you don't get kilt."

Hank offered Hugo a smile, though not a big one. "I can see how dying might take the fun out of it. What's with those two fellas walking into camp there?"

"The skinny one is one of the rustlers, but I don't feel his heart was truly in it."

"And the other one," Billy said, "is the deputy who was going to buy the stolen cattle. That poor fella didn't know what he was getting into when he headed over here this morning."

"Hey, help me up," Charlie said. "I want to get a look at things, too."

"You think you can stand?" asked Hank.

"Once I'm up, I can. It's the getting there that's giving me trouble."

Billy and Hank helped him to his feet.

"My word," Charlie said, "them cows running through the place kinda mussed things up a little, didn't they?"

Hugo chuckled at Charlie's understatement.

"You boys did a fine job of getting them going."

"Hell, Billy," said Charlie, "it didn't take much."

"Nah," Hank agreed. "Them bovines was eager to run." He craned his neck to look out into the desolate plains beyond Deer Creek and added, "Some of them critters are probably *still* running."

The deputy and Woodrow Bayliss had met in the center of the camp, and they stood, without talking, watching the four men watching them.

The deputy wore a dark-blue frock coat and a red cravat, which, along with his gold-rimmed spectacles and his elegant, gray city hat, made him look out of place here among the canyons, rocks, and streams of the Rattlesnake Hills.

"Hey, you, fancy dresser," called Hugo, "pull that coat back so I can see what you're totin'."

The deputy did as Hugo said, revealing a sidearm. The piece was strapped high around his waist in an awkward manner that suggested it was seldom worn.

"You pull that shooter and throw it back toward the chuck wagon." The deputy did it but was slow in the doing. "Hurry up, goddamn it."

"Now, Hugo," said Billy, "take it easy. I'm telling you, I think the man sprained something when he fell."

"I don't care. Serves 'im right." Hugo turned his attention to Bayliss. "Now, Woodrow, I want you and the dude-lookin' fella to drag that lump, Dale Jarrod, over here to the shade where we are. And be quick about."

The deputy and Bayliss met where Jarrod lay. Each took an arm and pulled.

"Earlier," Billy said, "you mentioned that you knew the deputy."

"I do. Don't remember his name, but me and the U.S. marshal met 'im a few months back when we went over to the Wind River Indian reservation."

"What was he doing over there?"

"His job, I reckon. These rustlers might've got it wrong when they called 'im a deputy. That may be his title, but I don't think so. The folks at the rez called him the clerk."

"Clerk for what?"

"The clerk for the Indian agent. That fella over yonder tuggin' on Jarrod's arm works for the man in charge of the whole reservation."

Chapter Thirty-Eight: A Hundred and Sixty Acres

Once the unconscious Dale Jarrod was deposited in the shade of Hank and Charlie's cover, Hugo said to the clerk, "I know who you are, Mister. I recognize you by them bushy whiskers on the side of your face, but I do not remember your name. What is it?"

The man recognized Hugo, too, and appeared hesitant to answer, but, after a tense moment, he did. "McClellan Walker," he said in a soft, quivery voice.

"McClellan Walker," repeated Hugo. "Why in the world, I wonder, does a fella need two last names?" Mr. Walker offered no explanation, and Hugo didn't press it. "McClellan," he said, "I want you to take that handsome gray hat of yours and go dip it in the crick."

"What?"

"Go fill it up with water and toss the water onto Jarrod's face. It's time this loafer's nap was over."

"I'll not do it. By God, this is a twenty-seven-dollar homburg. I purchased it in the finest millinery in Philadelphia."

"It's a hat of high quality, is it?"

"It is, indeed."

"Good," Hugo said, "then I doubt it'll leak."

"This hat, sir," said the clerk, "is *not* one to be dipped into water."

Considering all that had transpired since the clerk had first arrived in camp, the level of his indignation was surprising. Billy decided Mr. Walker must be very fond of his hat.

"The brim," the clerk added, continuing to argue his case, "is trimmed in silk."

Hugo squinted one eye at the man and aimed a finger at his head. "You know, McClellan, there is a chance you *might* not die this mornin'." Billy figured that to be about as subtle a threat as Hugo could muster, but the message made it through.

"It has," Walker whined to himself, "a feather in the band." It appeared for a moment he might cry. But with no more resistance, the clerk gimped his way to the creek, dipped his twenty-seven-dollar hat in the water, gimped back, and dumped the contents onto Dale Jarrod's upturned face.

It gave Billy pleasure to watch Jarrod cough and sputter after being drenched by a homburg-full of creek water. As sheriff, the man had been a worthless embarrassment. His losing the election last November was no surprise. His turning to rustling, however, was a surprise; though now, caught with the stolen cattle and lying wet-faced in the dirt looking up at Hugo, showed that Jarrod was as incompetent a rustler as he had been a sheriff.

"All right-y, now," said Hugo with a big smile, "ex-sheriff Jarrod is joinin' the party." He pointed to a large rock ten feet away and said to Bayliss, "Woodrow, go have a seat and make yourself comfortable." As Bayliss turned to leave, so did Walker. "Where d'ya think you're goin', Clerk?" asked Hugo. Walker stopped before his second step and stood motionless, holding his sodden hat.

Jarrod was now fully awake, and there appeared to be concern in his eyes as he rose onto his left elbow and with his right arm sleeved away water from his face and hair. Pushing himself to a sitting position, he let out a groan and looked out over the camp. "How many men did you and Billy Young kill today, Dorling?" He asked the question with a tone of confidence, but it sounded forced.

"Don't know yet. But however many it was, or will be, your boys fired the first shots."

"What are you saying? Your men were shooting when they came out of the canyon."

"They were firin' in the air, as anyone could plainly see. Your boys started shootin' to kill."

"You had attacked our camp. You stampeded our cattle."

"Well, of course, we did. Me and Billy're marshals. You're a bunch-a outlaws. What we did is what lawmen do. You'd know that if you'd ever done your job as sheriff." Hugo, offering a less-than-sincere tone of concern, moved in closer and said, "That was sure a nasty spill you took from your horse, there, Dale. Did you break any of your bones?"

"Go to hell." This also came out with an artificial note of bluster.

Hugo chuckled. "You ain't the first to make *that* suggestion. I hear you want to talk to me."

"Who told you that?"

"The late Earl Whitson. He said you wanted to talk to me and Billy and you sent him and his friend, Evelyn, to that little tent over yonder to find us. I'm guessin' Prophet Glatt told you we'd go there once we figured out he wasn't the fella sunnin' himself by the big tent." Hugo lowered his head and locked his feral eyes onto Jarrod's. "You told those two fools to either fetch us or kill us."

"Is that so?"

"It is. And I can't imagine what you'd think you and me had to talk about."

"Lots of things, Hugo."

"Really? And here all these years I counted us as havin' nothin' in common."

"One thing is I was curious how you came to find this place. I know you were following the big fella and the boy, but I never took you to be much good at tracking."

"Why, Dale, that ain't true. I'm a fine tracker. Ain't I, Billy?"

"You sure are, Hugo." Billy calculated his answer to be about two-thirds lie.

"This place ain't easy to find," said Jarrod. "Next to the Hole in the Wall, it's gotta be about the best hideout in the state."

"You'd think so, wouldn't you? It is one far-off, sorry location. I have to admit, though, Dale, I did not track Mr. Thorn. One of his many victims overheard him say he was headed to Deer Crick. Our friend

Charlie happened to know where the nearest Deer Crick was. We took a chance that this was the one Thorn meant, and we got lucky."

Jarrod gave a derisive snort.

"Real lucky. We not only found where Thorn and his captive, Abraham, was headed, but we also found that pretender Martin Glatt."

"You haven't found them."

"Not all of them, but we have found Glatt."

Jarrod's eyebrows moved some fraction of an inch closer together. "What do you mean?"

"Mr. Glatt is layin' in the little tent across the crick with his stomach flayed open and his guts piled up by his side, which is one of Elijah Thorn's specialties. You knew Glatt wasn't sittin' in a chair baskin' in the sun. Where did you think he was?"

"Gone."

"Well, you got that much right. Now we know where Glatt went; where's Thorn and the boy?"

Jarrod didn't answer.

Hugo waited a bit and said, "You aren't hardly in a position to be difficult, Jarrod. You'll be tellin' me where they went before we're through here this mornin'. And lots of other things, too."

Another one of Hugo's not quite subtle threats.

Jarrod cleared his throat and swallowed, though it did not appear to be easy.

"We got lucky findin' the right Deer Crick, and we also got lucky findin' us a full nest-a cattle thieves."

Though what Hugo said about cattle thieves was obvious, the saying of it out loud sapped Jarrod of whatever fake bravado he had left.

"Cattle thievery is an interestin' choice of occupations to go into after your retirement from sheriffin'. You know it's gonna take a lotta doin' to keep them Natrona County ranchers from stringin' you up once we get you back to Casper. I ain't sure that young fella who got your job'll be up to the task."

"I'm not sure he'll try," added Billy.

" 'Course, it is possible them ranchers you stole from might hold off on the lynchin' — for a while, anyhow. Could be they'll let you go to a trial and see if the jury'll think you're the fella who kilt young Joe Broom during that last batch of rustlin's you did."

"It is a fact," Billy said, "that the town'll be looking hard for someone to hang for that murder. Folks liked Joe."

"He always showed a quick wit, as I

recall," said Hugo.

"And he had a wife."

"By golly, that's right. And, ooh-wee, she's a smart, pretty little thing, and real good with words. I bet she'll have them twelve fellas on that jury plumb teary eyed once she tells how sad she is now that her poor husband's been kilt."

"You ain't funny, Dorling."

"No, sir, I'm serious. You, Mr. Ex-Sheriff, are a dead man. You may be breathin', but you are as dead as any one of them wretched fellas out there bloatin' in the mornin' sun. Here in the next few weeks — days, maybe — you're gonna be danglin' on a rope. Now it could be you'll end up that way from slidin' off the ass end of a horse and swingin' from a thick cottonwood branch — that'd be at the hands of irate ranchers — or it could be you'll end up danglin' after you fall through the trap door on a gallows. If I were you, I'd hope for the gallows. There, you'll have the able assistance of a professional hangman, and it'll be fast. With them ranchers, who knows how long it'll take you to die."

Charlie, who sat a few feet away with Hank, was stifling his laughter. Billy was enjoying the show himself. Hugo loved to taunt outlaws. Billy guessed next to whiskey and loose women, teasing outlaws regarding whatever horrible fate might await them was Hugo's favorite thing.

"But maybe, if you tell me a few things without makin' it too hard to get it, we could work somethin' out."

"Tell you what, exactly?"

"First, where we can find Thorn and the boy. I'll also be needin' to know what your plan was with this dandified fella here holdin' the wet hat. Simple trade. You help me, and I'll help you."

"What do you figure you could do for me?"

"I'd be willin' to do everythin' I can to help you avoid the noose. I'd talk for you, Dale. Hell, I'd even testify for you. Billy would, too. I expect if we tried hard enough, we could put a stop to any thoughts of hangin'."

"I s'pose we could try it that way, but it sounds like a big risk for me."

Hugo provided a what-can-you-do shrug, acknowledging that all of life had its risks.

"It don't have to be that way, Hugo," said Jarrod in a raspy voice. "You and your boys could help me round up them cows and get them delivered. There is plenty of money to be made."

"Are you offerin' me a partnership, Dale?"

"No."

"No?"

"No, I'm saying, once the chore was done, I'd go my own separate way, and you and your friends could have all the proceeds. If we do that, everybody's happy."

"How much money you figure we're lookin' at here?"

Jarrod turned toward Walker. "Well, sir, me and Mr. Walker have agreed on thirty-two dollars per head."

"My, my," said Billy. "You're getting quite a bargain, Mr. Walker."

"We had right at a hundred and eighty head before you boys came around," said Jarrod. "So, if we can find them all, that's just a bit this side of six thousand dollars."

"Five thousand seven hundred and sixty," corrected Mr. Walker.

"Who are you sellin' 'em to, McClellan?" asked Hugo. "I'm curious to know."

Walker's lips tightened. "That's my business."

"It's my business, too, if I take the ex-sheriff up on his handsome offer."

"Once you are paid," said Walker, "then what happens to them after that is none of your concern."

"For a fella whose gun is way over yonder by the chuck wagon, while mine is in my holster, you sure do like to split hairs."

"I expect I know what he's going to do with them," said Billy. "Sell them to the Indians. Or I guess it'd be more accurate to say sell them to the government and then to the Indians."

Hugo looked surprised. "How would you know that?" he asked.

"Have you ever heard of the Dawes Act?"

Hugo scratched behind his ear. "Let me think. Dawes. Are you talkin' about them three brothers in vaudeville who have that singin' an' dancin' act? Sometimes they tell jokes, too."

"What?" Billy was baffled for a second trying to decipher what the hell Hugo was talking about. After some quick thinking, he took in a breath and shook his head in wonderment, "No, Hugo, good God. Not that kind of an *act.* I'm talking about a law."

"A law, eh. The Dawes Act?"

"It's a law made by the Congress that takes reservation land from the tribes, divvies it up, and gives it back to all the individual Indians."

"Gives it to them? You mean like homesteadin'?"

"Each head of household will receive a hundred and sixty acres that they need to prove up before they get title, so, yes, it's sort of like homesteading."

Now it was Hugo who looked baffled. "What in God's name," he croaked through a boisterous peal of laughter, "would an *Indian* do with a hundred and sixty acres?"

Chapter Thirty-Nine: Farm

"Farm," answered Billy.

"Farm? An Indian farmer? I doubt it, boy. No Indian's gonna wanna farm. Why, hell, you'd be more likely to see a raccoon do the polka."

"There was Indian farmers," said Hank, "long before white men ever showed up. Haven't you heard the story about the Mayflower and them red men back east teaching the Pilgrims how to farm?"

"Well, them Indians back there ain't the ones we got here. These fellas do not farm. Most of 'em spent their younger years relievin' farmers of their scalps."

Billy turned to Walker and asked, "I don't think they're going to have a choice, are they, Mr. Walker?"

"It is the law, and it's for their own good."

"How do you figure that?" Billy asked.

"It takes them away from their savage ways. It helps to civilize them. Eventually they will become members of the society at large. It will make them Christian."

"So the Dawes Act, then, is doing them a favor?"

"It is."

"How much farming do you really think will get done on the reservation?" Billy asked.

"There's some fine farm land over there."

"I expect there is, especially with irrigation. And since the reservation was started in 1868, that must give the Shoshone and Arapaho water rights starting way back then, which would make their right senior to every one of the other users on the Wind River. Do I have that correct, Mr. Walker? Do they have an 1868 water right?"

Walker cleared his throat. "Well, no."

"Would you say it's hard to farm in this country without enough water?"

"They can also ranch. There's grazing land. And we, of course, will help."

Hugo asked, "Is that what you're buyin' these cows for, to help 'em?"

"Yes, as a matter of fact it is."

"That's good," said Billy. "I'm sure they'd appreciate all the help they can get."

"That's what we are here for."

Billy took off his hat, pulled a handkerchief from a back pocket, and ran it around the hat's sweat band. "I know that millions of acres make up the Wind River reservation. I don't know for sure how many Indians are living there these days. And I'm not worth a damn at arithmetic, but I'm pretty sure, even if every man, woman, and child, plus their dogs and cats, were to get a hundred and sixty acres, there'd still be millions of acres left."

If it had not been clear to Walker what Billy was getting at before he started talking acreage, it was clear to him now.

"What happens to all those left-over reservation acres, Mr. Walker?"

"Let me guess, Billy," said Hank. "The government puts them on the open market, and anybody with the money can buy them."

Billy didn't bother to tell Hank whether his guess was right. And neither did McClellan Walker.

"So, Billy," asked Hugo, "how does this Dawes thing work?"

"What do you mean?"

"We have Mr. Clerk here who decides to buy cattle from Mr. Rustler over yonder for the Indians because these Dawes Laws tell 'im to, right?"

McClellan Walker interrupted. "I want it

known that when I agreed to purchase these animals, I did not know them to have been stolen."

Everyone except for Dale Jarrod burst out laughing.

"And there is no way," Walker added, "that you could ever prove that I did."

With that, the laughter trailed off.

"I thought Dale Jarrod to be a legitimate cattle broker. That is how he represented himself, and I had no reason to believe otherwise. I did know him to have been, at one time, the sheriff of Natrona County, which is in itself a high recommendation as to the man's character. I had no reason to think he was anything other than a respectable businessman."

Hugo stared at the clerk for a long moment. He then turned to Billy and asked, "You're a smart fella, Deputy Marshal Young. Am I right about that?"

Billy knew Hugo did not expect an answer to this question.

"So tell me, Deputy, say Mr. Clerk here wants to buy cattle, or seed, or a plow, or anythin' else for the Indian farmers and ranchers, how would he go about doin' it?"

"I'm not sure of the process. I suppose if it was something the government didn't ship directly from the East, Mr. Walker, or someone else, would buy it locally and haul it to the reservation,"

"How would he pay for it?"

"Again, if the item didn't come straight from government sources, I suppose the funds for the purchase of anything the tribes might need would come out of the reservation's operating budget."

"So Mr. Clerk, here, would dig some money out of a safe at the Indian agent's headquarters, go to the feed store, or whatever, buy what he was after, and take it back to the reservation?"

"I can't imagine he'd be taking cash out of a safe, Hugo. They have to keep records. What they would do is pay for it with a bank draft, and the cost would then be billed to the tribes' government allotment."

Hugo turned to McClellan Walker and said, "Take off your coat, Mr. Walker."

Billy recognized a tone in Hugo's voice that he had heard before. "Easy now, Hugo," he said.

Walker didn't move.

"I'll tell you once more, Clerk," said Hugo. "Take off that coat."

Instead of taking off his coat, Walker asked, "Why should —"

But before the question was fully posed, Hugo's right fist lashed out and caught

Walker on the left side of his jaw, an inch before it curved around toward his chin. Walker's head snapped to his right, his body stiffened, he turned a half circle and hit the ground as rigid as a two-by-four. He was out before he landed, so no hands rose to break the fall, and he hit face first. Billy felt himself wince at the sight of it. He wasn't sure, but when Walker landed, Billy thought he'd heard the snap of nose cartilage, or it could have been the sound of cracking teeth.

Hugo stood above the clerk, and, when Walker didn't move, Hugo said, "Look at that, Jarrod. First you knocked this fella out and now I have. I gotta think a man gettin' hisself knocked unconscious twice in less than thirty minutes' time is somethin' rare. I know I've never seen it before."

Jarrod didn't say anything, but his expression showed that he did not like the direction things were starting to go.

Hugo straddled Walker's back and bent down. He shoved his hands under the man, and, grabbing both lapels, he peeled off the frock coat like he was skinning a rabbit. He held the coat up and inspected it. "My, oh my. This is one nice coat. Mr. Walker has good taste. You could learn a few things from him, Billy. Your wardrobe has been showin' neglect of late."

Hugo shoved a hand into one of the coat's side pockets but found nothing. He then stuck his hand into the pocket on the other side. Again coming up with nothing, he searched inside the left breast pocket. This time, when he removed his hand, it held a neat bundle of rectangular papers that were tied with a bright-blue ribbon.

Hugo looked at what he held and smiled. He then held it up for Billy to see. In the upper left corner of the first paper on the stack was the somber face of Abraham Lincoln. Arched across the paper's center were the words *United States.* Beneath that was written *Will Pay to Bearer One Hundred Dollars.* Billy took a guess that there were fifty-seven of those pale green papers tied together with that ribbon.

When Billy returned Hugo's smile, the old deputy said, "This ain't a surprise, Billy-boy. I never met a single rustler in all my many years who would agree to bein' paid with a bank draft."

CHAPTER FORTY: I BET YOU'D LIKE SOME COFFEE, TOO

Hank and Woodrow searched about the camp and located eight canteens, a couple of dozen biscuits, some bacon, and a bottle of whiskey. They also came back with a rope. Hank took the rope, pulled his folding knife from his pocket, and cut six three-and-a-half-foot-long strands. He and Woodrow used those to bind the hands and ankles of Dale Jarrod and McClellan Walker.

Neither man took to being tied quietly, so after a few minutes of screams, curses, and Jarrod's fervent attempts to strike a bargain with Hugo, Hugo left the shady area and crossed to the bloody body of the cowboy who had been trampled by the herd. Hugo dropped to one knee and removed the corpse's boots, tossed the boots away, and peeled off the dead man's socks. As he returned to the shade, he wadded the socks into balls.

"What the hell are you doing?" screamed Jarrod.

"You'll see," answered Hugo as he bent and rammed one of the socks into Jarrod's mouth. After doing the same to a squirming Walker, he tied Jarrod's neckerchief and Walker's cravat over their mouths to hold the socks in place.

"Gaggin' you two," said Hugo, "oughta tamp down the noise."

Once things were quiet, Billy and Hugo collected wood and built a fire. Billy fried the bacon while Hugo rummaged around for coffee. There was plenty of food besides biscuits and bacon in the chuck wagon, but the boys were in a hurry. After a bit, Hugo found a bag of coffee and set a pot to brewing.

As the boys made breakfast, Hank and Woodrow went back into the camp and loaded the dead men into one of the buckboards. Then they struck the tents and used the canvas to cover the bodies.

Charlie watched all this activity with a smile as he drank his whiskey.

After they'd eaten their bacon and biscuits, Billy and Hugo hiked up the hill to where they had camped the night before and saddled Billy's gray and Hugo's bay. On the way back, they spotted most of the horses that had run loose during the stampede. They brought Hank's and Charlie's horses back into camp. They also brought one for Woodrow Bayliss. Hugo told Hank and Woodrow to round up as many of the others as they could find. Not even Woodrow had an exact count of the rustlers' horses, but most were located and returned to the rope corral at the mouth of the canyon.

Back at the fire, Hugo poured two cups of coffee and crossed over to Jarrod. Standing above the hog-tied cattle thief, Hugo asked, "Care for some coffee, Dale?"

Jarrod was lying on his right side. His hands were lashed behind his back; his ankles were tied together, and the rope holding his ankles was tied to the rope around his wrists. When Hugo asked the question, Jarrod's eyebrows shot up, and he nodded with vigor. His head was the only thing he possessed that could move.

"That don't look comfortable, Dale. Let me help you." Hugo grabbed a handful of Jarrod's shirt and pulled him to a more or less sitting position. Jarrod still didn't look comfortable, but it had to be better than before.

Billy suspected Hugo would rather have hefted Jarrod by the hair than the shirt, but he knew Hugo wanted information, and he was trying his best to be nice.

"I got the feelin' when the boys were tyin' your hands and feet that you wanted to tell me somethin'." Hugo took hold of the neckerchief that covered Jarrod's mouth and pulled it down below the man's chin. Then, using two fingers, he dug out the ball of filthy sock. Once it was out, Jarrod sputtered and spit. He retched a couple of times in an effort to either hold his gorge or let it fly. It looked as though it could go either way. In the end, Jarrod didn't vomit, but, after watching Hugo pull the sock out of Jarrod's mouth, Billy better understood the meaning of the word "gag."

"Here, Dale, have a sip of java." Hugo held the cup to Jarrod's lips, and, as the ex-sheriff took a drink, Hugo glanced at Walker. The clerk lay on his side as Jarrod had been and watched Hugo's every move with eyes that bulged above his knotted cravat.

"I bet you'd like some coffee, too," said Hugo with a smile.

As with Jarrod, he also nodded with vigor.

"Well, you ain't gettin' any."

Being nice could last only so long. Billy knew Hugo had a mean streak, but its depth was sometimes surprising.

Though Jarrod had to be thirsty, instead

of swallowing the coffee, he swished it around in his mouth and spit it out.

"What's the problem, Dale? The taste of a dead man's sock don't appeal to you first thing in the mornin'?" Hugo chuckled. So did Charlie, who remained busy working his way through the whiskey bottle. "Here, have a little more." Hugo held out the cup again, and Jarrod took another sip. "Now, what were you sayin' before you got yourself sock-gagged?"

"I was saying don't you believe that bastard Walker. He knew what was happening here. He knew them cows was stole."

"I didn't figure otherwise. He looks to be a shifty fella. And then when you add to it that he came here today with a stack of fifty-seven pictures of Honest Abe instead of a draft from the First National over in Lander, that tells me for sure he knew what he was doin'." Hugo aimed an index finger at McClellan Walker and said, "We are on to you, Mr. Clerk."

Jarrod added, "I saw a false receipt he made up that said he paid five dollars and fifty cents per hundred for them cows. It came to eight thousand four hundred and fifteen dollars."

"And that's what he planned to bill the agency," said Billy.

Hugo took a sip of his own coffee. "Which figures out to a tidy profit of two thousand six hundred and fifty-five dollars."

"My God, Hugo," asked Billy, "did you do that ciphering in your head?"

"A-course I did. Didn't you?" Without waiting for an answer, Hugo asked Jarrod, "Would you be willin' to say all that to a jury?"

"You're damned right, Hugo. That is, I would be if your offer of vouching for me and keeping me from the noose remains on the table."

"We'll see. We've got some more talkin' to do before I decide. So was the clerk the only one in on this, or was the Indian agent himself in on it, too?"

"Just the clerk. Walker don't have any use for the agent. Says he can't stand the man. Walker told me he even done something with the bookkeeping at the rez so if anyone got to lookin' too close at things, it'd all fall right into the agent's lap. And it ain't just this deal, neither. No, sir. There's been other things that Walker's done to put feathers in his own nest. Lots of things. That Walker is a crafty one."

"Those're harsh words to say about your business partner, there, Dale."

"I done business with him, but I did not

like the man. The first time I met him, he was wearing spats. Can you believe that? *Spats.* Who could ever trust a man who wore spats?" Under his breath, he added, "I was a fool to even try."

"But the money was too good to pass up; isn't that right?" asked Hugo.

Jarrod nodded. "I had a pretty high overhead, though, Hugo. That money was gonna be split lots of ways. My boys were gonna get paid real good."

Billy glanced at the buckboard loaded with dead men and said to himself, *Not good enough.*

"Where's Elijah Thorn and the boy?" Hugo asked.

It looked as though Jarrod tried to shrug his shoulders, but the ropes wouldn't let it happen. "I can't say for sure. Maybe San Francisco, but I doubt it."

"San Francisco? Why there?"

"That's where Glatt was taking them. Though now that he's dead, my guess'd be they ain't going there."

"Did you know Glatt was dead before I told you he was?"

"No, though I did think something was odd. They were planning to put him into one of our buckboards and leave during the night. Glatt had already paid me for the wagon and a couple of horses. Since folks would be looking for them in Casper, they were going to Rawlins. From there they was gonna catch the train for California. Glatt said he wanted to go to San Francisco for the boy. Thorn didn't like the idea."

"Why do you say that?"

"I heard them arguing about it. I guess Thorn had thought all along that once they got the boy they'd be heading back to wherever they came from. From the sound of it, that was what Thorn wanted to do. It's funny that I didn't hear any screams when Glatt was getting hisself cut open. Thorn must've put a blanket over his face or something. But I could sure hear them fighting about where to go from here."

"Why were they across the creek in the small tent, anyway?" asked Hugo.

"Somehow Glatt knew you and Billy were around, and he figured you'd try something come daylight, if not before. That's why we moved him over there and posted Bayliss out front of the big tent. We figured that'd throw you off some."

"It sort-a worked, too, for a while, anyhow."

"Since we knew you were around, I had the boys keeping an eye out for you, but we weren't worried about you much, since we thought there was only you two 'gainst all of us."

"And since you sent Whitson and Jones out to bushwhack us," Hugo said.

"I'm sorry about that, Hugo. Mostly I wanted to talk to you and see what your plans was. And maybe the two of us make a deal. I didn't really want them to kill you."

Hugo responded with a skeptical snort, but he let it go. Turning to Billy, he said, "I'm surprised to hear this about San Francisco. I'm with Thorn on that one. My guess all along was they'd head back to the Community."

"Like I said before, Hugo, it sounded to me like things weren't going so good in Nebraska. Glatt told me he wanted to get the boy someplace else where his talents could grow. But he mentioned Philadelphia or New York, not San Francisco. He sure didn't want to go back to the Community, though. He realized some of the folks back there were wising up to him."

"I suppose even a fella as slippery as Glatt gets figured out after a while." He looked toward Walker. "Did you hear that, Clerk?"

"They were gonna leave sometime during the night," said Jarrod. "When I got up this morning and saw that both buckboards was still here, I wasn't sure what was going on, but before I had time to look into it, thanks to you, Hugo, all hell broke loose."

"Don't thank me. You got my clever young partner to thank for that."

Chapter Forty-One: The Spot Where the Mountain Ain't

After teams had been hitched to the two buckboards, Billy and Hugo helped Woodrow toss Jarrod and Walker, who remained tied hand and foot, into the wagon that was not filled to the brim with dead rustlers.

Hank and Charlie sat in the buckboard's shadow. Hank was changing Charlie's bandage, and, as he did, Charlie, feeling no pain, whistled a fine rendition of *Polly Wolly Doodle.* Once the bandaging was done, Billy and Hugo hefted Charlie into the wagon and placed him next to Jarrod.

"Hey, Rustler," Charlie said, with a scowl, "scoot the hell over."

"We'll load enough supplies from the chuck wagon to get us to Casper," said Hank, "and then we'll head out. We should get there before dark tomorrow. We found a couple of more bottles of whiskey, so I figure we can keep Charlie drunk the whole way."

Billy smiled. "By the time you get him into Doc Waters's clinic, his hangover will be worse than his gunshot wound."

"What are you fellas planning to do?" Hank asked.

"I guess we'll head toward Rawlins," answered Hugo. "With luck, we can run Thorn to ground before he gets there and lights out on a train."

Charlie was paying no attention to their conversation, and Hugo tapped the cowboy's shoulder. Charlie looked up with a smile and bleary eyes.

"How far do you think it is from here to Rawlins, Charlie?"

"Probably sixty or seventy miles, if you could go in a straight line."

"Can you go in a straight line?" asked Hugo.

"Nope."

"Why not?"

"Well, on second thought, I guess you could go in a straight line if you wanted to climb a mountain."

"Let's say we don't wanna climb a mountain."

"Then you'll have to veer off a bit and go through the Gap."

"What's the Gap?"

"It's the spot where the mountain ain't."

Hugo looked at Hank and said, "I'm thinkin' we might've given this cowpoke too much whiskey."

"I'm sure he's talking about Muddy Gap," Hank said. "You need to go back the way we came. Once you get to Split Rock, look toward the southeast. You'll see what he means about going where the mountain ain't. The Gap's obvious from there. Thorn don't know this country as good as you do, Hugo, and I expect even he'll be able to find it. After you get through the Gap, keep going to the southeast into Rawlins."

"We'll be going past Split Rock?" Billy asked.

Hank nodded. "You will."

"It could be," said Billy, "we may not have to go all the way to Rawlins."

"Why do you say that?" asked Hugo.

"Like before, Thorn's traveling with a boy on a mule, so he's not going to make very good time. It could be he'll hole up his first night at the Garvey place."

Hugo gave that thought some quick consideration. "You could be right." Turning again to Hank, he said, "Here, take this with you." Hugo had stuffed the cash into a gunny sack. "When you get to Casper, give it to Sheriff Gardner and let 'im know how much help Woodrow's been. Also tell 'im

Woodrow had no part in the gunfight, and he never made a dime at bein' a rustler."

Hank nodded. "I will. I don't think Woodrow has anything to worry about. What about Jarrod?"

"Tell Skip that Jarrod has been cooperatin', and if he keeps cooperatin' and is willin' to talk to the county attorney and a jury, we should all of us help 'im as much as we can not to get hanged."

"That might save him from the gallows," Hank said, "though I ain't sure it'll save him from the ranchers."

Noticing that most of the cattle had already wandered back into the two creeks's confluence, Billy said, "Once you tell them where their cows are, that might satisfy them."

"I think it will," agreed Hugo. "It's too bad we'll never know who killed poor Joe Broom. It could've been Dale Jarrod, but it's just as likely to've been any one of his men."

"Nothing could be proved either way," Hank said. "What about Walker?"

"Have the sheriff lock 'im up. After we finish with Thorn, I'll get word to the marshal and the U.S. Attorney down in Cheyenne lettin' 'em know we got us a crooked Bureau of Indian Affairs employee locked up in Casper. We'll all be lookin' into Mr. Walker's misdoin's. I expect that not-so-clever fox'll be spendin' a good chunk of the next decade or two in a federal prison."

Hank rubbed the back of his neck and let out a little groan. "That'd be a good place for him," he said. He turned away from the boys and looked out past the wagon full of dead men and over the destroyed camp. "It's too bad what happened here. There was lots of dying." The excitement Hank had felt right after the fight appeared gone. Now he looked tired. "I never killed a man before today. I fear it's a thing that'll stay with me."

"It will," said Hugo. "But what we did here was a good thing, Hank. It's not only brought these fellas to justice, but it has also put a stop to Martin Glatt, and soon Elijah Thorn will also be counted among the dead. I made that promise to Ivan Kradec back at Split Rock, and I aim to keep it."

"What are your plans, Hank," Billy asked, "once your chores in Casper are done? Are you headed back to the ranch at Devil's Gate?"

"No, I don't think so. It's a fine enough place to work" — he again looked out across the camp — "but I need a change. It's not only this." He jerked the back of his hand in an arc that covered everything in front of them. "I've been feeling restless since before I left the widow."

Though Hank had risen to the occasion and had handled himself well, Billy wished they had not gotten him into this. Like Woodrow Bayliss with the rustlers, Hank was not made for all that had happened here.

Hank returned his gaze to Billy and Hugo. "I suppose I'll keep on cowboying. There ain't much else for me. But I think I'll head to Jackson Hole. I hear it's nice up there, if you're willing to abide a bitter winter. I might even ride into the park and look at the geysers and the bubbling pots. I expect they're something."

"I expect they are," agreed Hugo, "though I've not seen 'em myself."

Hank climbed into the driver's box. "One thing's for sure," he said.

"What's that?" asked Billy.

"No matter what, I'm heading west."

Billy recalled what Hank had said the first day they met him at Tom Sun's corrals. "I'm sure you'll have good luck, Hank." Billy gave him a smile and shook his hand. "It's hard to go wrong if you keep heading west."

■ ■ ■ ■

Billy and Hugo loaded their saddlebags and Billy's burlap poke with enough food to last a couple of days. They filled only one canteen each. If they went back as they had come, along Deer Creek and the East Fork of Sage Hen, there would be plenty of water along the way. Should they not catch up to Thorn and have to continue on to Rawlins, there would be the Sweetwater and the North Platte. Having enough water available on a ride through Wyoming was a rare luxury. On this one, they were lucky.

Before they started out, they released the few corralled horses that were left. The animals would either stick around the camp for the water and grass as the cattle were doing, or they wouldn't. Either way, they would be fine. Billy expected the horses would have no trouble making a living on their own. They might even join one of the many groups of mustangs in the area. Billy wasn't sure if the dominant stallion leading one of the herds would allow geldings in, but why not? The geldings would be no threat.

Badger and the bay were well rested, and, once they were moving, the boys maintained a steady pace. They didn't take a break until they were beyond the East Fork and on the Sage Hen's main stream. Even then, they stopped for less than an hour — just long enough to loosen their horses' cinches, get them watered, and let them eat some grass.

There were a few canned goods left in the chuck wagon, and, before they headed out, Billy and Hugo both had grabbed a can of peaches, which they now ate without much conversation. Halfway through his can, though, Billy did ask one question. "If we don't catch Thorn before he boards a train in Rawlins, are we going to follow him all the way back to Nebraska?"

"Sure, we are," said Hugo.

"We could send a wire to the law back in Albion and let them handle it."

Hugo frowned and shook his head. "Hell, Billy," he said, jabbing his syrupy spoon in Billy's direction, "I couldn't hardly kill the man if we did that, now, could I?"

Chapter Forty-Two: It Could Go No Other Way

The shadows were long when they arrived at the Garvey homestead. Coming in from the north, there was much less cover than they'd had a couple of days earlier when they came in from the south along the river where the trees were thick. On this side, the only things taller than the many stands of sagebrush were a few scrubby pines and junipers growing in the shallow ravines draining off Split Rock. The boys rode into one of the ravines, tied off their mounts, and walked to the end where the draw washed onto flatter ground. They found a spot where they could remain hidden but were able to see all the homestead's buildings.

"Let's make ourselves comfortable, Hugo," said Billy, "and wait for the sun to go down."

As they had come out of the Rattlesnakes earlier in the day, Hugo had told Billy that they needed another one of his clever plans. "And you gotta come up with it before we get to Split Rock, Billy-boy; that's your assignment as my deputy in trainin'."

Now, as they waited for darkness to fall, Hugo asked, "So, are you done ponderin' a plan on how we're gonna do this?"

"Not so much, Hugo, but, before we do anything, we need to figure out if they're even there."

The sun, laying low in the sky, was no more than the width of a thumbnail above the distant western hills. Soon, it would be dark, but Billy could tell Hugo was already antsy waiting for the sun to set. The old goat loved a fight, but he wanted it when he wanted it, and he hated any delay. Patience was not high on Hugo's list of good qualities.

"Sure wish we had some whiskey," Hugo said in his usual refrain.

"You should've gotten some from Charlie before we all headed out this morning."

"I thought about it, but I figured he needed it more than me; though, now I'm thinkin' that was a big mistake."

As they talked, Billy stayed focused on the homestead below. "Their animals aren't in either of the corrals," he said, "so if Thorn and the boy are here, they must've stabled them. Once it's dark we can get to the barn and check it out. If the horse and mule are there, we'll wait 'til morning to do anything. If they're not there, we can bring our horses up and get them taken care of, then go into the cabin and rest a bit ourselves."

If Billy had been wrong about Thorn's stopping here for the night, that meant Thorn and the boy would continue on toward Rawlins at least until dark, and maybe longer, which would also mean he and Hugo were falling farther behind.

"If we do take a break," Billy added, "it can't be for long."

"If they're here, why the hell wait 'til mornin'? I'm for doin' whatever it takes to kill the son of a bitch tonight."

"What, are you thinking we should go up to the cabin and call him out like we did at the tent?"

"Maybe."

"Even when we did that, Hugo, I didn't think it was a good idea."

"Didn't hear you offerin' anythin' better."

"No, you're right. But then we didn't have much time. There was a gunfight going on, and we needed to get back to it so we could help Hank and Charlie. Here, we don't have to rush things. We have all the time we need. I'm counting us lucky that it was Earl and

Evelyn we had to face instead of Thorn."

"There's one of him and two of us. Those are good odds."

"We can't take chances with this man. Thorn's a lunatic."

"So what are you thinkin'?"

"The easiest and safest way to kill him is to wait 'til daylight. When he comes out of the house to take care of his morning business, you can shoot him as he heads to the privy."

This was an idea that violated their rule of no cold-blooded killings; but, after seeing what Thorn had done to Martin Glatt — his friend and mentor — in addition to all of his other horrendous murders, Billy decided their rule needed some flexibility.

"And," Billy added, "you can shoot him from the safety of the barn."

Billy caught himself before saying, "*We* can shoot him from the safety of the barn." He knew Hugo saw Thorn as the vilest killer he had ever hunted in his many years of vile-killer hunting. Billy also knew that the promise Hugo had made to Kradec was not the only promise he had made. He'd also made a promise to himself.

It could go no other way. Hugo would be the man who killed Elijah Thorn. And he would do it alone.

"Junior Deputy Young, maybe you weren't listenin' when I gave you your orders. I told you we needed somethin' *clever.* That idea ain't even close to clever."

"No, but it is an idea that will work."

"No, sir, I ain't doin' it that way, boy."

"Why not?" Billy asked, but, before Hugo could answer, Billy answered for him. "No, wait, don't tell me," he said. "Let me guess. You want to kill him up close so you can look into his eyes while you do it. Right? I've heard it all before, Hugo." Billy dropped his voice into a gravelly imitation of Hugo's. " 'I'm-a gettin' close 'nough to look inta the killer's eyes.' I don't know who's crazier — you or Thorn."

"You're right. There's been them times, and lots of 'em, when I've been exercisin' my duties against some evil wrongdoer, and I *have* wanted to look him straight in his murderin' eyes at the very second that justice got served." He shook his head. "But that's not my thinkin' this time, boy."

"Oh, really? What is it this time?"

"This time, I want the son of a bitch lookin' straight into *my* eyes."

The sun went down, and no lamp was lit inside the cabin — at least not one that shone through the window on the north side.

"Let's get goin'," said Hugo. "I wanna get this bastard kilt, so you can use that nice cook stove in the house yonder to whip us up a tasty supper."

Billy considered suggesting Hugo do the cooking for once but decided it was not the time.

Both men, in a crouch, made their way to the barn. Billy felt his insides flutter at the thought of what they had found the first time they crept into this barn. But, he assured himself, there would be nothing like that tonight. This time, the barn would hold only a horse and a mule, or nothing at all.

They inched around to the east wall and opened one of the large, double end-doors far enough to slip inside. The moon was growing brighter, but it sent very little light through these doors or through the loft. There was enough, though, to see that none of the stalls held animals.

"They ain't here," said Hugo. He sounded disappointed, and Billy felt the same.

"I would've bet anything they would be," Billy said. "Looks like I was wrong."

"Maybe. Let's go to the cabin and see if we can tell if they've come and gone."

They left the barn and started across the yard.

"Let's not go straight across," said Billy. "Let's stay in the shadows just in case." He was reluctant to accept his mistake.

They scuttled to the window and peered inside.

Nothing. Neither movement nor light.

Feeling more confident that the place was empty, they climbed the porch, and, with guns drawn, opened the door. Hugo, bending low, stepped into the dark.

A few seconds later, a match flared, and, as Hugo lit a lamp, Billy holstered his Colt and went in, too.

Hugo stood staring at the eating table that held the lamp he'd lit. "By God," he said, "you were right, Billy. They were here."

"How do you know?"

"The same way we knew they had been here before." Hugo nodded toward the table. Protruding from the lamp's base was an empty Hub Wafer wrapper.

With a smile, Billy said, "The kid did it again."

Chapter Forty-Three: Thumbed Back the Hammer

Hugo was to bring in wood from the pile out back and get the stove started while Billy returned to the ravine and fetched the horses. Before he left, Billy had told Hugo that it was time Hugo did some cooking. The old coot agreed with a grumble. And now, as Billy rode Badger into the yard and leading the bay, he called out to Hugo to come get their gunny sack of grub.

There wasn't much cooking to do, so Hugo should be capable of getting it done. The bag held elk jerky, a few of Hank's apricots, a couple of cans of beans, two or three slices of the smoked ham Hugo could heat up — probably — and the last two cans of peaches.

Billy dismounted, and, leading the horses into the barn, he shouted, "I am not bringing this food to you, Hugo. I'm leaving it right next to the barn door. You come out here and get it. And be quick about it. I'm hungry."

Billy put the horses into a couple of stalls, unsaddled them, and removed their bridles. He watered them and poured them both some oats. As he brushed Badger, he realized Hugo had not come for the food. Carrying the curry brush, he walked to the door. "Goddamn it, Hugo. Are you going to come get this chuck or not?" When there was no response, he let out another curse and tossed the brush onto a workbench.

He grabbed the gunny and headed for the house. Billy did not want to spend any more time than was necessary to eat, rest themselves and the horses a bit, and return to the trail. *There was no time,* he told himself, *for Hugo's usual dawdling.* As he walked through the door, he had every intention of giving Hugo hell.

But, once in the cabin, he saw Hugo wasn't there.

Billy set the sack on the table and went outside. "Hugo," he called, "where the hell are you?"

Billy looked toward the outhouse and figured that to be a likely spot. But if Hugo was in there, why didn't he answer? Billy headed in that direction and called again. There was no response, and, when he opened the privy door, he saw the place was empty.

He checked the springhouse. That was empty, too.

Expecting no answer, he called out once again. The only reply was the rhythmic chirp of crickets and the hoarse croak of frogs at the river.

Billy's mouth had gone dry. He tried, without success, to swallow away the clump of desert that now clogged his throat. He crossed to the pump for a drink, and, as he approached, he watched as a drop of water clung to the spout, and then, losing its grip, dropped to a puddle at the pump's base.

He knew Hugo had not used the pump. Even from inside the barn, Billy would have heard Hugo's working the handle. Also, though he hadn't looked around the cabin, he knew there had been no bucket of water at the table or near the stove.

The *stove.*

Neither, Billy realized with a start, had there been any wood. Hugo would have had plenty of time to collect wood and fire up the stove while Billy went for the horses.

He gave the pump handle a couple of cranks, and the water flowed without priming. It had not been long since the pump was last used, but Billy was convinced it had not been Hugo who had used it.

Without taking a drink, Billy lifted his short-barreled from its holster, thumbed back the hammer, and stepped into the shadows.

The moon was brighter now, and Billy expelled a long quivery breath as he scanned the yard.

Nothing.

He looked toward the river.

Nothing.

He turned toward the small corral on the hill. The only place Billy had not searched was the root cellar where he had found Ivan Kradec close to death.

There would have been no reason for Hugo to go into the root cellar on his own. If he was there, like Kradec, it would be because someone had put him there.

Still holding his forty-five and feeling uneasy, he started up the hill.

Before, when he had made this walk, he'd held a lantern. A lantern would be nice now, but this time he was more familiar with the layout of things. And, though not ideal, the moonlight would do.

He made it past the corral and stopped at the sloping dirt wall on the southeast side of the cellar.

Easing his head around, he could see the cellar's river-rock front. The door was closed, but its heavy steel hasp was disengaged from the staple and extended from its hinge straight out from the door's thick planks.

If Hugo was in there, he was likely in the same condition as Kradec had been. Billy shoved that thought aside and inched himself around to the door. Holding the Colt in his right hand, he took hold of the hasp with his left. He gave a tug, and, as the thick door opened, its rusty hinges let out a plaintive whine.

As before, the first thing Billy noticed when the door opened was the pleasant smell of cool, dry dirt. Now he needed a lantern or at least one of Hugo's wooden matches. The root cellar was as dark as the inside of a goat. Wishing his eyes would hurry and adjust, he pushed the door open a little farther, squatted low, and leaned into the cellar's black maw.

Even if there had been light, it happened too fast to see. But he felt it. Something large and hard struck him square in the face. The force of it snapped his head back and lifted him off his haunches. He went airborne. The Colt flew from his hand and disappeared into the darkness. When Billy landed, the back of his head smashed into the hard, rocky ground. Air exploded from his chest, and, looking into the night sky, he saw the stars twirl like the blades of a windmill.

Billy knew he was going out, but he could not allow it to happen. He shook his head in an effort to jar his senses back into operation. And, as he tried to find his feet, a vise grabbed him by the throat and the back of his neck.

An enormous man had him, and, with frightening ease, he lifted Billy straight up and held him at eye level. "How does a boot to the face feel?" he asked in a gentle, whispery voice that belied his size. The man's gray eyes were alert, but as empty as a fish's. And though he had not seen him before, Billy knew the giant who had him by the throat was Glatt's Enforcer, Elijah Thorn.

Chapter Forty-Four: Large, Mean Tree

Thorn knew him, too. "You're bigger than the other one," he said.

Trying to draw a breath, Billy struggled, but it was hopeless. As he dangled from the man's huge, beefy hands, a fog rolled in.

"You had to come to the cellar. There was nowhere else to look." Thorn smiled. And when his lips peeled back over his large, even teeth, the smile distorted an otherwise straight scar that ran from his left eye to below his chin. If not for the scar, the smile might have held a spark of innocence.

Holding Billy up, Thorn eyed him as though he were some small creature he'd caught in a leg trap. "The prophet said he owed you a favor, and I didn't have to kill you." His low brow furrowed, and he added with half a smile, "But the prophet is not here anymore."

Thorn pronounced his words with a quiet, unnerving precision.

His strange smile disappeared. He opened his left hand and released the back of Billy's neck. Continuing to hold Billy aloft with his right hand, he drew back an enormous left fist and slammed it into the right side of Billy's face. The sound of it connecting echoed through Billy's head like summer thunder. Thorn drew back the fist again, but, before he could throw the next punch, Billy, who was now desperate for air, held tight with both hands to the massive wrist at his throat. He extended his legs to the sides of Thorn's thighs, aimed the toes of his boots outward, and, with everything he could muster, drove the pointed rowels of his spurs into the meat of Thorn's upper legs.

The big man screamed, and his grip on Billy's throat loosened.

Billy went down hard onto his butt. Despite his violent gasps for air and the fog laying heavy in his head, he forced himself to his feet.

Thorn had dropped to one knee, and both his hands clutched his wounded thighs. As Billy staggered toward him, Thorn looked up just as Billy's fist plowed into his nose. Blood exploded, and Thorn flew backwards, his arms pinwheeling, grasping for purchase that wasn't there. This time it was the back of Thorn's head that smashed onto the rocky ground.

Billy bent over and gulped five quick seconds' worth of air. His brain was clearer now, and, as Thorn snarled like a wounded wolf, Billy bent to lift him to a sitting position so he could hit the bastard again. But, as he reached down, he reconsidered. If the fistfight turned into a wrestling match, Billy did not stand a chance.

Thorn rolled onto all fours, and Billy drew back a boot and kicked him in the ribs with everything he had. But, for all the good it did, he may as well have kicked the cellar's rock wall. Thorn continued onto his feet, and Billy hit him again. This time his fist landed on Thorn's eye. The big man's head twisted around, and Billy hit him hard in the mouth. Billy doubted he'd knocked out any teeth, but he felt a couple wobble. Thorn fell backward, his eyelids fluttering, and that appeared to be the end of it.

But it wasn't.

Thorn shook his head and spatters of blood shot from his nose and mouth like water off a dog. Smiling a red-toothed smile, he scrabbled to his feet and launched his shoulder into Billy's gut. Again Billy went down hard on his back. The side of his head landed within an inch of hitting a baseball-sized river rock. One no doubt left over from the root cellar's construction.

With a look of annoyed determination, Thorn said in his gentle, whispery precision, "You are harder than most." He moved in three steps closer, and, as he approached, Billy took hold of the rock next to his head and slammed it into Thorn's left knee. Except for the spurs to the thighs, Thorn had taken in silence everything Billy had dished out. Now, he shrieked in pain, and, bending over, he grabbed for his battered knee. When he did, Billy, still on his back, lifted his legs and, with both feet together, kicked the heels of his boots into the center of Thorn's bloody face. Thorn spun, staggered a dozen feet, and hit the ground face down.

Felled like a tree. *A large tree,* thought Billy. *A large, mean tree.*

Billy took a few seconds to catch his breath; then, with considerable pain, he pushed himself onto his feet.

He looked at Thorn. The Goliath lay unmoving where he had fallen. His face in the dirt. His arms tucked beneath his chest.

Billy lifted his head toward the sky and gulped in the night air. He filled himself up. The stars were no longer whirling, but he had to close an eye to erase one of the out-of-focus moons.

Sensing something to his left, he spun with clenched fists, as ready for whatever threat came next as his battered body would allow.

Sitting in the cellar's doorway was young Abraham Glatt.

Billy had to blink a couple of times to be sure of what he saw. "Abe, it's you. Thank God we've found you."

Abraham did not look up, and he gave no sign that he even knew Billy was there.

Billy staggered to the boy and knelt in front of him. He touched Abe's small right hand, which caused the boy to draw into himself even more.

"It's okay, Abraham. You're safe now. You don't have to be frightened anymore. I promise."

With that, Abraham lifted his eyes but would not look at Billy. He stared past him toward a place far away. Something in those wide, intelligent eyes made him appear a decade older than his years. *Or,* Billy thought, *a lifetime older. A dozen lifetimes older.* Billy could not describe what he saw in the depth of Abe's blue eyes. The look was haunted and, yet, in some strange way, appeared in control.

Billy was lost inside that mysterious gaze,

but, with great effort, he found the ability to look away.

He had to get Thorn tied before the giant woke. Standing, Billy unbuttoned his suspenders. He would use those to bind Thorn's hands behind his back. He'd then drag him into the cellar and lock him in.

He started for Thorn's prone, unmoving body, but stopped. Before getting any closer. He turned and retrieved the rock he'd used for knee bashing. If Thorn moved an inch, Billy intended to bring this rock down on the man's skull with everything he had. If this devil even twitched, Billy would crush its evil brains.

Taking comfort in that thought and the heft of the rock, Billy started toward the killer. When he was four feet away, Thorn rolled over, and, aiming Billy's already cocked Colt, he whispered, "Drop the rock, Mr. Young."

Chapter Forty-Five: Their Grim Situation

Though Billy's jaw ached and his throat throbbed, he was having an easier time getting down the hill than Thorn. Billy was in the lead, and every twenty feet or so Thorn had to stop to rest. A few times along the way he let out a groan, though he tried to stifle it. Thorn's attempts to hide any sign of weakness were obvious. What wasn't obvious was for whose benefit was this pretense — Billy's, the boy's, or his own?

With pleasure, Billy imagined blood flowing down the outside of Thorn's thighs, over his lower legs, and into the shafts of his boots. With even more pleasure, Billy thought of the discomfort a smashed knee might cause. Having never had a smashed knee, Billy was glad not to know the particulars of such a thing, but he expected the pain was considerable. And, since knees had a bunch of moving parts, Billy guessed the pain might well last a lifetime.

Especially a lifetime as short as Thorn's was apt to be.

Billy had no doubt that Thorn had gotten Hugo, but he also expected Hugo was alive. Thorn had not had time to do all the things he liked to do in the process of killing a man. And, if Thorn was fool enough not to kill Hugo when he had the opportunity, the chances of Thorn's not living to see much of tomorrow were high.

Billy told himself this in order to feel better about their grim situation and despite the assumption that, though not dead, Hugo was lying somewhere beat to holy hell.

As he gimped his way down the hill, Thorn called out, "Slow down." They were past the cabin, and Billy figured Thorn had left Hugo somewhere in the trees along the river.

"What's the matter, Thorn? Are your legs causing some trouble?" To be annoying, when he asked the questions, Billy chuckled.

Thorn didn't answer.

The boy followed a few paces behind the two men. "Abraham," Billy called out, "has this lunatic hurt you?" Billy was not surprised to receive no answer to that question, either. Not from Abraham, anyway.

"Stop," said Thorn.

Billy did as told and asked over his shoulder, "Already need another rest, do you, Thorn?"

Thorn shuffled down to Billy, and, without speaking, he slammed the barrel of the Colt into the top of Billy's neck, an inch below the base of the skull. A rocket exploded. Billy dropped to his hands and knees and struggled to keep from going all the way down. He didn't lose consciousness, but the fire ball in his head had scorched the backs of his eyelids. Billy gritted his teeth with the pain of it.

Thorn, in his icy manner, said, "I would never hurt the boy." And, even as crazy as Thorn was, Billy could tell this was the truth. "He," Thorn added, "is chosen, and I am his protector."

Like climbing out of a well, Billy made it to his feet. Once he found his voice, he asked, "Is that right?" From somewhere in his head — no doubt the very spot that had felt the barrel of his own gun — he heard the warning that it was unwise to continue baiting Elijah Thorn. But Billy couldn't help himself. Perhaps he'd been riding with the contentious Deputy Dorling for too long. "I heard you were Prophet Glatt's protector, too, yet, you emptied his guts onto the ground inside a tent next to Canyon Creek."

"Martin Glatt," Thorn said, "no longer

deserved his place."

Billy turned to look at the man behind him. The giant's expression was both indifferent and impassioned. Which made no sense. It couldn't be both. Yet Billy could see that it was. And, with that, he realized that neither he nor Hugo and probably not even Glatt himself understood the depth of this man's insanity.

Once they made it to the trees, Thorn moved past Billy and staggered through an open space. When he was at the river, he bent as best he could and scooped water into his mouth using his left hand. He continued to hold Billy's short-barreled in his right. After taking a drink, he ran his wet hand over his face and the back of his neck.

"What's wrong with that bastard?" grumbled someone from the darkness. The voice was hoarse and strained. It carried the sound of pain and exhaustion, but it was recognizable.

Even in the dim light, Billy could make out Hugo sitting at the base of a small tree. His hat, shirt, gunbelt, and boots were missing. His legs extended straight out. His arms stretched around behind him to the back of the tree's narrow trunk. His twisted position was awkward, unnatural. Billy couldn't see Hugo's hands, but they were no doubt lashed together.

"He hurt his knee," said Billy. He faked the sort of casualness that might be used to describe a base runner's banged-up leg after sliding into second.

"Gosh, that's too bad," said Hugo. "I hope it ain't serious."

Billy moved in a little closer and saw that, as he had expected, Hugo was beat to hell. But the good news was he had possession of both his ears and eyeballs, and his guts were not in a pile by his side.

"How are you?" Billy asked.

"Sittin' in this bunglesome way for this long has got my legs all stove up. I can't even feel the damn things. If I was blindfolded as well as tied, I wouldn't know they was there. Other 'n that, not so bad. He worked me over a bit, but he hits like a grandma."

Billy knew that wasn't true.

Thorn turned to Billy. "Stop the chit-chat and take off your gunbelt."

Billy decided since his gunbelt no longer held his gun, there was no reason to make a fuss.

"Now take off your boots."

"What? Take off my *boots*?"

"I don't want you running."

When Billy didn't move, Thorn leveled the Colt at Billy's chest. "I ain't fond of guns, so I'd rather not shoot you. But that doesn't mean I won't."

Billy took off his boots and let them fall next to his gunbelt.

"Abraham, if you please, toss his things over yonder with the gear."

Moving slowly, Abraham took the boots and gunbelt to a pile of saddlebags, saddles, tack, a couple of frying pans, and a sack of something Billy guessed to be food. There were other smaller items strewn about the pile, but Billy couldn't make out what they were.

Neither Thorn's horse nor Pearl, Abraham's white mule, were anywhere to be seen, but Billy could tell they were picketed back in the trees. From time to time he could hear the horse's nicker and whatever that annoying sound is called a mule makes.

"Now," said Thorn to Abe, "Please light the kindling, and start a fire." He held out four or five matches. The boy took them and crossed to a ring of rocks that contained a stack of cottonwood. The wood was split, so it had come from the woodpile behind the house. Billy guessed it was wood that Hugo had been fetching when he had the bad fortune to come across Elijah Thorn.

The logs and kindling must have been set up before Thorn had taken Abraham to the root cellar.

"This son of a bitch was hiding in the root cellar," said Billy. "I was looking for you. Why didn't you answer when I called?"

"I musta been sleepin'." A goose egg a half inch below Hugo's hairline suggested why he had taken a nap.

Once Abraham had the fire going, Thorn said, "That's better. We've got some light now. I like to see the faces of the men I'm talking to."

"I'd rather not look at yours," said Hugo. His usual bluster was there, but Billy could hear something else beneath the bravado. Fear. He doubted Thorn could hear it, but Billy could, and it was a thing he'd not heard in Hugo before.

"You're lookin' pretty bad, even not countin' that ugly-ass scar runnin' down your cheek." Hugo was either unaware or he didn't care that his own face looked no better. He turned to Billy. "Did you rough 'im up like that?"

Billy nodded.

"No foolin'?" Hugo squinted toward Billy, giving him a look-over. "You must be a whole bunch tougher than I thought, boy, 'cause you're hardly hurt at all."

"Well . . ." Billy said, clearing his throat. He rubbed a hand across his jaw and the spot at the back of his neck.

"Not as bad as Mr. Thorn, anyhow. So tell me, if you won the fight, how the hell come he's the fella holdin' the shooter?"

"Long story."

"We got time."

Billy wasn't sure about that, but he didn't say anything. Thorn was in the process of standing, and it was quite a show. Pain etched the big man's battered face, and, once he was erect, he swayed like he was standing in a canoe. He took in three deep breaths, and, as he exhaled the third one, his eyes squeezed shut.

After a while, he rallied and edged his way to the rear of the tree where Hugo was tied. Without bending, he leaned his weight against the trunk and used the toe of his boot to check Hugo's bindings.

Once he was satisfied Hugo wasn't going anywhere, he twirled the Colt on his finger and grasped it by its barrel. He turned to Billy and dragged his leg across the ten feet that separated them. The fire was going well now, and, as he approached, Billy noticed that Thorn's eyes caught the light like a cat's — or a devil's.

Thorn stopped behind Billy. The last time Thorn had come up behind him like this, a Fourth of July rocket had gone off in his head. Billy tensed himself and waited, but nothing came.

Thorn's breathing was shallow and wet. Billy thought maybe when he kicked the big bastard in the side that he had busted a few ribs. At the time, Thorn hadn't shown any sign that he'd even noticed the kick, but there was always hope.

"This is a mighty handsome Colt you have. Even so, here in a bit when I'm finished with it, it'll be going into the river with your partner's forty-four."

"That seems wasteful. You can keep it. Be my guest."

"I rarely use them. Since you two fellas are skilled gunmen, I have decided we will allow no guns around here."

Billy glanced at Hugo, and he saw in the tough old deputy's face the same fear he'd heard in his voice a moment before. Seeing his friend like that was a gust of frigid wind.

"I know what to do with the old one. He is a dead man, but, with you, I'm not sure." He leaned closer to Billy's ear. "I expect they'll have me kill you. But maybe not. I'll know soon enough, though. When the time comes, they always tell me what it is they want me to do."

Good Lord, Billy thought. *What have we gotten ourselves into?*

Billy looked from Hugo to little Abraham, who, after taking Billy's boots and gunbelt to the pile, had sat on the far side of the fire. The firelight danced around his face, and, though he didn't look in the men's direction, Billy could see the kid's ancient eyes staring at something in the distance, well beyond the river.

What, Billy wondered, could the boy see with those strange eyes.

That was Billy's final thought before the darkness fell.

Chapter Forty-Six: His Enforcer. His Protector

When Billy awoke, all his aches from earlier had been replaced by a single, searing, firestorm of pain raging in his head. He expected he carried a knot on the back of his skull the same shape and size as the butt of his Colt. He tried to lift a hand to touch it, but his hand wouldn't move. He, like Hugo, was lashed to a small cottonwood. He struggled against the bindings but soon gave it up.

The sun had risen, and, with surprised dismay, Billy realized he'd been out all night.

He turned his throbbing head and saw a fuzzy Hugo. Hugo's tree was ten or twelve feet to the right and a couple of feet to the rear of where Billy was tied. He thought Hugo gave him a nod, but he wasn't sure.

He looked out across the camp to see a blurry Abraham sifting through the pile of gear. Billy gave his head a shake, which at first didn't help much, but after a while the world began to inch its way into focus.

The firestorm, though, continued incinerating the inside of Billy's head, and he let go a weak breath. *How the hell hard did that bastard hit me?*

Billy turned again to Hugo, who was watching Abraham rummage through the gear. The boy moved things around until he came up with his battered violin case. He moved to the fire and sat down, took out the violin, and began to play. In an instant, the camp was filled with music.

Abraham moved his bow across the costly fiddle, and, with smooth, easy strokes, he coaxed from the instrument a beautiful, though mournful melody. Billy had no idea what sort of music this was, but it floated through the camp like fog and fit in well with the cool morning air.

Unlike Ivan Kradec, who played with clenched eyes and furrowed brow, Abraham played with eyes wide open. But he did not watch his arcing bow or the patter of his small fingers along the violin's neck. He locked his eyes on the flames dancing in the fire pit and, as was his way, watched something only he could see.

As Abe played, Thorn came down from the cabin and into the camp. Billy was pleased to see the bastard's limp was even worse than before.

It appeared Thorn, too, had just awakened. He dragged himself to the far side of the fire across from Abraham. As he eased to the ground, he said in a voice barely audible above Abraham's playing, "When I woke up, you weren't there. I was worried, but then I heard your music."

Abe didn't stop playing or even acknowledge Thorn's presence.

"I'm glad you got the fire going. Thank you, but you shouldn't be down here alone with these two. They're dangerous."

Abraham continued without looking up.

Thorn wore trousers, but had not yet put on his shirt, which he carried in his hand. His broad shoulders and strong chest were pale in the morning light filtering through the trees.

A discoloration of maybe six inches long and four inches wide ran across the ribs on his right side. That, Billy noted, was where he had kicked him the night before. Billy wished he could get a look at Thorn's knee. He expected that would be a sight to behold.

As Hugo pointed out, Thorn's face looked bad when they came down from the root cellar, but, overnight, it had gotten worse. He now sported a black eye with an iris as red as a Rocky Mountain sunset. Bruises painted his face and his swollen left jaw.

But, once he was sitting, Thorn paid his injuries no mind. The big man closed his eyes and with gentle, even graceful movements swayed in time to Abraham's playing.

While he listened, Thorn's lips moved as though he were either praying or carrying on a conversation with invisible visitors.

After a few minutes, the boy lifted his bow. The melody didn't end in a flourish or even taper off to silence. It just stopped. He laid the violin and bow across his lap and sat, still staring into the fire without expression.

When the music ended, so did Thorn's conversation.

"Thank you, Abraham," said Thorn. "That was beautiful." He pulled on his shirt. "Your music makes the angels smile."

" 'The angels smile'?" mocked Hugo. "This featherhead's a real poet, ain't he, Billy?" And to Thorn, Hugo called out, "What the hell would you know about angels, you sorry, human bein'-butcherin' son of a bitch?"

Hugo was back to his feisty self.

Thorn turned toward the two men he had lashed to trees, and to Hugo he said, "Martin Glatt told me about you."

"Did he tell you I was gonna kill you?"

"He told me you would try." He glanced toward Billy. "He said you would, too, but you had saved his life, and, if I could, I should let you live."

To the extent his bindings would allow, Billy shrugged. "That sounds fine by me." He smiled as though he'd made a joke, but the smile contained no warmth, which was all right with Billy.

"But Martin Glatt was not who he said he was."

"And that surprises you?" Hugo shouted. "You're not only crazy, you're stupid."

What Billy had seen and heard in Hugo the night before was gone.

"They stopped speaking to Glatt," Thorn said.

Billy and Hugo shared a look. The more they learned about Elijah Thorn, the more unnerving things became. Billy guessed whoever *they* were, to Mr. Thorn, the *they* were special.

The space between Thorn's eyebrows wrinkled as though something had only now occurred to him. He looked away, taking a moment to ponder this new insight. "I don't believe they *ever* spoke to Martin Glatt. He was lying all this time."

Again Hugo and Billy shared a bewildered look, and, to Billy, Hugo said, "Good, sweet God, I ain't never seen such an idiot. And for a while there you and me were thinkin' he was smart. Do you reckon that makes us idiots, too?"

"I fear it does," answered Billy with honesty. "Maybe even bigger idiots than he is. He's the one who has us tied to a couple of cottonwoods, not the other way around."

"Hey, imbecile, outta curiosity, what do you figure on doin' after you've sliced on me and my friend Billy Young?"

For a moment, Billy considered the possibility that Hugo had gone crazy, too. There was not a thing in all this world to be gained by provoking a man like Thorn.

To Billy's surprise, Thorn gave Hugo an answer. "I will take Abraham back to the Community. That was our plan all along. After I found Abraham, we were going to meet at Deer Creek and then go to Rawlins for the train. But Glatt changed his mind. He said I could go back, but he was done with our Community. He was taking the boy, and they were going to San Francisco."

San Francisco.

Billy gave a soft, derisive snort. Glatt had told him he was taking the boy back East. Maybe that was the real reason Glatt didn't want Thorn to kill Billy. If Glatt had somehow been able to survive all this, he knew he'd be a hunted man. So, Glatt wanted Billy alive to lead the law down the wrong trail.

Or, hell, maybe Glatt had lied to everyone, and he had no intention of ever taking the boy to any of the places he'd mentioned.

But, whatever Glatt's actual plan was, it not only depended on his not being killed by Hugo, but also surviving his infected bullet wound.

Glatt was a man who attempted to manipulate every situation and to be prepared for every contingency. But one thing he had not been prepared for was being field dressed by his disciple, Elijah Thorn.

"Maybe," Billy said, "Abraham doesn't want to go back to the Community."

Thorn's eyes narrowed. He had been oblivious to Hugo's insults, but Billy's comment caught the man's attention.

"Abraham was kidnapped, stolen from his home. Of course he wants to go back." With difficulty, Thorn pushed himself to his feet. He crossed to the pile of gear, opened a bag, and extracted a knife. A large knife. He held it at eye level and examined it. He looked at the knife as though it were a living thing. He turned to Billy and said, "Abraham knows who he is."

Billy couldn't take his eyes off Thorn's knife. His aching throat had gone dry, and he rasped out, "And who is that?"

"Why, he's the prophet," Thorn said, as though the answer was obvious. "I see it now. They have explained it to me. Glatt was a pretender. All along it has been Abraham. *Abraham* is the prophet." He then added with a smile of pure joy, "Abraham is our Messiah."

With a sound of wonder in his voice, Hugo said, maybe more to himself than anyone, "My God, this fool's as crazy as a shit-house rat."

Abraham still sat by the fire, staring into the flames. Listening.

"Abraham," said Thorn, "it's time for you to go to your place."

"What place is that?" shouted Hugo.

"I would guess the springhouse," said Billy, looking again at Thorn's knife. "The same place where Thorn put Abe when he murdered the boy's mother."

Abe didn't move.

"Please, Abraham," urged Thorn in his soft, precise tones, "the time has come."

Abraham stood, and, though he would not meet Thorn's eyes, the boy, carrying his violin, turned toward the springhouse and left the clearing.

Chapter Forty-Seven: Fourteen Words

Elijah Thorn limped across the camp toward Billy.

"What are you doin'?" asked Hugo.

Thorn didn't answer but continued in Billy's direction.

"Goddamn it," Hugo screamed. "What are you doin'?"

"I'd like to know the answer to that myself," Billy said. He heard a quiver in his voice.

"Look at me, you son of a bitch." Hugo, who now had been tied to a tree for well over fifteen hours, tried, for whatever reason, to get his stoved-up legs under him, but they wouldn't work. "What are you doin'? You were gonna kill *me*. You are supposed to kill me. There's no reason to hurt Billy. Please. Just kill *me*."

In his panic, or anger, or fear for Billy's life, Hugo continued struggling to get his legs beneath him, but he could not make it happen.

Thorn stopped and looked at Hugo. "They have decided that the young one has to die, too."

"Who the screamin' Christ are *they*? There ain't no *they*. There's just you and us, and you don't have to hurt Billy. Kill me. That's what you want."

"No, first the young one." Then, with what appeared to be an expression of kindness — even compassion — Thorn said to Billy, "Don't worry. It will be all right." He nodded, and as he approached, he offered Billy a sympathetic smile. "It will be quick, Billy. You'll see. It can't be so with the old one. They want him punished. But, with you, it will be all right."

Hugo continued to scream, but Billy couldn't make out Hugo's words. All Billy could see, or hear, or understand was the approach of Elijah Thorn, the gleam of his knife, and the soft, precise voice assuring him that it would be all right.

But he knew that was not true. Billy had to do something. He couldn't sit there and be butchered. But what? *What?* His brain raced.

He would kick the busted knee. He would kick the knee, and, when Thorn fell, Billy would keep kicking the bastard until he was dead. That was his only chance.

He hadn't been tied nearly so long as Hugo; even so, his whole body ached — throbbed — but if he could kick the knee, maybe . . . As Thorn moved in closer, Billy tried to twist around and lift his right leg, but he could raise it no higher than a mere few inches. He flexed every muscle. He gritted his teeth and clenched his eyes as he strained to fight the killer off, but, with rising panic, he realized his benumbed legs, as heavy as railroad ties, refused to obey. And, as Thorn moved in closer, Billy knew this was the end.

"It will be okay," said Thorn. "Don't worry, Billy." With a gentle touch, he took hold of Billy's hair and bent Billy's head back, exposing his throat. "It will be okay," he said again with his soft voice. "It will be —"

Before Thorn could use his knife to open Billy's throat, before he could even finish his last absurd, soft-voiced reassurance, Abraham stepped from the trees.

The big man stiffened. "Abraham. You should be at the springhouse. You shouldn't be here. This is not for you to see." He released Billy's hair.

Abraham found Thorn's eyes. For the only time since Billy met the boy on Center

Street in Casper, he saw Abraham look into another person's eyes. "They want you to kill him," said Abraham in his boy's voice, "but first you must kill the old one."

Not only had Billy never seen Abraham meet another's eyes, he'd never heard the boy speak.

But now Abraham did.

They want you to kill him. But first you must kill the old one.

Fourteen words all at one time. All fourteen laid end to end. One after the other.

With that, a darkness settled into Abraham's face. The saying of those fourteen words was a chore that had left him spent.

"Kill the old one first?" asked Thorn. He also appeared bewildered by the boy's speaking. He looked as astonished as he might have looked had those fourteen words come rolling down from the clouds or from a bush bursting into flame. "But it will take longer to kill him. It will take a long time."

Abraham didn't respond. He had depleted all the words he had.

Still not understanding, Thorn asked again, "First I should kill the old one?"

To that, Abraham nodded, and, when he did, Elijah Thorn straightened. His bewilderment was gone. "All right," he said, turning to Hugo.

The old deputy's lifeless legs were again extended in that awkward position. The rims of his eyes were scarlet. His cheeks and his stubble of whiskers were shiny with tears, but, as Thorn approached, Hugo smiled.

Thorn stopped over him and looked down. "For you," he said, "it can't be easy. This is how it has to be. It's the only way to make things right. Kradec, the mother and her man, the Pinkerton at the river, you and your friend have all tried to steal Abraham from us. That is the worst of crimes. The worst of sins."

Hugo's smile was gone. He lifted his head so he could look into Thorn's down-turned face. "Come here, you sick, sorry, son of a bitch. Bend closer. Do what you figure you gotta do. And then to hell with ya."

Wincing with the pains in his own legs, Elijah Thorn squatted next to Hugo and lifted his knife. But before he could begin whatever horror was in his sad, broken mind, Hugo's left arm flashed from behind the tree. He grabbed a handful of hair. And, as Thorn had done with Billy a moment before, Hugo twisted Thorn's head back, exposing his throat. In another flash, Hugo's right hand came from behind the tree. It held the toad-sticker Hugo had brought on his and Billy's manhunt — the one he had sent into the heart of the rustler at the Rattlesnakes — and with a furious, animal shriek, Hugo drove the knife into the underside of the big man's jaw. All six inches of the sharp blade passed through the bottom of Thorn's mouth, up through the tongue, through the mouth's roof, and exited Thorn's right cheek.

The Enforcer's shocked eyes found Hugo's and stared in disbelief.

"It's time for your reckonin', killer," whispered Hugo with a smile.

Thorn's knife fell. His hands flew to his throat. Without taking his eyes from Hugo's, he tried to speak. "How . . . how . . ." but nothing more would come out except a wet gurgle and a crimson freshet of blood.

As fast as Hugo had driven the knife in, he gave it a twist and jerked it free. He flipped it over, and, drawing back his arm, he slammed the steel into Thorn's left eye. Blood and a thick, clear goo exploded onto Hugo's bare chest.

Releasing his grip on Thorn's hair, Hugo grabbed the big man's shoulder and shoved. Thorn toppled onto his back, Hugo's knife still jutting from his left eye. The lid of his right eye blinked a dozen times before the blinking stopped.

■ ■ ■ ■

Hugo leaned his head against the tree and expelled a long, slow breath. Again, he tried to get his legs under him but soon gave it up. He reached across Thorn's blood-soaked body and retrieved his knife.

"Hang on, Billy," he said. "My legs still aren't motivatin' so good." Hugo rolled onto his belly, and, using his elbows, he crawled across the dozen feet that separated them.

Billy tried to ask the same question Thorn had tried to ask, but he wasn't having any better luck. "H-h-how . . ." he stammered, but that was all he could muster.

Hugo cut the rope that held Billy's hands.

"I got a little nervous there for a bit," said Hugo with a weak smile, "when I thought he was gonna slice you up before he came to me. I figured I was gonna have to get over here to fight 'im off, but I couldn't get my damned legs goin'." He doubled a fist and whacked his right thigh a couple of times. "I hope they don't stay like this forever. I'd hate to crawl around for the rest of my days. That could be hard on a fella's elbows." He jammed the knife blade into the dirt. "I guess it's just as well I couldn't get my blamed ol' legs movin', though. I figure in a straight-on knife fight with that big fella, I wouldn't fare too well even if my legs did work." He rolled onto his back. Exhausted, he stared straight up. With a smile, he aimed an index finger at the sky. "I can see a tiny patch-a blue up through all them cottonwood branches, Billy." He dropped his hand and laced his fingers behind his head. "I feared we might get some rain today; but, by golly, boy, it looks like it's gonna be nice after all."

Billy made it to a standing position before Hugo did. He leaned against the tree while the blood drained south toward his stockinged feet. Now that he was up and about, Billy's shoulders hurt more than his legs. He figured arms were poorly designed for being tied backwards all night around the trunk of a cottonwood tree.

"How did you do it, Hugo?"

"Do what?" Hugo asked, feigning ignorance.

Billy figured his legs were working well enough to give Hugo a good kick, but he decided against it. He should be nicer to the ol' coot for at least a day or so. "How did you get your hands free, of course? And how the hell did you get your *knife*?"

Hugo pushed himself up and sat with his useless legs extended. After Abraham had delivered his fourteen words, the boy had returned to the fire. Hugo jerked a thumb in that direction.

"This mornin', right after sunrise, little Abe came down from the house. Unlike you, I didn't get much sleep last night, and I watched as he walked straight to that pile of stuff over yonder and dug out my gun-belt, which, sad to say, was gunless, but it did hold my trusty toad-sticker. The boy brought it over, cut the ropes, and gave me the knife. Then he went to the firepit and built a fire."

"Why didn't you come over and cut me free?" Billy asked, rubbing his hemp-burned wrists.

"I considered it, but my legs was as dead as a corpse's. My butt and low back felt like a bucket of rocks. While I was pullin' myself together, Abraham started playin' his fiddle, and I knew Thorn'd be down shortly. I decided to wait until he came over to do his worst on me, and then I'd give 'im a great big surprise. The plan was a good one, too, until he decided to cut you up first. Lucky for us, little Abe had the good sense to not go direct to the springhouse."

Abraham, sitting at the fire, lifted his

violin and began to play.

"My, oh, my," said Hugo. He took hold of the tree Billy had been tied to and used it to pull himself onto his wobbly bare feet. "Ain't little Abe's music pretty?"

Chapter Forty-Eight: Young Abe Is His Nephew

Billy made breakfast while Hugo went to the pump by the house and washed off Thorn's blood and eyeball juice. Once he'd cleaned up, he saddled their horses and led them back to the clearing. He then located Pearl, the mule, and saddled her, too. He turned Thorn's horse loose to fend for himself, which would be easy here along the river.

"You think we should risk goin' into the water to try to find our shooters?" asked Hugo once he was back at the fire and eating a biscuit. "It don't look deep here along this stretch, and the current's not too bad this time of year."

"My guess is the only thing we'd get from that river is wet. The odds of finding those guns are next to nil. Too bad, too. Pa bought me that Colt when I was not much older than Abraham."

"Well, he sure bought you a nice one,"

Hugo said. "I always liked them pearl grips. I'd had my ol' forty-four for a long while as well. Fine piece. But I suppose you're right. It'd be a miracle if we found 'em. We'll put in a voucher to the marshal and have the United States of America buy us a couple-a new ones. How does that sound?"

It sounded fine, but it wouldn't be the same.

After breakfast, they packed things up. "I don't mind tellin' ya, Billy. I'll be glad to leave the Lost Hope Ranch."

"I agree. Although after all that's happened, maybe folks'll go back to calling it New Hope." Billy knew that after avoiding Elijah Thorn's knife, if he ever had a reason to mention this place again, he would sure call it New Hope.

They were about to leave when Billy walked over to Thorn's bloody body. Looking down, he said, "I suppose we should give him a decent burial before we go. It'd be the Christian thing to do."

Hugo lifted Abraham and sat him on the mule. As he crossed to his bay, he said, "Mount up, Billy. Let the critters eat 'im."

Billy and Hugo decided what they needed to do was get young Abraham back to Ivan

Kradec. Kradec was the boy's only living relative, and, since there were no more Garveys left, and Seth and Marlene were as much as married, the boys wondered if Kradec and the boy were in line to get possession of the ranch.

"I don't expect Kradec'll want to run cattle for a living," said Billy.

"Or farm alfalfa, neither," Hugo added.

"Do you think Tom Sun would be interested in buying the place?"

Hugo snapped his fingers at the idea. "By golly, I bet he would, and that'd make a nice nest egg for the boy and his uncle, if he did, wouldn't it?"

"Yes, sir, it surely would. We'll mention that to Mr. Kradec when we see him."

They knew Matthew or Mark had taken Kradec to a nurse by the name of Sally Barker. They'd look for Kradec there. They expected to have no trouble finding her ranch. According to Charlie, it was on the lower slopes of Whiskey Peak no more than fifteen miles away.

As they approached the big mountain, they located the largest creek coming down. Considering the amount of water it carried, the creek probably had a name, but neither Billy nor Hugo knew what it was. The stream was sizable, though, and made it all the way to the Sweetwater. Since the surrounding area was sparsely populated, the boys guessed those few who had settled here would choose a spot with the most running water, so they followed the creek upstream.

In the early afternoon, they came to a likely looking, well-tended place. It had a nice barn and corrals. A log cabin was near the stream. The cabin was rough, but large by log cabin standards. Up the hill, and twenty feet below a wide stand of aspen, there were the beginnings of an even larger house that was in the process of being built. The place was far from finished, but a brick and mortar foundation was in, and the framing was well along.

"Nice spot," said Hugo as they rode into the yard.

Billy led the way to the cabin. "With luck, it's the nurse's place," he said, "but if it isn't, whoever is here will be able to tell us where she lives."

He dismounted and allowed his reins to drop. As he approached the door, it opened, and a woman of maybe fifty stepped outside. She was handsome with dark hair that showed a frosting of gray.

"Good afternoon, strangers," she said, wiping her hands on a dish towel. She had straight, very white teeth and a pretty smile. Billy removed his hat and was about to introduce himself and the others, but, before he could, the woman asked, "So what brings you boys around? None of you look sick, and I don't see any broken bones or bullet holes."

Nurse Sally Barker led Billy, Hugo, and Abraham around the cabin to a shady area next to the stream. The spot had a rough, hammered-together table with long benches on both sides. There were also five wooden chairs scattered about the grassy yard. Despite each chair holding a cushion, they didn't look very comfortable.

Ivan Kradec sat in one. He was asleep, so maybe the chairs were more comfortable than they appeared.

"We probably shouldn't wake him," whispered Billy.

Nurse Barker checked a small watch pinned to her rose-colored blouse. "No, no, it's about time he woke up. If he doesn't, the poor dear won't get any sleep tonight."

Hugo walked over to Kradec and leaned forward. After he'd taken a closer look, he returned to the others. "Sure has lots of stitches."

"Forty-seven," said the nurse.

"How's he doing?" Billy asked.

"Very well, considering. Nothing is life threatening. He does have six broken ribs that are giving him plenty of pain. There's not much to be done with broken ribs. I have him taped in a snug corset of gauze, but I sometimes fear that does more harm than good. I think I'll remove it tomorrow and see how he feels. You fellas are his friends?"

"We are acquainted," said Billy. "Young Abe is his nephew."

"Oh, how nice," she said, turning her pretty smile on Abraham. When he offered her no response, her brow furrowed, and she glanced at Billy.

Billy shrugged and said, "He's shy."

"I have coffee made. You gents make yourselves comfortable, and I'll fetch it. If Ivan hasn't awoke by the time I return, we'll give him a little shake. I'm sure it will cheer him to see you're here."

"Thank you, ma'am," Billy said. "Coffee sounds fine to me, and Hugo has never turned down a cup of coffee in his life." Or a glass of whiskey, either, thought Billy, though he doubted whiskey was in the offing.

"George, my husband — who's around here somewhere — was in Rawlins yesterday, and he brought home some lemons, if you can believe it. They came in on the train, and not three days ago they were hanging on a tree in California. The three of you have a seat and make yourselves comfortable. I'll be right back with the coffee. And then I'll squeeze a glass of lemonade for Abraham." She smiled at Abe, but, again, to no avail.

Billy and Hugo sat down, and, to Billy's surprise, the chairs were much more comfortable than he had guessed. Also to Billy's surprise, Abraham took a chair and scooted it closer to Kradec.

"I bet it's good to see your uncle again," said Billy.

No response.

"In spite of all them stitches," said Hugo, "he looks lots better than when we saw the poor soul last."

Billy agreed. The swelling around Kradec's face was there but close to gone. Billy rubbed his own jaw and looked at Hugo. "I bet if we had a contest to see whose face had the least swelling, Mr. Kradec would win the prize."

Nurse Barker came out carrying a tray holding four cups, each with strong-smelling coffee filled to its brim. She set the tray on the table and started again for the cabin.

"It'll take just a few minutes on the lemonade."

Even though the nurse said it was time for Kradec to wake, Billy noticed when she spoke she kept her voice low. So he kept his low, too. "I've had lemonade before," he said. "Once when I was in Cheyenne, they were making it at an apothecary's shop. You're in for a treat, Abe."

"I don't know," said Hugo. "I figure Abe ought-a be drinkin' coffee with the rest of the menfolk. I bet if we asked her, that nice nurse would bring you out a hot cup of java, too."

Of course, Abe didn't respond, and, for once, Billy didn't blame him.

"You should try it," encouraged Hugo. "It'll put some hair on that young chest of yours."

Hugo looked to Billy and smiled.

"Why don't you offer to roll him a shuck?" asked Billy. "Bad habits are your specialty."

"If it weren't for bad habits, Billy, our existence in this harsh world would be plumb without meanin'."

Billy could tell Hugo was about to go on, which was no surprise, but, before he could get rolling, Kradec began to stir. He didn't come fully awake, but it was the first sign of life he'd shown since they arrived.

When Kradec moved, Abraham turned and watched. He showed no expression, but he locked his eyes onto Kradec the same as he had the flames in the firepit earlier in the day.

Billy and Hugo shared astonished expressions.

After a moment, Abraham turned away from his uncle and stood. He crossed the narrow space to Hugo. When he was standing next to the old deputy, the boy dug into a pocket and produced his third and what had to be his last roll of Hub wafers. He lifted out the wafer on top of the half-empty tube and slipped it into his mouth.

Though he didn't say anything or meet Hugo's eyes, he extended the roll of Hubs to Hugo.

"Why, thank you, Abe. And lookie here, by golly. The next one up is green. My favorite." He peeled the wafer out and handed the tube back to Abraham, who tucked it into his pocket and returned to his chair beside his uncle.

When Abe had first sat down, he had placed the violin, still in its case, next to his chair. He now picked it up and rested it in his lap.

The Pinkertons would not have stopped their hunt for that costly fiddle, but Billy expected once Kradec returned it to its owners, they would forgive and forget. Despite all it had been through, the violin was in the same fine condition as it had been when Ivan Kradec had . . . borrowed it.

Kradec again stirred. He awoke slowly, his lids fluttering open. Once he was focused and realized he was not alone, he gave a startled jerk. When he did, Abraham turned in Kradec's direction.

"Abra . . . ham," Kradec said, his voice breaking. He moved his hands onto the arms of the chair and, with a soft groan, pulled himself toward the boy. "Abraham," he repeated, and, as he said it, his eyes brimmed with tears. "Is it really you?"

Abraham didn't respond or smile or even lift his eyes; but he did extend his small hand and place it atop his uncle's.

ABOUT THE AUTHOR

Robert McKee's short fiction has appeared in numerous commercial and literary publications. One of his stories was selected for the prestigious anthology *Best American Mystery Stories,* edited by Otto Penzler with the assistance that year of visiting editor Michael Connelly. He was also a recipient of the Wyoming Art Council's Literary Fellowship Award, as well as a three-time first-place winner of Wyoming Writers, Incorporated's adult fiction contest, and a two-time first-place winner of the National Writers Association's short fiction contest.

He was the author of four novels. His first, *Dakota Trails,* was awarded the 2016 Will Rogers Silver Medallion for Best Western. His other three novels, *Killing Blood, Out of the Darkness,* and *Gypsy Rock,* were all finalists for Western Fictioneers Peacemaker award for Best Western. *Gypsy Rock* also received a Will Rogers Bronze Medallion in the Western Maverick category.

The employees of Thorndike Press hope you have enjoyed this Large Print book. All our Thorndike, Wheeler, and Kennebec Large Print titles are designed for easy reading, and all our books are made to last. Other Thorndike Press Large Print books are available at your library, through selected bookstores, or directly from us.

For information about titles, please call:

(800) 223-1244

or visit our Web site at:

http://gale.cengage.com/thorndike

To share your comments, please write:

Publisher
Thorndike Press
10 Water St., Suite 310
Waterville, ME 04901